The Nakano Thrift Shop

Hiromi Kawakami

Translated from the Japanese
by Allison Markin Powell

Portobello
BOOKS

First published by Portobello Books 2016
This paperback edition published by Portobello Books 2017

Portobello Books
12 Addison Avenue
London
W11 4QR

Originally published in Japan in 2005 under the title *Furudogu Nakano Shoten* by Bungei Shunju, Tokyo.

A CIP catalogue record for this book is available from the British Library

9 8 7 6 5 4 3 2 1

ISBN 978 1 84627 602 6
eISBN 978 1 84627 601 9

www.portobellobooks.com

Typeset by Avon DataSet, Bidford on Avon, Warwickshire

Printed and bound by CPI Group (UK) Ltd, Croydon, CR0 4YY

Contents

Rectangular #2

You know what I mean? Mr Nakano had a habit of saying this.

I was caught off guard when he said abruptly, 'You know what I mean – pass me that soy sauce pourer.'

The three of us had gone for an early lunch. Mr Nakano ordered the gingered pork set lunch, Takeo the simmered fish of the day, and I went for the curry rice. The gingered pork and the simmered fish came right away. Mr Nakano and Takeo each drew a set of disposable chopsticks from the box on the table, snapped them apart, and began eating. Takeo muttered under his breath, 'Excuse me,' but Mr Nakano just started bolting down his lunch without a word.

My curry rice arrived eventually, and the moment I picked up my spoon was when Mr Nakano spoke up with his 'You know what I mean . . .'

'When you say, "You know what I mean," isn't it, well, out of place?' I asked.

Mr Nakano set down his bowl on the table. 'Did I say, "You know what I mean"?'

'You did,' Takeo affirmed in a murmur from just beside him.

'You know what I mean – I don't say that.'

'You just said it again.'

'Ah.'

Mr Nakano scratched his head in an exaggerated gesture.

'It must be a verbal tic.'

'It's a strange one.'

I passed the soy sauce pourer to Mr Nakano, who doused his two pieces of pickled daikon with it and then munched away on them.

'I guess it's part of a conversation that I have inside my own head.'

He went on, For example, in my mind I think: if A happens, then B, so that must mean C, and it follows with D. But when I start speaking, I just say D, so then 'You know what I mean' comes out unintentionally.

'That what happens?' Takeo asked as he poured the broth from his fish over his leftover rice.

Takeo and I were working in Mr Nakano's store. For the past twenty-five years or so, Mr Nakano had been running his thrift shop in a western suburb of Tokyo that was full of students. Apparently, his first job was at a mid-sized food company, but he quickly lost interest in working for a corporation so he quit. This was around the time when the phrase 'corporate dropout' was gaining traction but, he said, he would need to have worked at the company longer in order to be considered a 'dropout'.

In any case, he explained to me in his slight drawl as he tended the store, I hated it and quit my job – I was humiliated at the time.

'These are not antiques. They're second-hand goods. That's what I sell here,' Mr Nakano had stated plainly during my interview.

Pasted in the window of Mr Nakano's store was a notice written in sloppy calligraphy: PART-TIME HELP WANTED, INTERVIEWS NOW. Although the sign said that they were interviewing now, when I went inside to enquire, the shopkeeper told me, 'Interviews start on the first of September at two in the afternoon. Punctuality is of the essence.' With his beard and knitted hat, the trim shopkeeper made an odd impression. That had been my first encounter with Mr Nakano.

With its second-hand goods (not antiques), Mr Nakano's shop was literally filled to overflowing. From Japanese-style dining tables to old electric fans, from air conditioners to tableware, the shop was crammed with the kind of items found in a typical household from the 1960s and later. In the mornings, Mr Nakano would raise the shop's shutter and, with a cigarette between his lips, he'd arrange the goods intended to tempt customers outside the front of the store. Bowls and plates that had any kind of fancy pattern, arty task lamps, onyx-like paperweights shaped like turtles or rabbits, old-school typewriters and the like – these were all attractively displayed on a wooden bench set outside. Sometimes ash from his cigarette fell on the turtle paperweight's back, and Mr Nakano roughly brushed it off with a corner of the black apron that he always wore.

Mr Nakano stayed at the shop until the early part of the afternoon, and from then on I usually minded it by myself. In the afternoons, Takeo and Mr Nakano went out on pickups.

Pickups were exactly what they sound like – they would

go to clients' homes to pick up goods that they had acquired to sell. The most common situation was when the head of a family had passed away and the household belongings were being disposed of. Mr Nakano's shop collected everything in bulk – be they items not regarded as mementos or keepsakes, or entire wardrobes. For the price of anything from a meagre few thousand to at most 10,000 yen, he acquired enough goods to fill his small truck. Clients usually called for a pickup because they figured that it was better to set aside the items they thought were worth something and get rid of the rest, rather than having to pay for it to be hauled away as oversized garbage. Most of them accepted the token amount without complaint and were happy to see Mr Nakano drive away with his truckload, but once in a while things got awkward when the client grumbled about the offer being too low, or so I heard from Takeo.

Takeo was hired to help with pickups only a short time before I started working there. When it seemed like a light load, Takeo would go out on a pickup by himself.

'What to do about the price?' Takeo asked with a hint of anxiety, the first time Mr Nakano ordered him to go out alone.

'You know what I mean – whatever you think is appropriate. You see how I do it, don't you, the way I decide how much to offer.'

Whether or not he had watched how Mr Nakano came up with his offers, at that time Takeo had only been working there part-time for a little more than three months. Mr Nakano seemed to me like the kind of person who said wild and random things, but when I saw what a surprisingly brisk business the shop seemed to be doing, I wondered if maybe it was because he simply inhabited this very recklessness. In any case, Takeo appeared quite nervous when he left, but by the time he returned he was back to his normal self.

'Was no big deal,' he said casually. Takeo said he had offered 3,500 yen for the pickup, to which Mr Nakano nodded repeatedly; however when he actually looked at the haul, his eyes grew wide.

'Takeo, you know, that was a steal. This is exactly the kind of thing that's scary about amateurs,' Mr Nakano said, laughing about it.

The haul included a jar that must have been worth 35,000 yen. At least that's what Takeo told me. Mr Nakano's shop didn't deal with those kinds of things, so he had sold the jar at an antique market that was held in the grounds of a local shrine. The girl Takeo was dating at the time had tagged along with him to the stall at the market, under the pretext of helping out. Apparently, once the girlfriend saw that such a dirty-looking jar could fetch a price like that, she had pressured Takeo incessantly – why not get into the second-hand business professionally himself? That way he would be able to leave home and get his own place. Whether or not it was because of that, Takeo broke up with the girl soon after.

It was unusual for the three of us – Mr Nakano, Takeo, and me – to eat together. Most of the time, Mr Nakano was running around buying things at markets or auctions, or else meeting with people, and Takeo went straight home after he finished with pickups; he never hung around. The three of us had gathered together that day because we were going to see an exhibition by Mr Nakano's older sister at a gallery.

Masayo was single and in her mid-fifties. Long ago the Nakano family had been one of the original landowners in this part of the city, and although their fortune was already considerably in decline by the time of Mr Nakano's parents' generation, apparently there was still enough left for Masayo to be able to live off the income from rented houses. 'Because she's an artist, you know.' There were times when Mr Nakano said things to make fun of his sister, but he certainly had nothing against her work as an artist. Masayo's one-woman show was being held at a tea shop called Posy that was by the train station and had a small gallery on the second floor. This time it was an exhibition of her doll creations.

I had heard about her previous exhibition, which had been held shortly before I was hired, a show of 'various wood-dyed items'. She had gathered leaves in a small forest that still stood on the edge of town, and had utilized these materials for dyeing fabric – Masayo used the word 'chic' to describe the colours this produced, but according to Takeo, shaking his head in puzzlement as he thought back on the exhibition, the colours reminded him of those found in the toilet. From the ceiling of the gallery, Masayo had hung the branches from which she had plucked the leaves for her creations, and they had fluttered in suspension. Perhaps because of the dangling branches and dyed pieces of cloth, the space felt like a labyrinth, and with every step, the fabric seemed to envelop your head and arms and hold you in place – that had been Mr Nakano's account.

This time, the dolls featured in the exhibition were not

hung from the ceiling, but instead appropriately arranged on tables lining the space, and placed under title cards such as DRAGONFLY AT NIGHT or STANDING IN THE GARDEN. Takeo made a quick and absent-minded pass through the exhibition, while Mr Nakano looked around, carefully picking up and turning over every doll. Daylight streamed through the window, and Masayo's cheeks were flushed in the heated room.

Mr Nakano bought the highest-priced doll there, and I bought a small cat from among the dolls that were heaped in a basket by the reception desk. Masayo waved goodbye from the top of the stairs, and the three of us went out onto the street.

'I'm going to the bank,' Mr Nakano said as he disappeared behind the automatic door of the bank in front of us.

'As usual,' Takeo said, thrusting both hands into the pockets of his baggy trousers and starting to walk.

That day Takeo was supposed to go on a pickup all the way out in Hachioji. Mr Nakano referred to the clients in Hachioji as 'the spinster sisters' – two elderly sisters who telephoned almost every day to complain about how no sooner had their eldest brother passed away than relatives upon whom they had never before set eyes started showing up, one after another, each of them trying to steal away the artworks or rare books or other such things that their brother had collected. 'Yes, well . . . Yes, this is a terrible loss,' Mr Nakano politely responded each time. He never once tried to cut short their phone calls.

'That's how it goes in this business,' Mr Nakano had said with a wink, after spending more than thirty minutes listening to them complain. Despite the fact that he seemed to pay such close attention to the spinster sisters' grievances, he made no attempt to go out to the old ladies' home for the pickup.

'All right for me to go alone?' Takeo asked, and Mr Nakano stroked his beard as he replied, 'You know what I mean – make sure your offer is at the lower end. The old ladies might be flabbergasted if the bid is too high, and if it's too low, well, then too.'

We reached the shop and opened the shutter, and while I was trying to arrange the goods on the bench like Mr Nakano always did in a way to lure customers, Takeo manoeuvred the two-ton truck out from the garage at the back. See you later, I called out, and Takeo revved the engine as he waved with his right hand. He was missing the part from the top knuckle to the tip of his little finger on his right hand. That was the hand that he waved to me with.

Apparently, during his interview with Takeo, Mr Nakano had asked, 'Does that mean you're one of them?' He was referring to the yakuza practice of finger shortening.

After Takeo had been working at the store for a little while, he said to Mr Nakano, 'Be pretty dangerous, wouldn't it, if I really were one of them.'

Mr Nakano laughed, 'When you work in this business, you tend to get a sense of what kind of person you're dealing with.'

Takeo's finger got caught in an iron door: that's how he lost it. A classmate had slammed his finger in the door; it seems he had bullied Takeo for all three years of secondary school, saying that the sight of Takeo 'made him want to puke'. Takeo dropped out six months before finishing secondary school. Because, he said, ever since the incident with the iron door, he felt like 'his life was in serious danger'. Neither his teachers nor his parents seemed to pay any attention. They pretended that Takeo dropping out was his own lifestyle choice or the result of a fundamental lack of self-discipline. Even so, Takeo claimed, 'Dropping out of school was lucky for me.' Meanwhile, he heard that the guy who had made him feel that his life was endangered had gone on to a private university and last year had got a job right away with a corporation.

'Aren't you angry?' I asked, but a look crept across Takeo's face – one corner of his mouth sort of curled up – as he replied, 'What difference does it make for me to be angry?'

'What difference?' I repeated, and Takeo chuckled to himself.

'Hitomi, you don't understand,' he replied. 'You like books, you have a complex mind. Me, I'm just simple.' That was how he put it.

'I'm simple too,' I said, and Takeo laughed again.

'In that case, you must be *really* simple then,' he said.

The tip of my little finger is smooth, Takeo explained. The doctor at the hospital told me I didn't have a predisposition for keloids, so it would be a perfectly clean scar.

After I watched Takeo drive away in the truck, I sat in the chair by the till and read a paperback. Over the course of an hour, three customers came in; one of them bought a pair of old glasses. I wondered why anyone wanted to buy glasses that weren't the right prescription, but it turned out that old glasses were a sleeper bestseller at Mr Nakano's shop.

'People buy things exactly because they're of no use,' Mr Nakano liked to say. Is that how it is? I said.

'Hitomi, do you like useful things?' Mr Nakano asked with a grin.

'Yes, I do,' I answered, and Mr Nakano snorted, before suddenly breaking into an odd little melody. '*Useful plates, useful shelves, useful men . . .*' He surprised me.

There was a lull after the customer who bought the old glasses left. Mr Nakano had yet to return from the bank. Seems like he's got a woman, Takeo had let slip sometime recently. When he says he's at the bank, I bet that usually means he's with a woman.

A few years before, Mr Nakano had got married for the third time. With his first wife, he had a son, who was a university student; with his second wife, he had a daughter, who was in primary school; and with his third wife, he had a six-month-old son. And now, he had yet another woman?

'Hitomi, do you have a boyfriend?' Mr Nakano had asked me. He hadn't seemed particularly curious about it. He had asked while he was standing by the till, drinking coffee, the same way he might comment on the weather. He pronounced 'boyfriend' in the kind of monotone that was current nowadays.

'I had one for a bit, but I don't have one now,' I answered, and Mr Nakano just nodded and said, I see. No further questions about what the guy had been like, or when we broke up, or anything else.

'How did you and your current wife meet?' I asked in reply.

'It's a secret,' he answered.

'Saying it's a secret will only make me keep asking, won't it?' I went on.

Mr Nakano just looked me straight in the face.

'Why are you staring at me like that?' I asked.

In a serene voice, Mr Nakano replied, 'Hitomi, there's no need for such banalities.'

He was right – I wasn't particularly curious about how Mr Nakano's romance with his wife began. The shopkeeper was inscrutable. Probably what makes women like him, Takeo whispered furtively in my ear later.

Mr Nakano wasn't back from the bank, Takeo had gone to Hachioji, there were no customers. With nothing else to do, I went back to reading my paperback.

Lately, there was a man who came in when I was tending the store on my own. He looked like he was about the same age as Mr Nakano or a little older. I had thought it was a coincidence that he always seemed to show up when I was alone, but apparently not. If he saw that Mr Nakano was there, he darted out of the shop. When Mr Nakano disappeared from sight, he rushed back inside.

That guy, does he come here a lot? Mr Nakano asked one day, to which I nodded. The next day, Mr Nakano had spent the whole afternoon rummaging around in the back storeroom. The man came by late in the day and was hovering about, between the front door and where I was sitting at the till; Mr Nakano was steadily observing him from the storeroom. Just as the man approached the till, Mr Nakano sprang forward with a beaming smile and struck up a conversation with him.

That was the first time I heard the man's voice. In the course of chatting with him for fifteen minutes, Mr Nakano found out that he lived in the next neighbourhood over, that his name was Tadokoro, and that he was a sword collector.

'I don't sell old things here, you know,' which seemed like a strange thing for Mr Nakano to say, since the sign outside read THRIFT SHOP.

'I see. But you have some interesting things, don't you?' Tadokoro pointed to a corner that displayed plastic Glico toys from the 1930s along with women's magazines.

Tadokoro was a bit of a charmer. He had thick stubble on his cheeks, and if he were a little thinner in the face, he might even have resembled a certain French actor whose name I can't remember. His voice had a slightly shrill quality that put me on edge, yet his manner of speaking was calm and composed.

A short time after Tadokoro left, Mr Nakano proclaimed, 'That guy won't come by here again for a while.' Even after such a friendly conversation, I murmured, and Mr Nakano shook his head. Why not? I asked, but Mr Nakano didn't answer. I'm just running out to the bank, he said as he left the shop.

Just as Mr Nakano predicted, Tadokoro didn't make an appearance for about two months. But from that point on, he again started showing up as if he intuited exactly when Mr Nakano wouldn't be there. When our eyes met, he would say, 'Hello,' and then when he left, he would call out, 'See you later.'

There wasn't much else to say to each other besides that, but whenever Tadokoro was in the shop, the air seemed to grow heavier. We had various regular customers, all of whom came in and went out uttering the same sort of greetings, and yet Tadokoro's presence was altogether different. Takeo had only met Tadokoro twice.

'What do you think of that customer?' I asked him.

Takeo thought about it for a moment and then finally, all he said was, 'Doesn't smell too bad.'

What do you mean, doesn't smell? When I asked him, Takeo just dropped his gaze and fell silent. While he was watering down the area in front of the shop, I thought about what he meant by smell. I thought maybe I understood, but then again, it was entirely possible that Takeo's idea of smell and my idea of smell were not at all similar.

Takeo finished watering and as he was carrying the empty bucket, on his way to the back, I heard him mutter, "Cause only a total idiot like me smells that bad.' But I really didn't know what he meant by 'an idiot like me'.

The next time Tadokoro showed up, I was reading a book because there was nothing else to do. The air in the store instantly grew dense. After a young couple who bought a crystal vase had left, Tadokoro came up beside the till.

'You're alone today?' he asked.

'That's right,' I answered cautiously. Even more than usual, the air around Tadokoro seemed to cloak him in heaviness. He talked for a while about the weather and about recent things in the news. It was the longest conversation I had ever had with him.

'Listen, there's something I want you to buy from me,' Tadokoro suddenly blurted out.

Customers often brought items that they wanted to sell directly to the shop, and if they were small, commonplace things, I could name a price and strike a deal. But for tableware or electrical appliances or geeky things like those plastic Glico toys, Mr Nakano was the only one who could decide the price.

'This here,' Tadokoro said as he held out a large brown kraft paper envelope.

'What is it?' I asked.

He set the envelope next to the till and said, 'First take a look.'

Now that I had been told to do so, I knew I wouldn't be able not to look. With this kind of thing, shouldn't the shopkeeper be the one . . . I tried to say, but Tadokoro was peering at me as if he were about to nestle up closer to the till. But you haven't even seen what kind of thing this is yet, have you? he said. Anyhow, take a look first. Okay?

Reluctantly I reached for the envelope. Inside there was a piece of cardboard the same size as the envelope. The cardboard fit within perfectly, so it was quite difficult to withdraw it. And I was conscious of the fact that Tadokoro was watching me closely, as the movement of my fingers grew more and more clumsy.

Once I was able to pull it out, I saw that there were two pieces of cardboard stacked together and fastened with tape. Something was sandwiched between them.

'Please open it and have a look,' Tadokoro urged in his usual calm and composed tone.

'But, it's taped . . .'

'It's all right,' he said. Somehow without my noticing, he now held in his hand a utility knife. He clicked out the blade and deftly slit open the tape that held it together. The utility knife seemed like an extension of his hand. It had been such a graceful gesture. I felt the slightest flutter in my stomach.

'See, look! You ought to learn something from this,' Tadokoro said enigmatically as he slit open the rest of the taped sides. I wondered whether he would also turn over the piece of cardboard, but he made no further motion. Slowly I reached out and spread open the cardboard pieces to reveal the monochrome photographs within.

They were of a man and a woman, naked and intertwined.

'What the hell are these?' This was Mr Nakano's initial response.

'Seem like some kind of old photos' was Takeo's impression.

Having been caught by surprise, I was struck dumb, still holding the cardboard, when Tadokoro called to me over his shoulder as he briskly walked out, 'I'll be back again. Decide on a price. See you.'

I had let out a gasp the moment I saw the photographs, and in the same instant I felt as though I were being drawn towards Tadokoro. I had the illusion that his slight frame was billowing outward.

Once Tadokoro had departed and I took another look, I saw that the composition of the photos was innocuous enough. The man and woman who were acting as models seemed to have a similar kind of air. There were ten photographs. I held each one as I studied it.

There was one photo in particular that I liked. It was taken in daylight, and the man and woman were clothed, their buttocks the only part of their skin exposed to the camera as they made love. In the background was an alley filled with small bars. Each bar had its shutter closed, with a large plastic bucket set out in front. It was in such a forlorn setting that the man and woman bared their fleshy buttocks and plump thighs.

'Do you like art, Hitomi?' Mr Nakano asked, his eyes widening when I pointed to this photograph. In his hand, he held another photo of the man and woman, completely naked, seated in front of a dressing table.

'I think I prefer classic ones like this,' he said. The woman sat on the man's lap with her eyes tightly shut, her hair perfectly coiffed.

'The man and woman aren't too pretty,' Takeo said, putting the photos back in order and setting them on the table after carefully examining all ten.

'What should we do with them?' I asked.

'I'll return them to Tadokoro,' Mr Nakano replied.

'You think you could sell them here?' Takeo asked.

'They don't really seem finished, do they?'

The conversation ended there, and Mr Nakano placed the photographs between the cardboard again and put them back in the envelope, which he set on top of a shelf in the back room.

For a while, the brown kraft paper envelope on top of the shelf weighed on my mind. It almost pained me to turn my head in that direction. Every time a customer came into the shop, I nervously checked to see if it was Tadokoro. Mr Nakano had said that he would return the photographs himself, but there the envelope remained, still left up on the shelf. No one even knew Tadokoro's exact address. In the meantime, the new year arrived.

Masayo came by the shop on the day after it snowed.

'Such tidy snow shovelling!' Masayo said in a cheerful voice. Masayo always sounded cheerful. When Takeo first started working here, the sound of her voice used to give him a start. He seemed to have grown accustomed to it now, but I was aware that he still kept his distance from her.

'Our dear Takeo is the one who did the shovelling, right?'

Takeo gave another little start when he heard her refer to him as 'our dear'. The previous day it had snowed more than twenty centimetres. Once it had started to accumulate, Takeo had taken care to shovel in front of the shop repeatedly, so that it was clear down to the asphalt. As usual, Mr Nakano had put out the bench and arranged the goods by the road which now glistened, black and wet.

'I love snow because it isn't sad,' Masayo chatted away. She had an unguarded way of speaking. Takeo and I listened to her without saying a word. While she was talking, people began to come in. Despite how much it had snowed, I knew there would be a lot of customers on a day like today. Three people bought space heaters, two more people bought *kotatsu* heaters, we sold two mattresses – even Masayo was enlisted to help with customers. By evening, when it finally slowed down enough for me to look outside, most of the snow that had been exposed to the sun had melted. There was no longer any distinction between the ground where Takeo had shovelled and where it had simply melted away.

'Shall we get some soba noodles?' Mr Nakano suggested. He closed the shop and we all filed into the tatami room in the back. There had been a *kotatsu* heater there but it had been sold only a little while ago and now, in place of the table with its inbuilt heater, just the *kotatsu* cover was laid flat on the tatami. Mr Nakano brought in a largish Japanese-style dining table from the shop and set it on top of the cover.

'Warm us up, huh,' Takeo said as he sat down on the cover.

'Eating together will warm us right up,' Masayo remarked, somewhat randomly.

Mr Nakano lit a cigarette while he phoned the soba restaurant. Still standing, he was tapping the ash into a chipped ashtray on top of the shelf.

Next thing I knew, I heard him shout, Look what I've done! I turned and saw Mr Nakano holding Tadokoro's brown kraft paper envelope, flapping and waving it around. He must have touched the tip of his cigarette to the envelope. A thin line of smoke had risen, but the shaking had extinguished whatever flame there had been. The edge of the envelope was charred black. Pulling out the cardboard to check, it seemed everything inside was unharmed.

'What is that? An art print or something?' Masayo asked. Without saying anything Mr Nakano handed her the cardboard. She opened it and gazed closely at the photographs.

'Are these for sale?' Masayo asked.

Mr Nakano shook his head. 'They're terrible, aren't they?'

Masayo nodded, somewhat delightedly. 'My work isn't quite as bad as these.'

Takeo and I exchanged glances. It was surprising that Masayo would have such objectivity towards her own artwork. Artists are inscrutable. And Masayo said even more inscrutable things than most.

'Were these photographs taken by Tadokoro, by any chance?'

What? Mr Nakano cried out loudly.

'Tadokoro was my form teacher in middle school, you know.'

Masayo said this quite calmly, and just then there was a rapping sound on the front shutter. Both Takeo and I started with surprise.

'It's the soba delivery,' Mr Nakano mumbled, and headed for the front with a cigarette between his lips. Takeo followed him, and Masayo and I were left in the back room. Masayo pulled out a cigarette from Mr Nakano's pack and, with her elbows propped on the table, lit it. The way Masayo held the cigarette in her mouth was exactly the same as Mr Nakano.

'Tadokoro looks quite young, but he must be almost seventy by now,' Masayo explained as she slurped from her bowl of soba noodles topped with tempura.

Tadokoro had been her form teacher during her third year of middle school. Though today he was still a bit of a charmer, back then – practically forty years ago – he had been 'movie-star handsome', according to Masayo. He wasn't an especially good teacher, but certain female students swarmed around him, like bees to honey. Among those who were drawn to Tadokoro, one girl in particular stood out – a classmate of Masayo's named Sumiko Kasuya. Rumour had it that the two of them had even been spending time together at a place that supposedly had a hot spring.

A place that had a hot spring, meaning what? Takeo asked, and Mr Nakano replied with a serious look on his face, She means a love hotel.

The rumours about Sumiko Kasuya and Tadokoro spread far enough that Sumiko dropped out of school and Tadokoro was dismissed. In order to put some distance between her and Tadokoro, Sumiko was sent away to the countryside to live with her grandmother, but she patiently awaited contact from Tadokoro, and a year later they eloped. After that, apparently she and Tadokoro wandered all over Japan together, and once the excitement about their affair died down, they came back to a neighbouring district where Tadokoro took over his family's stationery business.

'That's pretty daring.' Mr Nakano was the first to voice his opinion.

'Weren't playing around, were they?' Takeo chimed in next.

'But, how could you tell that they were Tadokoro's photographs?' I asked.

Masayo nibbled at the fried tempura batter which she had peeled off and set aside at first and murmured, You see . . . I like to eat the tempura batter by itself. It soaks up the broth well, and it's surprisingly delicious. She kept up this chatter as she picked up the fried coating with her chopsticks.

It seemed that, while he and Sumiko Kasuya were wandering all over the country together, Tadokoro made money by selling his photographs. Even after they eloped, there was no dearth of women for Tadokoro. It was through his connections with such women that he began taking erotic photos, and these sold well on the black market. Still, since he was just an amateur, the local thugs and yakuza were soon after him. Gradually it became too dangerous and he quit selling his pictures but – whether taking those kinds of photographs just suited him or it came naturally – after that he started using Sumiko Kasuya as his model and selling them at a price near cost, only to people he knew.

'The woman in those photos is Sumiko Kasuya,' Masayo said, gesturing with her chin at the cardboard package on top of the shelf. 'I have a print of one of these same photos.'

'Which one?' Mr Nakano asked.

'The one with the buttocks,' Masayo answered.

After that the four of us slurped our bowls of soba noodles without saying anything more. Takeo finished eating first and carried his bowl to the sink, and Mr Nakano stood up next. I followed Masayo's lead and scooped up the pieces of tempura batter that were floating in my broth.

'I like the one with the buttocks too,' I said, and Masayo laughed.

'That cost a pretty penny. But Sumiko was so broke, the least I could do was shell out ten thousand yen.'

I wouldn't pay even a thousand yen for all ten of them, Mr Nakano said breezily as he sat back down after putting his bowl in the sink. Takeo nodded in agreement, a deadpan expression on his face.

Mr Nakano and Takeo went into the garage to have a look at the truck, so I washed up the bowls alongside Masayo. While the water was running, I asked about what happened to Sumiko Kasuya afterwards. She died, Masayo answered. Tadokoro was a terrible womanizer, and they had a son who was killed in an accident when he was eighteen, so she ended up having some kind of nervous breakdown. Tadokoro isn't such a creep. But, Hitomi, don't let yourself be fooled by a guy like that.

Masayo scrubbed the bowls vigorously with the sponge.

I won't, I replied. I recalled that heavy feeling that Tadokoro seemed to carry around with him, and it wasn't quite fear I felt but a shiver went up my spine. Like the shiver one feels before catching a cold.

When Takeo and I left the shop together, I told him, 'Masayo says that Sumiko Kasuya is dead.'

'That so?' he said, rubbing his hands together.

Tadokoro did not come into the shop for a while, but then he unexpectedly appeared, two days after the next time it snowed.

'I've decided not to sell the photographs after all,' he said.

I held out the photos sandwiched in cardboard, and as Tadokoro brought his face in closer, he asked, 'What happened to the envelope?'

Takeo had just then returned from a pickup and had come back into the shop. 'I'll run right out to buy a new envelope,' he said, taking it upon himself.

Tadokoro swivelled in his direction. 'You need a rectangular #2 envelope,' he directed in his calm and composed tone as Takeo dashed off.

'Learn anything? From looking at the photos,' Tadokoro asked after Takeo had gone, once again drawing closer.

'You used to be a teacher, didn't you?'

I might have thought he would be surprised, but Tadokoro only moved in closer, completely unfazed.

'I did that for a spell,' he said, now so close I could almost feel his breath. The snow that was left in the shade was glittering outside.

Got a rectangular #2, Takeo said as he returned. Tadokoro,

ever calm and composed, moved away and slowly pulled the new envelope out of its cellophane wrapper before carefully sliding the cardboard inside.

'See you,' he said and left the shop.

Immediately afterwards, Mr Nakano came in, muttering, 'You know what I mean – Takeo, the price was too high today.' Takeo and I both found ourselves staring at Mr Nakano's beard.

'What is it?' Mr Nakano asked with a blank look.

Neither Takeo nor I replied, until a moment later, Takeo said, Didn't know that envelope was called a rectangular #2.

'Yeah?' Mr Nakano asked in response, but Takeo didn't say anything more. I remained silent, staring at Mr Nakano's beard.

Paperweight

Once the rainy season arrived, Mr Nakano had a bit more free time. The rain prevented the weekend vendors from setting up their stalls in the outdoor antique market, and because there were fewer house moves in the humid weather, there were also fewer pickups.

'Why so many good finds at the pickups when people move?' Takeo asked Mr Nakano as he drank from a can of coffee.

Mr Nakano pressed his cigarette butt through the opening of the now-empty can, his head slightly to one side. He had let the butt fall through only the top of the narrow hole, so the ash piled up as it burned down and was now on the verge of spilling over. Even when there was an ashtray right in front of him, Mr Nakano preferred to use anything else as a receptacle for his cigarette butts.

One time I asked Takeo furtively why Mr Nakano didn't use any of the ashtrays in the shop. Takeo replied, Must be he plans to sell them. Surprised, I said, But that ashtray isn't particularly old, it's just an ordinary freebie from somewhere. Takeo said impassively, Just shows that Mr Nakano is an avaricious businessman. Avaricious? That's a pretty old-fashioned word for a young guy to know, Takeo. C'mon, Hitomi, they say it all the time on *Mito Komon*. You watch period dramas like that? I asked. I like the actress Kaoru Yumi, he explained.

I chuckled at the idea of Takeo intently watching Kaoru Yumi on television. Now that I think about it, sometimes ad posters for mosquito coils displaying her photo come into Mr Nakano's shop. At one time they had been a bestseller, and the posters would sell within a week of arriving in the shop. But lately it seemed like the demand had run its course, and they didn't move as quickly.

'You know what I mean? When people move to a better place, they want better things for inside their home too,' Mr Nakano answered Takeo's question.

He added, 'That's why we get so many cheap-n-goodies.'

'Cheap-n-goodies,' Takeo parroted after him, and Mr Nakano nodded perfunctorily.

'So then, what happens when they move to a worse place?' Takeo continued.

'What do you mean by "a worse place"?' Mr Nakano asked, laughing. I laughed too. Takeo didn't crack a smile, his face solemn.

'Running away in the middle of the night, or the break-up of a family,' he offered.

'You know what I mean? In urgent situations like that, there's no time to request a pickup, is there?' Mr Nakano said as he stood up, brushing off the cigarette ash that had fallen on his black apron. Takeo said tersely, Right, and got up too.

It had been pouring with rain since the early part of the afternoon. The bench that always sat out at the front had been brought inside, making the shop feel cramped. Mr Nakano ran a feather duster over the items for sale.

These things are old, so you can't let them collect dust, Mr Nakano often said. Because they are old, they must be immaculate. But not too perfect. It's a fine line, a fine line, he would say, chuckling as he passed the duster over everything.

Takeo had gone out to throw his coffee can into the recycling bin next to the vending machine that was nearby. He had gone out without an umbrella. When he came back, he was soaking wet. Mr Nakano tossed him a towel. It had a frog pattern on it. They had got it from the last pickup. Takeo used it to rub his hair roughly, then hung the towel off a corner of the desk where the till was. The frogs turn a brighter green when they are wet. The strong smell of the rain wafted from Takeo's body.

Come to think of it, I hadn't seen Masayo around for a while.

What made me realize this was hearing Mr Nakano say her name while he was on the phone at the back of the store.

'Masayo has what?'

Really. You're kidding. Come on. Hard to imagine. Mr Nakano was continuing to interject these kinds of responses as he listened.

'I wonder what's going on with Masayo,' I said to Takeo, who was sitting idly on the bench, which was still inside the shop.

'Hmm,' Takeo replied. He was drinking another can of coffee.

You must like that kind of coffee. When I had said this to him previously, he had looked at me with surprise.

Do I like it? Takeo had repeated back to me. Because you're always drinking the same kind, aren't you? I had said. I never really thought about it, Takeo had replied. You pay attention to such odd things, Hitomi.

Even after we had this conversation, Takeo continued to drink the same brand of coffee. Just once I had gone so far as to try that brand, to see what it tasted like, but it was too sugary for me. Sweet, milky coffee. Takeo was lounging on the bench, sitting with his legs spread wide.

'See now, time for work!' Mr Nakano said, coming out from the back room. Takeo slowly stood up from the bench. He went outside, jangling the keys to the truck. As usual, he didn't take an umbrella. Mr Nakano sighed exaggeratedly as he watched Takeo's retreating back.

'What's the matter?' I asked. It seemed like Mr Nakano wanted me to ask him about it. Sighing deeply and muttering to himself was Mr Nakano's way of showing that he wanted to talk about something. Regardless of whether or not I asked him, eventually he would start talking, but I could do without the little lecture that always seemed to precede these chats.

At some point I had seen Takeo pre-empt Mr Nakano's lecture by asking him, 'Something happen?' and ever since, I had started doing the same. Once prodded, Mr Nakano would start talking, spouting forth like water from a hose. Not prompting him meant that only a strange sermon would sputter out, as if the end of the hose were packed with hardened soil or something.

'Well, you know.' It started to gush from Mr Nakano. 'Masayo has . . .'

'Your sister, Masayo?'

'It seems that Masayo has fallen for a man.'

'What?'

'And it appears that this man is shacked up with her.'

'You mean, he's her live-in?'

'Live-in, is that what you young people call it? It's like they're playing Sachiko and Ichiro.'

'What do you mean, Sachiko and Ichiro?'

'That is just what I can't stand about young people!'

The phone call had been from Michi Hashimoto, Mr Nakano and Masayo's aunt. Michi was the youngest sister of their father, who had passed away; she had married a young man who ran a sporting goods shop in their home town. Of course, this was all long ago – that young man had now retired and his son, who was the same age as Mr Nakano, had taken over the shop.

A few days ago, Mr Nakano said, Aunt Michi had paid a visit to Masayo's house, bringing some cakes from the Posy tea shop as a present. The cakes from Posy were not particularly remarkable or even very tasty, but Michi always chose to patronize old local shops.

'Tradition is important,' Michi had once said to Mr Nakano. He had nodded his head at her in agreement, but later had said to me with a laugh, 'In those high-street shops, nobody gives a damn about tradition.'

Aunt Michi had bought two pieces of cheesecake from

Posy and called on Masayo. She rang the doorbell, but there was no answer. Thinking that Masayo must not be home, Michi tried the doorknob and found it unlocked. The door swung easily inwards. Concerned that there might be a burglar inside, she checked for signs. She heard a faint noise. She thought she might have imagined it, but then she heard it again. It didn't sound like a person's voice. Nor was it music. It was a muffled, heavy sound. As if one or two people or things were slowly moving about in the next room.

Michi braced herself, in case it really was a burglar. From her handbag, she took out a bell that she carried to ward off gropers, ready to ring it loudly if necessary.

'Imagine – an old lady carrying a bell to ward off gropers!' Mr Nakano stopped to mutter in the middle of his explanation.

'There have been a number of disturbing incidents lately,' I replied, and Mr Nakano just shook his head.

'You know what I mean? So then, what is she doing, going into such a dangerous situation? If she thought there was a burglar, why didn't she just run off, eh?' he said, letting out a deep sigh.

And if Aunt Michi had run off, she never would have discovered the 'man' at Masayo's, Mr Nakano seemed to be implying.

Michi had been standing for a moment inside the front door, when she began to hear some kind of moaning.

'Moaning?'

'You know what I mean . . . Masayo . . . and that . . . man,' Mr Nakano said with vexation as he continued to swish around the duster.

'You mean they were doing it?'

'Hitomi, a young woman shouldn't ask things so bluntly.'

Mr Nakano let out another sigh, seemingly oblivious to the fact that he was the one who had started such a blunt conversation, which had led to such a blunt question.

Sliding open the paper door, Aunt Michi barged into the room. Masayo sat facing an unfamiliar man. In between them, there was a cat.

'They weren't doing it. At least not at that moment. It was the cat.' The moaning sounds had come from the cat.

'Isn't that better, that it was the cat?'

'Yes, good thing it was the cat. If Aunt Michi had caught them in the act, it would have been quite a scene,' Mr Nakano said, as if Masayo had committed a crime.

'But, since Masayo is single, she can have someone over whenever she wants, can't she?' I said.

Mr Nakano frowned. 'There is such a thing as appearances.'

'I see.'

'It's not easy, when so many relatives live around here too.'

'But is this man really, I mean, as you say, does he have a relationship with Masayo?'

'I don't know for sure.'

Here Mr Nakano's story grew vague. Aunt Michi had pressed Masayo for answers, he said, but Masayo had been nonchalant, remaining perfectly tight-lipped when asked who this man was, or what she was doing with him. Michi had even questioned the man, but she got nothing more than evasive responses from him too.

Finally, he said, Michi had practically thrown the box of

cakes from Posy at the two of them and left. And I was looking forward to eating them with her, Aunt Michi had apparently fumed over the telephone. She had then dispensed a vehement lecture to Mr Nakano who, as the only brother, she said, had better keep a closer eye on his older sister.

'It's because she only bought two pieces of cake. With stingy little pieces like that, she should have got ten – or twenty even.'

'Even so . . .'

'You know what I mean? Masayo's a woman in her mid-fifties, there's really nothing to see to about her, is there?' Mr Nakano furrowed his brow again. 'What is to be done about it, Hitomi?'

I wanted to tell him that it was none of my business – not in the least – but I couldn't say so, certainly not to my employer. I liked my job. And Mr Nakano wasn't a bad boss. The hourly wage wasn't much, but it was consistent with the amount of effort required.

'You know, Masayo is fond of you, Hitomi.'

What? I asked in reply. I had never once heard anything to the effect that Masayo felt any particular fondness for me, nor had I ever got that impression from her.

'Do you think you could . . . pay a visit to Masayo's?'

What? I asked in reply, my voice rising.

'See what this man is like,' Mr Nakano said with forced casualness.

'You're asking me to?'

'There's no one else I can rely on.'

'But . . .'

'My wife, you know, she and Masayo don't get on well.'

All you have to do is just check out the scene. I'll even pay you overtime. Mr Nakano put his hands together, as if he were praying. What do you mean by overtime, I asked, and Mr Nakano winked at me. Just don't tell Takeo or my sis, he said as he opened the till, pulled out a 5,000-yen note, and thrust it into my hand. I can't do anything, you know. I'm just going to go over there, I said as I hurriedly stashed the 5,000-yen note in my wallet.

That evening, at the convenience store where I stopped on my way home from Mr Nakano's shop, aside from the chicken bento that was usually my only purchase, I added two cans of beer to my basket. I also threw in a packet of Cheechiku – short tubes of fish paste *chikuwa* stuffed with cheese – along with a packet of 'mayo-flavoured' fried squid snacks. After wavering, I added two cans of *chuhai* as well. And an eclair and a carton of vegetable juice. When I finally made it to the till – not before grabbing a weekly manga magazine – the total came to just over 3,000 yen.

You know what they say, I murmured as I walked along the street that night. Easy money. The cans of *chuhai* and beer clinked against each other in the bag from the convenience store, making a metallic noise. I sat down on a bench in a park along the way, took out one of the beers, and started drinking it. I tore open the packet of Cheechiku, but only ate three of them. The bench was damp from the rain that had kept up until the afternoon. If Takeo were here now, I could share my beer with him, I thought fleetingly, but then I quickly changed my mind. He would annoy me if he were really here.

The dampness had soaked through my jeans, so although I was still drinking my beer, I stood up. I sipped the beer as

I walked along. I decided that I would pay a visit to Masayo's house tomorrow, in the morning. The moon was high in the sky, enveloped in mist. It was a thin crescent moon.

Come to think of it, Masayo's eyebrows resemble crescent moons.

Masayo hardly wore any make-up, just a bit of lipstick, but she was always glowing. There is that phrase, doll-faced, which is exactly what her features called to mind, her eyes and nose perfectly placed in her oval face. No doubt she was very beautiful in her youth. Mr Nakano's and Masayo's features resembled each other's closely, but his face was more angular and tanned, so that if Masayo's face were carved from porcelain, his seemed etched in brown sugar soap, perhaps.

On Masayo's mostly unmade-up visage, only her eyebrows were perfectly groomed. They were thinly drawn gentle curves, like in a poster of a Taisho-era beauty from the early part of the twentieth century. Masayo had once told me that she used tweezers, arranging her eyebrows one hair at a time.

'At my age, I'm long-sighted, so sometimes my aim goes astray,' Masayo had laughed. 'But having plucked my brows all these years, I hardly have any left.'

Listening to Masayo, my hand had instinctively touched my own brows. I hardly groomed them at all, so they sprouted above my eyes, thick and untamed.

I rang the doorbell, and Masayo soon appeared.

Above the shoe cupboard by the front door, there was a pair of dolls, a tall and spindly man and woman, which had been on display at the exhibition of her doll creations six months ago. Stepping into the slippers that were laid out, I followed Masayo. After much deliberation, I had bought four pastries from Posy to bring with me. When I handed them to her after we had entered one of her rooms, Masayo giggled, covering her mouth with her palm.

'Haruo must have sent you,' she said.

Yes, I answered.

'How much of a bonus did he pay you?' she pressed me.

N-no, it's not . . . I faltered, and Masayo raised those crescent-moon eyebrows at me.

'Haruo doesn't want to stir up a hornets' nest, that's why he won't come himself,' she said. 'Hmm, 5,000 yen, I bet. He can be cheap,' Masayo guessed, poking her fork into the lemon pie from Posy.

Before I knew it, I had told her all about the 'extra over-time pay' from Mr Nakano. Although it may be disingenuous to say that I didn't realize I was spilling the story; I think I had the subtle intention of wanting to see the expression on Masayo's face when I confirmed the amount – I still couldn't figure out if it was too much or too little.

'I'm sorry,' I said, casting my gaze downward as I picked at my cherry pie.

'Hitomi, you must like pie.'

'Excuse me?'

See here – cherry pie, lemon pie, millefeuille, and apple pie. Like a bird singing, Masayo cheerily recited the different pastries I had brought from Posy. Then she stood up, opened the cupboard that was beneath the telephone, and took out a wallet.

'Make up whatever you want to tell him,' she said, as she

wrapped a 10,000-yen note in a tissue and placed it beside my plate of cherry pie.

'That's not . . . I don't need that,' I said, pushing back the tissue, but this time Masayo stuffed it into my pocket. The tissue had bunched up, and the top half of the note was exposed.

'Keep it. Haruo thinks everything should stay the way he likes it.'

Have the apple pie too, if you like, Masayo encouraged, as she tapped my pocket twice. The tissue swayed gently. The nerve of him, I wish he would leave me alone, a woman well past fifty. Masayo muttered to herself, in the same manner as Mr Nakano, as she busied herself with the rest of her lemon pie. I too applied myself to my cherry pie. When Masayo had finished the lemon pie, she immediately moved on to the millefeuille.

While she ate her millefeuille, Masayo began telling me about the man. His last name was Maruyama. Just as Mr Nakano spouted like water from a hose, once Masayo started talking, her torrent of words gushed at full blast.

I dated Maruyama a long time ago, you see, but I broke up with him, Masayo explained brightly. After that, he married Keiko, the rice dealer's daughter from the next neighbourhood over, and they set up house, but just recently they got divorced. I wonder if it was one of those divorces that happen after the man retires. Apparently Keiko served him with a letter of divorce, and he simply agreed to it. It seems that Keiko was a bit taken by surprise. I don't think she expected Maruyama to give her a divorce so easily.

Masayo's words flowed ceaselessly. Judging from the

photo she showed me, Mr Maruyama was a man of average height and medium build with drooping eyes. He and Masayo stood next to each other in front of a shrine. That's Hakone Shrine, Masayo said in an excited voice. We bought some Hakone mosaic woodwork on that trip too.

From the interior room, Masayo brought out a *yosegi* puzzle box. I see, it's beautiful, I said, and Masayo smiled, lowering the tips of her eyebrows. Traditional things are nice, aren't they? Isn't it beautiful? I nodded ambiguously. The Nakanos certainly liked things with tradition.

Please save the pastry for Mr Maruyama, I said, sliding back the apple pie that Masayo had placed before me. Really? Masayo said as she carefully put it back into the box. Then she covertly ran her fingers over the Hakone puzzle box.

'What should I tell Mr Nakano?' I turned to ask Takeo.

'Whatever you see fit,' he replied, sipping his lemon sour. With the 10,000 yen I got from Masayo, I had ended up going out drinking with Takeo.

Even with a little booze in him, Takeo still didn't say much. Do you ever watch movies? What video games do you like? Mr Nakano's shop is a good place to work, isn't it? This liver *sashimi* is pretty good, don't you think? I dropped questions, one by one.

Not much. The usual. Yeah, it is. That was about all I could get out of him. Yet I could tell that he didn't really mind, because from time to time he would look up and our eyes would meet.

'Masayo seemed as if she was on cloud nine, for some reason.'

'Why wouldn't she be, she's got a man,' Takeo said unemotionally.

I couldn't help but blurt out, 'Takeo, whatever happened with your girlfriend?'

'Nothing happened.'

Been without a girlfriend for four months, Takeo said, taking another sip of his lemon sour. Been without a boyfriend for two years, two months, and eighteen days, I retorted. What are you talking about, eighteen days? Takeo gave a slight laugh. There was something about the way Takeo laughed that made him seem more callous than when he didn't.

He's heavy, Masayo had said. Maruyama is heavier than he appears. She murmured as her fingers stroked her souvenir from Hakone. By heavy, do you mean his weight? I asked. Masayo seemed to raise her crescent-moon shaped brows as she stifled a laugh and replied, Hmm, well, I guess you could say that.

Seeing Takeo's callous expression had reminded me of the sound of Masayo's stifled laughter. As if from deep within her throat – how should I describe it? Yes, there was something obscure about it. Subtle. A mysterious sound.

'Takeo, do you think you'll keep working at Mr Nakano's shop?'

'Who knows.'

'Mr Nakano is a strange guy, isn't he?'

'Hmm, guess he is.' Takeo had a slightly faraway look in his eyes. Then he touched his left little finger with his right hand. Takeo's right little finger, with its missing first joint, was stroking the intact tip of his left little finger. I watched this movement for a moment, then asked if I could touch it, and he let me feel the tip of his damaged right little finger.

While I did this, with his left hand Takeo lifted his glass mug and, tilting his head back, he drank down what was left of his lemon sour.

'A paperweight, she said,' I said, as I let go of Takeo's little finger.

'A paperweight?'

Maruyama was like a paperweight. That's what Masayo said. Don't you think so, Hitomi? When a man is on top, don't you ever feel like paper being held down by a paperweight?

By paperweight, do you mean like the thing that comes with a calligraphy set? I asked in response, and Masayo furrowed her brows. This is why I can't stand young people! They've barely ever used a paperweight! I'm not talking about calligraphy paper – this is something that's used to hold ordinary things down, Masayo said, poking her fork at the slivers of millefeuille scattered on her plate.

There are paperweights in Mr Nakano's shop. That's right. Paperweights are very practical. I use one to hold down papers in the box where I keep receipts. Otherwise, when the receipts pile up, they'll go flying out of the box and all over the place. That's why I hold them down with a paperweight, you see.

As Masayo said this to me, I recalled the times when I myself had felt like a flimsy piece of paper, being held firmly in place by a paperweight.

'I wonder if you're heavy, Takeo.' I seemed to be getting drunker. Seeing as I was the one who had asked that question.

'Want to give it a go?'

'No, not right now,' I said.

'Anytime you want to try, fine with me.'

Takeo's eyes looked drowsy too. He didn't seem like he

was very heavy. Mr Nakano too, he seemed pretty light. That night, I had spent almost 6,000 yen. Both Takeo and I were totally wasted, and on the way home we kissed twice. The first time was just before we reached the park, our lips brushed against one another's; the second time was next to a shrubbery in the park, and when I tried to use my tongue, Takeo seemed to draw back slightly.

'Uh, sorry,' I said, and Takeo replied, 'No problem,' as he dutifully stuck his tongue in my mouth. He said it as he was doing it, though, so it sounded like, 'Ro robrem.'

What does that mean, no problem? I started laughing, so Takeo laughed too, and sadly, we stopped kissing. Bye-bye, I said and waved my hand. Instead of 'Thanks,' his usual parting words, he replied in turn, repeating my 'Bye-bye.' But there was something terribly unconvincing about Takeo's version of 'Bye-bye.'

Masayo was by herself. The man wasn't there. At least not when I visited, I reported back to Mr Nakano. Hmm, that's very good, he said. Takeo was carrying the bench outside the shop.

It had been a long time since the weather was fair. Mr Nakano expertly arranged the usual task lamps, typewriters, and paperweights on top of the bench.

'Ah, the paperweights,' I murmured, and Takeo cast a glance in my direction.

'There're the paperweights,' Takeo echoed quietly.

'What, is "paperweight" some kind of password between the two of you?' Mr Nakano cut in.

'Not really,' Takeo said.

'Not really,' I echoed.

Mr Nakano shook his head and turned towards the back of the shop, where they kept the truck. There were supposed to be three pickups that day. Takeo, he called out. Takeo quickly followed him.

Perhaps because of the fine weather, there were customers coming and going all day long. On a typical day, most customers just came in to browse and then left, but today there were several who approached the till to make a purchase. Whether it was a small dish or a second-hand T-shirt – small price-tag items, all of them – the *ka-ching* of the till rang out incessantly throughout the day. It got dark during the rush, and yet the flow of customers did not ebb. Even when the usual closing time of seven o'clock came around, people who seemed to be on their way home from work continued to trickle into the shop. By eight o'clock, Mr Nakano and Takeo had finished the last pickup and returned, but there were still two customers in the shop, so I had pulled the shutter only half-closed.

'We're back,' Mr Nakano said as he came in. Takeo followed him in silence.

Hearing the sound of the shutter, one of the customers left, and the other one brought his purchase to the till.

The customer had an ashtray and a paperweight; it was the ashtray that Mr Nakano always made sure not to use, a typical freebie from somewhere.

'Mr Nakano, how much is this?' I asked, looking from the ashtray to Mr Nakano. He came over to the till.

'I can see, sir, from the fact that you have selected that paperweight, you have a good eye,' Mr Nakano laid it on chattily. Is that right? the customer responded, not without a certain satisfaction.

'As for the ashtray, five hundred – no, you can have it for four hundred and fifty yen,' Mr Nakano went on smoothly.

With no expression on his face, Takeo was stacking the miscellaneous cardboard boxes stuffed with assorted items acquired from the pickups near the entrance to the shop.

After the customer left, Mr Nakano rattled the shutter all the way closed. I'm starving, he said. So am I, Takeo replied. I'm hungry too, I added last. How about three bowls of *katsudon*? Mr Nakano said as he reached for the telephone receiver.

While we were eating the pork cutlets over bowls of rice, Mr Nakano asked us about the paperweights, but both Takeo and I feigned ignorance. The smell of sweat rose from both Mr Nakano and Takeo. After Takeo finished eating his *katsudon*, he suddenly burst into laughter. Hey, what are you laughing about? Mr Nakano wanted to know. Takeo managed to say, 'The ashtray,' before breaking into peals of laughter again. Annoyed, Mr Nakano stood up and started rinsing the dishes.

On a shelf next to the cardboard boxes that Takeo had stacked up earlier, the turtle paperweight – the one that was always displayed as a pair with the rabbit paperweight that the customer had bought – was left all by itself. The steady sound of the water that Mr Nakano was running echoed through the darkened shop, while Takeo just kept on laughing.

Bus

'I'll be damned – there are tickets for two here,' Mr Nakano said as he pulled a pair of airline tickets from a registered mail envelope. The opening of the envelope was torn to shreds. On the whole Mr Nakano tended to handle things a bit roughly, despite the fact that being the owner of a thrift shop requires a certain degree of carefulness.

'Tamotsu Konishi's father-in-law died,' Mr Nakano went on.

I see, Takeo said, nodding in the perfunctory way he always did. I see, I had also replied, our voices in unison. This was the first I had heard of Tamotsu Konishi.

'Tamo has always seemed like he was brought up well, come to think of it. Exactly the kind who would send airline tickets for two.' Mr Nakano was deeply impressed.

'He wants me to come all the way to Hokkaido. This coming weekend. It would be for work, in theory. For a pickup, or more likely, a valuation,' Mr Nakano explained, his eyes opening wide as he held the airline tickets – two round trips, four sheets total – lightly between his fingers. First he looked at Takeo. Then his gaze shifted in my direction.

Professional valuations – is that something you do, Mr Nakano? I asked. Mr Nakano shook his head slightly. Not really. I don't have much of an eye for it.

'Why would Tamo have asked me to do a valuation?' Mr Nakano grumbled, as he spat into a tissue. My lungs, these days, they're not so much. This had become a refrain of his lately. Takeo and Hitomi, you both should be glad you don't smoke. As for me, I could quit whenever I want to, but . . . I want to honour my right not to quit, or something. That's what it's like at my age.

Whether or not Takeo was listening to what Mr Nakano was saying, he took the keys to the truck and went straight out the back.

Who is Mr Konishi? I felt obliged to enquire.

'A friend from secondary school.'

I see, I said, nodding again. I had a hard time imagining Mr Nakano in secondary school. Had he worn a school uniform with a stand-up collar? Had he and this buddy of his walked home together while bolting down croquette sandwiches or some other snack? Had the whites of his eyes been clear – maybe even bluish – rather than cloudy, like they were now?

'That Tamo, never without a woman, even back then,' Mr Nakano said with a gentle inhalation. Then he spat into the tissue again.

'He played the field quite a bit, then married a rich girl and ended up living with her family up in Hokkaido.'

I see, I said, nodding for the third time.

'And she's quite a looker too.'

I gave up on nodding along and looked him straight in the face. Mr Nakano seemed as though he was about to say something else, but I began to turn the pages of the notebook we kept for the shop, and he got up. Takeo, Mr Nakano called out as he headed towards the back. The two of them were going for a pickup.

This pickup was at the home of an acquaintance of Masayo's. They were long-time landowners, so there were sure to be some good finds, Masayo had said, but Mr Nakano had replied, as he slowly made his preparations, 'With landowners' homes, it can be either very good or very bad, you know.'

At the sound of Mr Nakano and Takeo pulling away in the truck, I let out a sigh for no particular reason. Takeo and I had plans to go out that night. I had been the one to invite him.

'Been a long time since I had a date,' Takeo said as he took a seat. Takeo had chosen to meet at this cafe, which seemed as if it had been around for more than thirty years.

'The guy who painted the murals on the walls, what's his name again?'

'Seiji Togo.'

'There's something nostalgic about them, isn't there?'

'I don't know much about them.'

'But you know his name, don't you?'

'Sorry, was just by chance.'

'You don't have to apologize to me.'

'Is a habit, sorry.'

'There you go again.'

'Right.'

When Takeo had returned to the shop earlier that evening, the back of his T-shirt had been soaked through with sweat, but as he sat before me, a faint scent of soap wafted from his body.

'Do you not hear from your ex-girlfriend any more?'

'Sorry, not at all,' Takeo said flatly.

'There you go again.'

'Right.'

Takeo ordered black tea. With lemon. As he spoke, he bowed his head slightly at the lady who ran the cafe. Either he bowed his head, or he tucked in his chin. There was always something awkward about Takeo's movements.

'Do you come here a lot?'

'It's cheap, and not too crowded.'

I gave a little laugh. Takeo laughed too. He may be awkward, but then again, I'm awkward too. Do you want to get something to eat? Takeo asked. Sure, I replied.

We went to a yakitori restaurant, where we ate salted liver, wing tips, and *tsukune* meatballs. Something called 'crispy vinegared chicken skin' was on the menu, so I ordered it, and when I did so, Takeo murmured, 'Vinegared?'

'Do you not like pickled things?' I asked.

'I used to have to drink vinegar every day,' Takeo replied.

Who made you? My ex-girlfriend. Why? She said it worked.

That's strange – what did it work for? I asked with a laugh, but Takeo didn't respond.

At the end of the meal, Takeo ordered a bowl of rice,

and I watched as he polished it off with the crispy vinegared chicken skin and some pickles. I nursed what was left of my lemon sour. I invited you so it's my treat, I said, but Takeo immediately stood up and walked to the till with the bill in hand. At first his steps were light, but when he reached the till he stumbled, even though there didn't appear to be anything there to stumble over. I pretended not to see.

Once we left the restaurant, I said, 'That was like a real date.' Takeo knit his brows together as he parroted, 'A real date?'

The night was still young, and the club barkers in their black suits were chattering away, shoulder to shoulder in the street. Should we get another drink? Takeo asked, and I nodded. We went into a seedy-looking bar that was off the main drag, where Takeo ordered the cheapest bourbon with soda, and I drank a pina colada. I had asked for a white drink, and that was what had arrived.

We each had two drinks, and then we left. While we were walking, Takeo took my hand. We walked along, awkwardly, hand in hand. When we neared the station, Takeo let go of my hand. See ya, he said, and went into the station. I saw him off at the ticket barrier, but he didn't turn around, not even once. I was still hungry, so I stopped at a convenience store and bought a pudding. When I got back to my apartment, the light was blinking on my answering machine. The message was from Takeo. 'Sorry, that was fun,' was all that he said.

There was no modulation in his voice. In the background I could hear the station announcements. While I listened to the recording, I tore the lid off the pudding and ate it little by little. I rewound the message three times, listening to the sound of Takeo's voice. And then, I carefully pressed the erase button.

*

Mr Nakano left for Hokkaido at the weekend.

'Takeo, do you want to come along with me?' Mr Nakano had asked, but Takeo declined.

It's a free trip to Hokkaido – why wouldn't you go? I asked Takeo furtively afterwards. He fixed his gaze on me and said, 'I'm afraid of aeroplanes.'

You're joking? I laughed, but Takeo continued to stare fixedly at me.

'Also bet Mr Nakano would most likely ask me to pay for my own hotel, and maybe even a bit of the airfare too.'

He wouldn't do that! But even as I said those words, I had to admit that Mr Nakano might do just such a thing, and I admired Takeo's foresight.

Unaware of our speculations, Mr Nakano left for Haneda airport early on Friday morning. Presumably he had already been refunded for the extra airline ticket. He told us that he planned to meet up in Hokkaido with a colleague in the business, and the two of them would arrive at Tamotsu Konishi's house as if they had travelled there together from Tokyo.

'That's pretty tight-fisted, Mr Nakano.'

'Hitomi, you should appreciate the fact that I am so honest with you,' he replied. I would never understand him.

The ticket that Tamotsu Konishi sent had an open return.

'Only God knows when I'll be back,' Mr Nakano had crowed, and Masayo, who had arrived at the shop just as he was leaving, let out a laugh.

'We don't get many customers, so I might just retire and

leave the whole shop up to Hitomi and Takeo,' Mr Nakano went on.

'In that case, I'll take over,' Masayo declared breezily.

'Sis, we'd go bankrupt in no time with you running the shop – such as it is.'

'"Such as it is?" – it doesn't sound like you think much of your own shop.'

'You know what I mean. This place is built on my miraculous flair for business – in spite of it being such as it is.'

As brother and sister, they were quite a pair. In any case, Mr Nakano set off on his trip. Masayo came every day to check the safe. Inside the safe were the proceeds from the day's sales and the receipt book, along with an amulet from the Toyokawa Inari temple. Masayo had bought the amulet; it was supposed to bring prosperity in business. Hang it from the lintel, Masayo had said, but Mr Nakano firmly refused to put the amulet anywhere in plain sight. I mean, come on – I grew up listening to Janis Joplin! Mr Nakano had once said to Takeo, with a sidelong glance at the amulet, which he now kept in the safe. Takeo had replied, I see, with the same expressionless look as always.

On the third day after Mr Nakano left on his trip, a postcard arrived. It was addressed to Nakano & Co.

'Is the name of this shop Nakano and Co.?' I asked.

Masayo shook her head. 'I've never heard it called that before now,' she replied.

Masayo read the postcard first, then passed it to me. After

I read it I passed it to Takeo, who stared at the postcard as if his eyes were glued to it.

> *Just a quick note. I'm here in Sapporo. I ate some ramen. I also ate some Genghis Khan barbecue.*
>
> *Unfortunately something came up with Ishii, and I'm stuck in Sapporo until the day after tomorrow. Hokkaido is vast, but it's spread out like a big-boned woman.*
>
> *Cheers to everyone. Haruo Nakano*

Takeo read the contents of the postcard in a low voice. Guess Ishii must be the colleague in Hokkaido who was supposed to travel with him, Takeo said, his head tilting to one side.

Just then, we happened to be in the midst of eating ramen ourselves. Masayo had made *tanmen* for us. It was filled with bean sprouts, garlic chives, and bamboo shoots. There had been hardly any customers. If you're busy, Hitomi, I can mind the shop, Masayo said occasionally. No, it's okay, I'm fine, I replied. Masayo would smoke one or two cigarettes and then go back home.

At eleven o'clock, when I opened the shop, and again around seven, when we closed, Masayo always showed up. She was much more punctual than Mr Nakano, and more importantly, whenever she was minding the till, things sold very well.

'There must be something about me that puts people at ease,' Masayo said.

Exactly one week had passed since I went on something like 'a real date' with Takeo. During that time, I had sent two emails and phoned him once in the evening. Takeo's email reply – both times – was 'I'm fine. Hope you are too.' As for the phone call, it was difficult to keep the conversation going for even five minutes, so I hung up soon after.

'How does one go about having a carefree conversation with a boy?' I decided to ask Masayo one afternoon when Takeo wasn't around. Masayo was in the process of going over the receipt book, but she looked up and thought about it for a moment.

'If you can get them into bed, they tend to relax a bit.'

I see, I said in response.

'You know, it's amazing this shop doesn't go under,' Masayo said with awe. Then she snapped the notebook closed. Maybe Haruo really doesn't plan on coming home, Masayo said, stifling a laugh. Business is getting worse and worse, and that woman is bleeding him dry.

What, is that true? I asked. Masayo narrowed her eyes. She's a strong-minded woman. But he always goes for that type. She shrugged as she said this. I wonder why that kid only ever falls for exactly the same kind of woman. It's ridiculous.

I didn't know whether by 'woman' she was referring to Mr Nakano's wife (his third) or perhaps to yet another mistress. I was too embarrassed to question Masayo about it. And when it came to having sex with Takeo, I had a hard time imagining it. Maybe I should rearrange things? I said as I went outside and changed the position of a lampshade and an ashtray that were placed oddly on the bench. The rainy season had not yet ended, but there had been a string of hot days that felt like summer, and the blazing sunlight was glinting off the ashtray.

*

Just a quick note. The valuation went well. Ishii has a way with words and he saved the day.

Tamotsu and I are going to travel together for a few days. Despite the fact that he lives in Hokkaido, he can't drive, so we have to get around by bus. We could take the train, but there are fewer transfers on the bus.

It takes about two hours to go from one town to the next, so if I have to pee along the way, I'm out of luck.

Tonight we're staying at a hot spring spa that faces the sea along the main road. We had planned to get off at the last stop, but Tamotsu suddenly suggested that we stay here. There are no other places to stay around here besides the inn – no town, no shops, no seaside homes – nothing.

I was hoping we could go to the cave at the tip of the cape, where they say there are white crabs (they're white because they don't get any sun), but Tamotsu was afraid. Tamotsu may be bald and fat, but he still gets the women.

Cheers to everyone. Haruo Nakano

Takeo slowly read the postcard out loud. It was a hot day. When it first gets hot, I always feel like the heat might drive me mad, but once that passes, I get used to it again and it doesn't bother me – why is that, I wonder?

'Want some ice cream?' Takeo asked.

Sometimes, when Takeo and I were alone together in the shop, he would speak to me familiarly, without his idiosyncratic stiffness. Sure, I said, and Takeo ran over to the convenience store across the street. He came back with cola-flavoured ice cream. This acceptable to you? he asked, reverting to his peculiar form of polite speech as he handed it to me.

'Mr Nakano is a good correspondent,' I said, and Takeo nodded. His mouth was filled with ice cream, so he couldn't reply.

Takeo had just returned from a pickup at the house of a family who were planning to move. Nobody had died, they were simply moving, so there wasn't that much stuff. Takeo had not paid anything for doing the pickup. There were two cardboard boxes filled with odds and ends. The moment he had brought them into the shop and set them down on the floor, an old sweet tin rolled out of the larger box. The tin was light green and had a pretty design. I tried to open the lid but it was tightly rusted shut and wouldn't budge.

Takeo deftly took it from my hands. With a little grunt, he gave it a jerk and the lid came off easily. Inside, it was chock-a-block with monster-shaped erasers and suchlike.

'Hey!' Takeo said.

'What?'

'These might actually be worth something.'

The garish yellow and red and orange of the monsters wasn't faded at all. It's great that you got these for free, I said, and Takeo nodded lightly. Glad I didn't know about them. Would feel funny about it if I had.

Glad I didn't know about them. Takeo's words echoed vaguely in my mind. Takeo, do you want to have dinner together again? I asked without really giving it much thought. Yeah, sure, he replied on the spot. Then you should come to my place, I continued. Tonight, even. Yes, I will be there tonight. Takeo again reverted to stiffness. I chewed on the stick from my ice cream. It tasted of wood mingled with a sweet liquid.

*

It was just before the shop's closing time when I realized that my place was a total mess. Takeo had already gone for the day. Once he finished his duties, he always left in a hurry. As soon as Masayo arrived, I rushed out of the shop.

Back home, I shoved my discarded clothes and CDs and magazines onto the bottom shelf of the cupboard, ran the vacuum cleaner around in record time, scrubbed the toilet, decided the bathroom floor and bath would have to do because there was no time, and then finally, I looked around the apartment. It seemed unnaturally tidy to me, like I had overdone it, so I took out a few CDs and magazines from the cupboard and scattered them around.

Takeo arrived, again smelling of soap. For a moment, I wondered if I ought to have taken a shower, but I quickly pushed that thought aside, since had I done so, he might have thought I was expecting something. This was what made love so difficult. Or rather, the difficult thing was first determining whether or not love was what I wanted.

Let's just go with the flow, I murmured as I held up one hand to welcome Takeo. Hey, Takeo said. It was a greeting midway between friendly and brusque.

'What flow are you talking about?' Takeo asked. Y-you have good hearing, I stuttered. Takeo was no longer just Takeo; he looked to me like 'a man named Takeo'. 'Should we get something, like pizza?' I asked cautiously.

'Do you like pizza, Hitomi?'

'In general.'

Hmm, Takeo said. What kind of pizza should we get? I asked. With tomatoes, I guess, he said. Oh, I said, I want to get it with anchovies. Mmm, he replied, that sounds good.

Takeo was sitting in a chair. Actually, it was a yellow stool that had no backrest. I bought it cheap from Mr Nakano's shop. I got it because I liked the frivolity of the yellow. I made a cucumber salad (I just cut it up and poured dressing over it), took beer glasses from the cupboard, set out plates, and there was nothing left to do. It would be twenty minutes or so until the pizza was delivered – just how were a young man and woman expected to pass the time? I thought with a faint sense of desperation.

So, I got a postcard from Mr Nakano, Takeo said and, remaining seated, he felt around in his back pocket. Out came a postcard folded in half, which Takeo read slowly, in his usual manner.

Dear Takeo, just a quick note. How are you?

I've been drinking. Since I've been here, alcohol seems to have a strong effect on me. Maybe because all I've been doing is riding along in the bus.

During the day, there are lots of flies on the beach. They must be newly hatched. They fly around in swarms, and I just stare at them. The flies don't seem to notice me at all.

Hokkaido is really vast. I wonder if that has anything to do with the saké taking effect more quickly.

I really don't understand women. Takeo, even though you're young, it seems as if you are indifferent to women, and I envy you.

I think Tamotsu will spend the night tonight with a woman he met here, and then go home tomorrow.

Takeo, you know, don't get involved with women.

Sincerely, Haruo Nakano

Huh, I wonder if Mr Nakano is all right? I said.

Takeo's entire body swayed vertically. 'He was just drunk, right?'

But doesn't it sound like he's in some kind of trouble?

'Someone who was really in trouble wouldn't have time to write a postcard like this.'

Takeo's tone was light, which made me look at him suddenly. It was the first time today that I had really looked at his face. Takeo's eyes were closed. In contrast to his light tone, his expression was like that of a small animal crouched down in its burrow. Takeo's entire body appeared to be coursing with energy, as if it were emitting a faint electrical charge.

Are you angry? I asked softly.

'Why would I be angry?' Takeo said in the same light tone, but the electrical charge was still there. Takeo's mind may not have been worked up, but his body definitely was. I looked away from him. Just who was this Takeo? I no longer knew.

'Nice to be so happy-go-lucky,' Takeo murmured. It was only his tone of voice that was still light. I wondered why I had invited Takeo over. I sincerely wished that the 'happy-go-lucky' Mr Nakano were here instead.

Since we saw each other every day, I had been under the impression that I knew a little about Takeo. But now I realized that was not the case at all. The thought had even occurred to me that maybe I should just throw myself at him. Masayo had made a valid point: once two people start sleeping together, all sorts of things become hazy and unsettled.

Takeo was dangling his legs from the stool. Eventually the sound of the doorbell rang, and I paid for the pizza, a little over 2,000 yen. Let's eat, Takeo said and then he dug in. We emptied several cans of beer. After we had eaten everything, Takeo smoked a cigarette. I didn't know you smoked, I said. Every once in a while, he replied. Without anything much to say, we just sat facing each other. We each drank another can of beer. Takeo looked at the clock twice. I looked three times.

Well, then, Takeo said and stood up. At the front door, he brought his lips near to my ear. I thought he was going to kiss me, but I was wrong. With his lips close, he said, 'I, uh, I'm not one for sex and all. Sorry.'

While I was standing there astonished, Takeo closed the door behind him as he left. After a few moments I snapped out of it. Thinking about it while I washed the glasses and plates, it occurred to me that Takeo had chosen to eat the pieces with the least amount of anchovies on them. I couldn't decide whether I should be angry or sad about it, or just laugh.

When I went to the shop the next day Takeo had already arrived. Masayo was there too. I looked at the clock and said that it was almost one o'clock. I was the one who was late.

Masayo left as soon as I got there. It took me a little while to realize that, come to think of it, Takeo didn't have any reason to be at the shop that day.

'Here,' Takeo held out 2,000 yen. 'The pizza and beer last night, that was good,' he said.

Uh huh, I said, nodding absently. For some reason I had a hard time falling asleep the night before, and had ended up watching television until dawn. I would never understand why television shows in the middle of the night were so stilted.

Without saying anything, I put the 2,000 yen in my

wallet. Takeo didn't say anything either. As usual, there were no customers in the shop, and after an hour had passed, still no one had come in.

'Vinegar,' Takeo said suddenly.

Huh?

'My girlfriend heard somewhere that vinegar helps with impotence, and she made me drink it every day.'

What?

'I, uh, that isn't the problem, I just don't have that much interest in doing it.'

Uh, okay.

'I can't really explain it. It just got to be too much trouble.'

That was all he said before falling silent again.

I wonder if another postcard from Mr Nakano will arrive today, I said to break the silence. Takeo gave a little laugh.

I wonder if he's still riding around on the bus. I glanced across furtively to see Takeo's expression.

What do you think Mr Nakano looks like, on the bus by himself? In turn, Takeo looked at me from under his brows.

I had the feeling that Mr Nakano might walk through the door at that moment, but still, nobody appeared.

Hitomi, I . . . I'm not very good at this, I'm sorry, Takeo said softly.

Not good at what?

Everything and nothing.

That's not true. I'm the one who's no good at this.

Really? I mean, Takeo said, looking me straight in the eyes for a change. You're not one for, for getting through life either?

Takeo took out a cigarette from the crumpled packet that

Mr Nakano had left on a corner of the shelf and lit it. Could I have one too? I said, and gave it a puff. Takeo spat into a tissue, just like Mr Nakano. Without answering Takeo's question, I asked instead, When do you think Mr Nakano will come back? Takeo replied, Only God knows. Then he pursed his lips and inhaled the cigarette smoke.

Letter Opener

Tch. The sound of a quick click. An electronic flash lighting up everything.

'You know what I mean? These digital cameras scare me,' Mr Nakano said, pointing at it without seeming particularly frightened.

'What do you mean, then?' Masayo asked, looking up with the camera still in front of her face.

'It makes no sound.'

'What do you mean, sound?'

'The sound of the shutter.'

There's a little click, Masayo replied, bringing the camera's display up to her eye once again and crouching. She was taking a shot, head on, of a glass vase that was set directly on the floor alongside the wall. Then, turning it to the side, another shot. Lastly turning it upside down, another shot, this one a close-up of the bottom. The wall was slightly yellowed. A little while ago Takeo had carried to the back the goods that were usually stacked up in disarray along the wall. Within the jumble of Mr Nakano's shop, the only calm space was the wall where the vase now sat, as if bathed in soft light.

From here on, it will be online auctions! Masayo had first said this around the time that Mr Nakano returned home from Hokkaido. With Tokizo posting photos on the website he made for us, stuff will sell like hot cakes! Masayo would say, coming by religiously every week to photograph what she called 'featured items'. Whenever she did this, Takeo and I had to follow her instructions, which involved tidying things up along the wall, or holding up a reflector board (this was what Masayo called the piece of simple white cardboard – Ever the artist, Mr Nakano would grumble when Masayo wasn't around) at a forty-five-degree angle.

The Tokizo whom she mentioned was a Western antiques dealer, a friend of a friend of Masayo's live-in, Mr Maruyama. Tokizo seems to specialize in watches, Mr Nakano said, which had surprised Masayo.

How do you know anything about Tokizo?

I've seen him a few times at swap meets. You mean to tell me that wiry old crane knows how to use the Internet?

He may be wiry, and he may look like a crane, but Tokizo has a very enterprising spirit – unlike you! Masayo said bluntly, still peering at the camera display.

Come to think of it, Mr Nakano had returned home from Hokkaido a bit fatter. Never mind cranes, he looked more like a goat, his body scrawny with only his belly that looked as if it was swathed in a few towels. His face and limbs looked the same, and his chest was lean enough to be concave, so only his belly bulged out.

'I wonder if he's got some kind of terrible disease?' I asked Takeo furtively.

Takeo shook his head. 'Nah, just ate too much.'

'Really?'

'My grandfather looked exactly like that when he gained weight.'

'Do you think he just ate a lot of *hokke* and potatoes?'

'Genghis Khan barbecue,' Takeo supposed.

Mr Nakano was soon back to his former self. The belly which had looked as if it was swathed in three bath towels went from two towels down to one towel, until finally he was even somewhat thinner than he had been before.

'Now he's suddenly too thin. He definitely has some kind of disease, right?' I said to Takeo, who laughed.

'Hitomi, you must really like Mr Nakano.'

'Huh?'

'You care about him, don't you?'

I harboured no particular affection for Mr Nakano. It was sheer curiosity. I don't, I told him later, but I couldn't manage to add that I was only having a laugh, because for some reason I felt embarrassed. Takeo had just finished unloading a pickup; sweat ran from his temple down his cheek. I stole a glance at Takeo's sweat. I closed my eyes and, as I was just about to experience a tender moment – one that might make me want to squeeze my legs together – I hurriedly opened the notebook.

There were various messages written in the notebook. *204 Heights Kitano. Bid up to 20K. Call from vehicle inspection. Complaint, woman, whetstone.*

Whetstone was written in light blue marker. *Woman*

was in orange, the *Com* in *Complaint* was black, the *pla* was blue, and the *int* was red. Mr Nakano must have done this while he was on the phone. Whenever he was on a long call, he always opened the notebook and doodled. So that in between the words *Call from vehicle inspection* there was a drawing of a young guy who looked like Takeo from behind, some nonsensical lines, and a sketch of a vase. Mr Nakano's drawings were rubbish, but somehow, it was perfectly clear what he had drawn.

The vase was the one that Masayo was now photographing with the digital camera. 'Might be a Gallé,' she was saying, but Mr Nakano laughed at the idea.

'What's a Gallé?' Takeo asked.

Mr Nakano thought for a moment and then replied, 'A man who worked in glass with designs of things like dragonflies and mushrooms stuck on them.'

'Sounds awful.'

'Well, I guess it's a matter of taste.'

You people don't appreciate the beauty of this vase, Masayo said, this time clicking the shutter from an upward slanting angle. *Tch*, goes the faint click. Digital cameras are definitely not for me, Mr Nakano gripes. If it doesn't make any sounds or say anything, how am I to know? he muttered.

Would call that a sound, Takeo tilted his head. Mr Nakano stood up and headed for the back. Haruo really is conservative, Masayo said as she gently moved the vase, and then set up an unidentifiable animal figurine in front of the wall. It's a dog, she said as she shifted the angle of the figurine this way and that. Maybe it's a rabbit.

It's a bear, Takeo said.

You could hear the sound of Mr Nakano starting up the truck's engine through the wall. But the truck simply wouldn't start. Just when you thought you heard the sound of the ignition, right then it would fall silent. Battery might be dead, Takeo said as he too headed for the back.

I couldn't hear the *tch* sound as Masayo clicked the shutter; it was drowned out by the noise of the engine trying to start. The push of the shutter on the digital camera was shallow, so it was hard to even know when Masayo was snapping away with her finger. As she lowered the camera, then started moving again, I became confused about where to focus on her silhouetted movements.

Slowly my gaze returned to the notebook. I stared at the light blue letters of the word *whetstone*. For the umpteenth time, the rough sound of the truck's ignition echoed from the back.

'What do you think?' Mr Nakano asked.

There had just been a trio of middle-aged women in the shop. They were about the same age as Mr Nakano or perhaps a little younger, and I thought they had probably taken the train to visit this neighbourhood. As Masayo had recently commented, ever since they renovated the building that housed the train station about two years ago, the clientele had changed a bit.

'One of the women was pretty.' Two of the three were decked out in rings and earrings and had been wearing T-shirts featuring unusual lace designs or drawings of cats – it was hard to imagine where they had bought them – but the other woman had been dressed in a simple beige summer sweater worn over a pair of narrow trousers, accessorized with only a luxurious-looking gold wristwatch.

'That watch was pricey. Probably an antique.'

The things on sale at the Nakano shop are second-hand goods. We don't deal in vintage or antiques. I recalled the words Mr Nakano had said to me on the first day I started working there, and gave a little laugh.

'In the end, those three women didn't buy anything.'

The one with the gold wristwatch had picked up the turtle paperweight and deliberated for a moment. Then she had gently put the paperweight back down, and next looked at an Imari bowl that had come from a pickup at an acquaintance of Masayo's. In the meantime, the two overly accessorized women had been making comments laced with criticism about the menu at the place where they had apparently had lunch.

It said they were truffles, but I thought that bit of black powder was dust that had fallen into the sauce. And the lychee sorbet, I bet they just added the flavouring to it. Lychee essence – the kind of thing they sell in Hong Kong or somewhere. I mean, we might have been better off going all the way to Hong Kong. Of course, they sell that here in Japan too. The two of them had kept up this torrent of conversation, while one of them picked up a bag of dyed grasses made by Masayo and stuck her nose inside to smell it.

'I thought she was going to buy the Imari bowl,' I said, and Mr Nakano nodded.

'So, what do you think? That was like the moment when you go into a love hotel, you know?'

What? I cried. As usual, Mr Nakano's comment was completely out of the blue.

'What do you mean by "that"?'

'You know what I mean? The things a woman says. Like, you know, darling, you have impeccable timing when it comes to entering a love hotel.'

What? I retorted. Is that what the woman with the gold wristwatch said?

'Why does that happen?' Mr Nakano furrowed his brow and looked at me. I was the one who wanted to furrow my brow.

Mr Nakano soon unknit his brows and began to speak raptly, That woman from just now looks like the type who would say something like that to me.

'Is it a bad thing to have good timing?'

'She said it's unbecoming to have timing that is too perfect.'

I burst out laughing at the word 'unbecoming'. Mr Nakano kept a straight face as he went on.

'In the city, the entrance to a love hotel is always along a street where there are lots of people coming and going, right?'

Outside the city, you can drive a car to a love hotel that's by the side of the road, so you don't have to worry, but when you walk into a love hotel in the city, you have to be concerned about attracting attention. Especially during the daytime. Mr Nakano explained all this.

As I nodded along, listening, I realized that, whereas I hadn't been before, I was now completely familiar with this manner of Mr Nakano's, and I let out a brief sigh. Paying me no heed, Mr Nakano resumed what he was saying.

'You take a quick look behind you and ahead of you, and then you dart inside. And that's about all there is to it,' Mr Nakano said as he looked straight at me. He wore a serious expression.

'Right when we went inside, there was a step, and she, well, she tripped.'

But you didn't trip, Mr Nakano? I asked, and he nodded in assent.

'Because I have sharp reflexes.'

'You said that she did trip, though.'

Right, Mr Nakano said. Then, we went to a room, we did this and that, and afterwards, in the midst of saying that it had gone well, she started to give me a hard time.

As I listened to Mr Nakano's stop-and-start style of chatter, I was reminded of Masaki, a classmate from my third year of primary school. Masaki had a ten-yen-sized bald spot on his head, and even though he was short, his feet were too big for his body – he was not very good at dodgeball. He was always the first to get hit with the ball and then he was out. I was usually the second or third to be out, so I spent a lot of time just standing there next to Masaki on the sidelines.

Masaki and I hardly ever said anything to each other, but one time he blurted out, 'You know, I have a bone.'

Almost all of the other kids were out, and only the two or three strongest players were still in the game. Masaki and I were all the way back by the gymnastics bars, watching the ball as it went back and forth from one court to the other.

I have my older brother's bone, Masaki said. What are you talking about? I asked. My older brother died the year before last, Masaki replied. But how come you have his bone? I asked. I stole it from the urn – I really loved my brother. That was all Masaki said before falling silent again, leaning against the bars. I didn't ask him anything more about it.

I ran into Masaki right before finishing secondary school

– we hadn't seen each other for a long time. He had grown super tall, and what was more, he said that he was trying for admission to a really selective university. University of Tokyo? I asked. Masaki laughed and nodded briefly. Hitomi, I bet Todai is the only selective university you know of, right? he said, using the abbreviated name for it. Sure is, I replied smugly, as I stared at Masaki's head. His bald spot was hidden by his hair and I couldn't see it.

'When you say she was giving you a hard time, what did she do?' I asked Mr Nakano.

'You know, it was like I was too skilful at certain things, and she didn't like it.'

And were you proud of that? I asked. That's not it, Mr Nakano said with a bemused expression. I usually take my time, I try to make sure she comes more than once, I change my underwear every day.

'What?'

'And then, I mean, along with her telling me all those things are unbecoming – I mean, what's more – when she comes, she doesn't say anything. Not even a moan or a sigh. Most people make a little sound, don't they? I can't seem to figure this woman out. She's just like that digital camera, isn't she?'

'I see,' I said dryly. There was no other way for me to respond.

A customer had come in. It was a young man. He glanced impatiently around the shop's interior, and in what seemed like a haphazard fashion, he grabbed a few sets of *menko* playing cards from the 1960s or '70s. When he brought them to the till, I realized he had in fact chosen the cheapest of the Showa-era *menko* sets, which were among the most expensive items in the Nakano shop. Thank you, I said as I put the *menko* cards in a paper bag. The customer was looking blankly at my hands. When I first started working here, it made me nervous when people watched my hands, but by then it didn't bother me in the least. Thrift shop customers, on the whole, watch hawkishly at the till during payment and receipt of goods. Mr Nakano let out a sigh as he went outside. The customer left the shop shortly after Mr Nakano. It was damp and humid; the sky looked like rain.

It was pure chance that I met Mr Nakano's 'bank'.

By his 'bank', I mean Mr Nakano's lover. Ever since Takeo had at some point told me that when Mr Nakano would say, 'Just off to the bank,' he was most likely meeting his lover, the two of us had been in the habit of referring to this woman of Mr Nakano's – whom we had never seen – as 'the Bank'.

I happened to come across 'the Bank' on the street near the bank.

As usual Mr Nakano had gone out while it was still early in the afternoon, saying 'Just off to the bank,' so right when Takeo came back after finishing a pickup, I asked him to mind the store while I myself went to the bank to pay my rent.

Even though it was only the beginning of the month, the bank had been crowded. The Nakano shop paid my monthly salary in cash. The portion for any days missed was deducted from the monthly total, and the final amount was handed over in a manila envelope at the end of the month. Occasionally Mr Nakano made mistakes in his calculations, so I always made a point of taking the money out of the envelope right then and there and checking the amount. So far, twice there had been too little and once there was too much. Even when the error was in my favour, I informed Mr Nakano of it promptly. You're so honest, Hitomi! To go to such trouble for that, Mr Nakano said in a strange voice, magnanimously accepting the 3,500 yen I held out to him.

The queue did not seem to be moving at all, so I decided to go and buy some stockings first. I had just remembered that my cousin's wedding was next month. My cousin, who was the same age as I was, had been working at a travel agency for three years after graduating from university, but she worked herself so hard that she fell ill. Nevertheless, she was so industrious by nature that it seems she couldn't bear to sit idle, so she registered with a staffing agency, and after all that, was now basically working again day and night. When I heard that the guy my cousin was marrying was the chief of the company she had been placed with, I had to admire her. It really was just like my cousin to find a husband with such an ill-defined title as 'chief'. I bet the wedding favours will be from among 'Your Choice of Items Worth ¥4,000', I thought to myself as I made up my mind to head over to a clothing boutique just a little way beyond the bank. No sooner had I stepped outside than Mr Nakano and 'the Bank' appeared before my eyes.

Mr Nakano and 'the Bank' were turning the corner in front of me. Just a little way along that street was the entrance to a love hotel. I never imagined he would go to a love hotel this close to the shop. I followed Mr Nakano more or less without thinking. 'The Bank' had nice legs. She wore a tight skirt that was cut just above her knees with a close-fitting T-shirt, and a thin scarf was wound loosely around her neck and trailed behind her. 'The Bank' looked around and for a moment I froze, but she quickly turned back without seeming to notice me.

'The Bank' was pretty. To call her a beauty might have been going too far, but she had a delicate complexion – she seemed to be wearing hardly any make-up yet her skin was flawless. Her eyes may have been narrow but her nose was straight. There was something inexplicably vibrant about her lips. At the same time, she had a purity about her.

So this pretty woman was the one Mr Nakano couldn't figure out, the one who didn't make a sound. I followed them, my mouth agape. Mr Nakano and 'the Bank' kept going straight ahead. When they reached the entrance to the love hotel, Mr Nakano turned a full circle. He surveyed the entire street with a covert glance. At first, Mr Nakano seemed not to register that it was me. But then immediately after that, he opened his eyes wide. His lips formed the shape of my name.

Just like that, Mr Nakano was drawn into the entrance of the love hotel. He appeared to have been literally swept inside, regardless of his own will, whether he wanted to or not. 'The Bank' was also drawn within. Well, well, he was pretty good at that. I had to admire him.

I pulled myself together and went to the clothing boutique, where I bought some stockings. After wavering, I chose fishnets. I recalled browsing through an article in a fashion magazine that said, 'Guys go crazy for a glimpse of fishnet stockings between your boots and your skirt.' After buying them, I realized that it was summer so I wouldn't be wearing boots, not to mention the fact that I didn't own a skirt that was the right length for catching a glimpse of stockings. And in any case, I had virtually no occasion to wear skirts other than this wedding, so it really didn't matter. Maybe I could try them on when Takeo came over to my place, like some kind of cosplay. But what kind of costume anyway? With this nonsense in my head, I walked along the street back to the store.

It was just before Mr Nakano came back to close up that I realized I had forgotten to do the bank transfer for my rent. Welcome back, I called out to him as he returned. As if nothing had happened, Mr Nakano replied, Here I am! In the notebook, I wrote down the word *bank* in blue ballpoint pen. The letters looked scruffy lined up below the word *whetstone* in thick light-blue marker.

Is a whetstone the same thing as a grindstone? I was about to ask Mr Nakano, but he had retreated to the back. Goodbye, I called in that direction as I set out to leave. Goodnight! Mr Nakano's voice drifted from the back. See you tomorrow, I heard him add. His voice flickered brightly, like a ghost in the daylight.

I think someone's been stabbed in the neighbourhood! shouted the owner of the bicycle shop two doors down as he burst into our store.

He told us that the only thing known so far was that 'a middle-aged man was stabbed'. The incident happened in an alley at the end of the shopping district, and the man was taken away in an ambulance. There were no witnesses, and apparently the guy who was stabbed dialled the emergency number himself. It was only once the ambulance arrived that anyone realized the man was lying there, and by the time curious onlookers began to gather, both the man and the ambulance were already gone.

The bicycle shop owner, in his work clothes, was stout and fat – the exact opposite of Mr Nakano. That guy doesn't even drink or smoke, so Mr Nakano once said. Mr Nakano always seemed as if he was trying to keep his distance from the bicycle shop owner, but the guy would call in at the Nakano shop from time to time, putting on a patronizing air as an older and wiser business owner.

Mr Nakano said that he and the bicycle shop owner had gone to the same primary and middle schools. You know Higonokami? – they make really good penknives for sharpening pencils. I mean, they're not just good for sharpening – they will carve up a pencil nib like the imperial battleship *Yamato* – they're ridiculously good! Yet still, the time when I forgot my pencil case and asked to borrow one, the only thing he lent me was this amazingly stubby pencil, even the lead was worn down to a nub. Meanwhile, he must have been hiding a pencil like the *Yamato* or like a Zero fighter in the palm of his hand. That's the kind of guy he is. This was how Mr Nakano once described the bicycle shop owner.

Soon after the bicycle shop owner's visit, we found out that the man who had been stabbed was someone from the shopping district, and it was close to evening when we learned that the person who had been stabbed was none other than Mr Nakano himself. The telephone had rung, I had taken my time answering (Let it ring at least three times before answering it, Mr Nakano would say. If you rush to answer it, you lose the customer, along with the chance for us to sell the thing they were calling about, he had explained as he smoked a cigarette); it was Masayo calling.

Don't be alarmed, Masayo said in a tone that sounded even more composed than her usual calm voice.

'Haruo has been stabbed.'

What? I asked, in shock. The bicycle shop owner had just come rushing into the store again, making a lot of noise. He took one look at me with the phone in my hand and nodded vigorously.

'But it's not serious at all. There was hardly any blood.'

I see, I replied, at the same time aware that my own voice was betraying me. As if in inverse proportion, Masayo grew more and more composed. Whether your voice betrays you, or becomes deliberately calm, in the end it amounts to the same thing, I thought in a corner of my mind.

'So I will close up the shop today. I might be a little late, but I hope you don't mind waiting for me.'

Yes. This time I replied in a normal voice. The bicycle shop owner was watching my mouth and the back of my hand gripping the receiver, a piercing glint in his eyes. What do you think you're looking at? I wanted to shout at him, but since I wasn't one to shout, I couldn't bring myself to do so. Instead I replaced the receiver quietly and looked straight in front of me.

'It was poor Nakano who got stabbed, wasn't it?' the bicycle shop owner asked.

Well, I said. I don't know.

After that, no matter what the bicycle shop owner asked me, I maintained a sullen silence. A little while later, Takeo came back. The bicycle shop owner was chattering on about the details of what had happened in 'the shopping district's dead-end assault'. But there were too many things that were still unknown, and Takeo wasn't asking the right questions, so the conversation went nowhere.

'Hitomi, should I go to the hospital?' Takeo asked soon after the bicycle shop owner had left.

'Oh, I didn't ask which hospital.'

'I could ask the police.'

Takeo then picked up the shop phone and proceeded to call one place after another. With one hand on the receiver and an elbow holding the notebook open, he wrote down the names and telephone numbers of the hospitals in blue ball-point pen. The words *Satake Clinic, 2 Nishimachi* were lined up under *bank*. I'll go then, Takeo said, and he trotted off towards the back. The truck's ignition sounded a few times until finally the engine started, and Takeo beeped the horn once. Then he lightly raised his hand to me, adjusted his grip on the steering wheel, and stared straight ahead through the windshield.

The Satake Clinic was difficult to find. I had not yet paid a proper visit to Mr Nakano's hospital room since having gone along with Masayo to see him that night when she had come to close the shop.

Even on the day when he was stabbed, despite having only just awakened from the anaesthesia, Mr Nakano had been in fine form, grasping the banana that Masayo had brought him tightly in one hand and peeling it halfway, then munching on it.

'While I'm here, they're going to do all sorts of examinations,' Mr Nakano said blithely.

'What about your injury – is it all right?' I asked, and Masayo replied instead of Mr Nakano.

'Sure – after all, something like that doesn't cause a proper injury.'

'A proper injury?'

'Here I am, thinking it was a knife, but turns out it was just a letter opener.'

Masayo took the banana in her own hand and peeled the rest of it. Her gesture was polite but – just like Mr Nakano – she had a messy way of peeling the banana.

That's right – Mr Nakano was stabbed with a letter opener, Masayo explained.

A letter opener? I repeated.

That's right – a letter opener, of all things!

Can a letter opener be used to injure someone?

No, as you can see.

But he was bleeding, wasn't he?

Wouldn't you know – that's just like Haruo!

When Masayo told me on the phone that Mr Nakano had been stabbed, my first thought had been that it was 'the Bank' who had stabbed him, but that was not the case.

'Do you remember, the other day, I was on a long phone call?' Mr Nakano chimed in.

'A long phone call?'

Two or three times a day, Mr Nakano would be on the phone for an extended period. Mostly it was with customers who were calling for the first time. When it comes to old things, whether buying or selling, why is it that people act so cautious? Mr Nakano would grumble every so often. With something brand new, they have no problem just ordering it from a catalogue, no matter how expensive it is.

'When was this long phone call?'

I think about a week ago? There was a woman who called in a complaint, something that she wanted sharpening with a whetstone. As he spoke, Mr Nakano took another banana, this time peeling it smoothly all the way to the bottom and then shoving the entire thing in his mouth. You're going to choke if you try to eat that all at once! Masayo said. What the hell are you talking about? Mr Nakano exclaimed, his mouth full of banana. Don't you see the articles in the newspaper about people choking on bananas? Masayo said. Come on, that's only at New Year's, with *mochi* rice cakes, Mr Nakano replied.

'Wait – was that, by any chance, written in the notebook?' I asked, remembering *complaint* written in black and blue and red letters.

That's right. The woman was really persistent. She was quite angry, demanding that I sharpen the letter opener she had bought because it wouldn't cut anything.

'Is a letter opener something you usually sharpen?'

One that's top quality, sure you do. But the kind of flimsy ones like we sell? Probably not. Mr Nakano tilted his head as he said 'not'. For a moment he wore an expression as if he were gazing at somewhere off in the distance. But you know, there was something rather nice about her voice, Mr Nakano went on.

The woman with the nice voice called again. This time, she wanted him to bring the whetstone and meet her at the edge of the shopping district. It was a strange phone call. In this business, Mr Nakano explained, one encounters all sorts of weird things so one becomes inured to it, but still, 'the edge of the shopping district' struck him as odd. It was not the kind of place where one usually met up with someone. But, charmed by the voice, he went anyway.

'My dear!' Masayo uttered these two words softly. Mr Nakano cast a glance at her and shrugged his shoulders.

Mr Nakano took the whetstone, without even bothering to wrap it up in anything, and made his way to the edge of the shopping district at the appointed time. The woman was there. She was wearing a bibbed apron over a knee-length skirt, she had on white socks with sandals, and her hair was in an updo. What stuck in his mind was how the front of her sandals were like some sort of mesh. Right – they were like the ones that were sold up until the mid-1970s. Of course a thrift shop owner would notice such a minute detail.

The woman appeared to be about the same age as Mr Nakano. She wore heavy lipstick. Beware, Mr Nakano thought to himself. There was something dangerous about this woman. It was his instinct as a thrift shop owner. Or rather, it was what any normal person's instinct would have told them too.

Squat down! she ordered him. Huh? Mr Nakano replied.

Squat down there and sharpen my letter opener, the woman said. It was the same pleasant voice that he had heard on the phone. It sounded even nicer in person. I got a little hard-on, Mr Nakano muttered. Masayo clucked her tongue.

As if under her spell, Mr Nakano squatted. He set the whetstone down on the ground and poured over it some mineral water from a small plastic bottle that the woman gave him, and he began to slowly sharpen the letter opener that she held out to him. The woman was standing in the middle of the street, her feet set apart and her hands on her hips.

Mr Nakano continued to slowly sharpen the letter opener.

Perhaps from the lingering effect of the anaesthesia, Mr Nakano had suddenly fallen asleep after that, and no matter how Masayo shook or pushed or pulled him, he didn't wake up. Since then, amid the hectic rush of the Nakano shop without Mr Nakano, neither Takeo nor I had gone to visit him. Whereas things had been slow when Mr Nakano was off gallivanting in Hokkaido, lately the shop was doing a brisk business.

When our day off finally came around, Takeo and I decided to meet up in the late afternoon to pay a visit to the Satake Clinic. I had missed hearing about how Mr Nakano had been stabbed by the woman after he sharpened her letter opener. I considered asking Masayo, but I was reluctant to have that conversation in the store. The bicycle shop owner from two doors down might be watching carefully and could burst in at any time.

We should bring some fruit to the hospital, Takeo said. Doubt that Mr Nakano cares much for flowers.

Takeo chose strawberries. They're expensive, I said from his side. He's in hospital, after all, Takeo replied. We took two punnets of enormous strawberries, but when we got to Mr Nakano's private room, he wasn't there; he had already moved to a six-person ward.

It won't be easy to get the whole story of the stabbing in a six-person ward, I thought to myself as we opened the curtain to Mr Nakano's corner bed – and there was 'the Bank'.

I caught my breath in surprise, and 'the Bank' smiled.

Indeed, the contrast between her tapered eyes and her full lips was alluring. This is Sakiko from the Asukado, Mr Nakano cheerfully introduced her. This is Hitomi and Takeo, he says, turning to Sakiko.

The Asukado – you mean, the shop with all the pots and jars? Takeo asked, and Sakiko nodded. They're a real antiques dealer, Takeo went on. Sakiko shook her head slightly. Her gesture could have been interpreted as either yes or no. She had an air about her that was completely incompatible with someone like Mr Nakano.

Hey, Hitomi, I bet you want to hear the rest of the story from the other day, Mr Nakano said without even lowering his voice. Even in front of Sakiko, his attitude was exactly the same as when it was just Masayo or the two of us. Sakiko offered chairs to Takeo and me.

No, well, I said, but Mr Nakano grinned. Don't hold back – it's not good for your health! If all you do is deprive yourself, the first thing to happen is impotence!

I was curious to see the look on Takeo's face, but I didn't dare turn my head.

'So I sharpened it,' Mr Nakano began, back to his usual abrupt manner.

I sharpened it. Slowly and carefully. Then when I finished, I stood up and handed it to the woman. The letter opener. Will it cut now, I wonder? the woman asked. Will it really cut something? It will cut now, I assured her, and without any warning, she thrust the letter opener into my side. She didn't make any kind of motion beforehand to pull back or to hold up the blade – she jabbed it into my side, as naturally as if she were swatting an insect in front of her – just like that.

Mr Nakano chatted away as if he were speaking lines that he was used to repeating over and over. Takeo and I were dumbfounded.

I had done such a good job sharpening the damn thing – normally it couldn't have been used to stab a person, but now this letter opener cut very well!

The moment that Mr Nakano finished saying this, Sakiko let out a little 'Ah!' Then she suddenly burst into tears.

I thought her tears had just spilled over, flowing from her eyes and running down the curve of her cheeks, but once she started there was no end to it. Sakiko simply cried, without making a sound. I guess this is what is meant by the phrase, a flood of tears. In the midst of it, Mr Nakano said to me, 'Give her a tissue,' and then to her, 'Here, take this,' as he passed the packet of tissues advertising a personal loan company that I handed him, but otherwise, nobody said anything. Sakiko went on crying, without making any noise at all. She didn't use the tissues, she didn't even wipe the mucus from her nose – she just kept on crying.

When she had seemingly cried her fill, her tears ended as abruptly as they had begun. It's all right, the woman has been arrested, I'm sure she will be charged, Mr Nakano said, even though Sakiko seemed not to hear him as she sat as still as a statue. I suddenly had a fleeting memory of the statue of a dog or a rabbit or a bear or I don't know what that Masayo had photographed with her digital camera. If Sakiko were photographed from every angle, I'm sure those pictures would sell. This thought also flitted through my mind.

You're right, it's my fault, Mr Nakano apologized. It was the kind of apology that sounded like he had no idea why he was the one apologizing. Sakiko said nothing. Finally, as she reached into the packet of tissues and blew her nose quite loudly, Sakiko looked Mr Nakano sternly in the eye and said, 'From now on, I'll make sounds.'

What? Mr Nakano said in a wild voice.

I'll make sounds. So from now on keep your hands off anyone other than your wife, Sakiko said, speaking softly but with distinct pauses between her words.

Oh, Mr Nakano replied. His voice is like that of a sumo wrestler who has been overpowered and pushed out of the ring.

Uh huh, right, I promise. Of course, Mr Nakano said timidly.

Remaining stern, Sakiko stood up and left the ward. She walked away, just like that, without turning back.

Takeo and I soon left the ward as well, walking with quick steps towards the lift.

Sure seemed like a tough one, Takeo muttered.

Masayo said as much. She said Mr Nakano always goes for the tough ones.

But she was pretty, that one.

Is that the type you like? I asked Takeo. I had done my best to feign nonchalance but had not been very successful.

Don't really have a type, Takeo replied. Just what did she mean, about making sounds?

She meant when she comes, she'll make a sound.

What? Takeo said loudly.

We fell silent for a while after that. We were totally quiet, and then, as if with finality, I sighed deeply.

Hey, you know. Even if I were reincarnated, I wouldn't want to come back as Mr Nakano, I said.

Takeo chuckled. There's no way that could happen.

Sure, but nevertheless.

But, have to say, I don't dislike Sakiko, Takeo said.

Me neither, I didn't dislike her. And, of course, I don't dislike Mr Nakano, I thought to myself. There are plenty of people in the world I don't dislike, some of whom I almost like; on the other hand, I almost hate some of those whom I don't dislike, too. But how many people did I truly love? I wondered, as I clasped Takeo's hand lightly. Takeo was in his own world.

When we left the hospital and I looked up at the sky, there was a star whose name I didn't know but which was always visible at this hour during that time of year; it had enough brightness to shine palely in the sky. Takeo, I said. Yes, he replied. Takeo, I said once more, and Takeo kissed me. It was a simple kiss, without any tongue. I didn't use my tongue either, I just stood still. Such warm lips, I thought to myself. Somewhere I heard the sound of an engine starting, and then it quickly stopped.

Big Dog

'You know what I mean? That, uh, huge, what do you call it?'
Mr Nakano asked as he took off his black apron. There weren't
any pickups scheduled for that day, but a customer had called
a little while ago to request a valuation. Valuations were not
Mr Nakano's strong suit, but the customer had been most
persistent, and now it seemed he had no choice but to go over
and take a look.

'A big what?' I followed up.

As usual, Mr Nakano's conversation was unexpected.

'With long hair, and kind of . . . like a woman who is a bit
hard to approach,' Mr Nakano went on, unfazed.

'Do you mean a woman?'

'No, no – I'm not talking about a person.'

'Not a person?'

'A dog – I'm talking about a dog,' Mr Nakano said impatiently as he tossed his apron into the shop's tatami room at
the back.

A dog, I repeated.

Right, a dog, you know. One of those – what do you call it – like those tall, long, and thin ones that are always frolicking around the gardens of aristocrats.

I laughed at Mr Nakano's words. The expression 'frolicking around' didn't seem to go with the idea of 'aristocrats'.

'All right, I'll be off then,' Mr Nakano said as he ran his hands through the many pockets of his nylon waistcoat.

See you later, I responded.

I heard the clear sound of the engine. Last week, the Nakano shop had, in the parlance of Mr Nakano, done a 'full change-up' on the truck's engine. It wasn't just the battery that was kaput; the drive belt was practically ready to snap, as they had found out during the last vehicle inspection.

Takeo and I were used to driving this truck, so we were pretty good at getting around using the belt as it was. Mr Nakano went on, grumbling endlessly to himself as he eyed the bill from the repair shop. Can he really be serious when he says that? I tried to ask Takeo furtively; he nodded with an earnest look. He's definitely serious, Mr Nakano.

In any event, the truck's engine had come through its 'full change-up' without a hitch, and Mr Nakano was completely recovered from his injury as well. Having undergone a thorough examination while he was in the hospital, he had been diagnosed with a predisposition for diabetes, which resulted in a tendency to spout copious and dubious information about calories at mealtimes. Otherwise Mr Nakano seemed quite back to himself again, as he manipulated the truck's steering wheel with one hand, making a wide turn onto the street.

The rays of midsummer sunlight came into the shop, high and strong. I sat on a chair and massaged my own shoulders.

*

The incident with the dog frolicking around in the aristocrat's garden had all started with Mr Maruyama, Masayo's whatever-he-is (that was Mr Nakano's name for him).

'You know, I hear Maruyama lives in an apartment in the next neighbourhood over,' Mr Nakano had said, a hint of displeasure in his voice. Really? I replied.

'I mean, if he's my sister's whatever-he-is, they ought to live together. Her house is big enough.'

Masayo lived in the house left by Mr Nakano's and her late parents; it is an old but quite magnificent home.

'There's something cheeky about them insisting on living apart, isn't there?'

I always suspected that Mr Nakano might have a bit of a sister complex. Perhaps, I offered reasonably.

'And, you know, there's the landlord at his apartment building . . .' Mr Nakano said and then paused meaningfully. I ignored his suggestive silence and continued to busy my-self with pasting rough paper together to make bags. When customers bought large items, we put them in paper shop-ping bags with handles that came from department stores or boutiques, but for things that weren't so big, like smaller delicate items, the Nakano shop provided simple paper bags – flat square ones like you used to get at the greengrocer's.

'Hitomi, you make pretty bags,' Mr Nakano said, admiring my work.

Really? I replied.

'Yeah, you are good with your hands. I think the bags you make may even be that much neater than my sister's.'

Really? I said again. The reference to his sister had

brought Mr Nakano back to the topic, and he started off again about 'the dog in the aristocrat's garden'. This was the gist of the story.

The landlord of Mr Maruyama's building was a heartless miser.

The apartment block was called 'Maison Kanamori 1' and, first of all, despite it being a forty-year-old building that was showing its age, the landlord shamelessly charged rent that was almost the same as for a newly constructed building. He even paid careful attention to refreshing the paint and changing the wallpaper – the kind of work that keeps up outward appearances – so that inside and out it bore enough of a resemblance to a new construction.

Tidy rooms with a spacious layout like you used to see, plenty of cupboards. His modus operandi was to trick foolish tenants into paying a deposit right away, before they noticed the hidden truths of 'Maison Kanamori', such as the voices from neighbouring apartments that could be heard distinctly, the floors that were on a slant, and the numerous cockroaches that came up out of the drain as soon as night fell to run rampant around the apartment.

What made things even worse was that Maison Kanamori was blessed in its surrounding scenery. Even tenants who had steeled themselves against the sloping floors or the vague signs of vermin would, nine times out of ten, break into a smile the instant they laid eyes on the landlord's garden – his 'pride and joy' – which was directly opposite Maison Kanamori. Verdant was the perfect word to describe it.

Buildings one to three of Maison Kanamori were built

in a row on the landlord's property. These buildings as well as the main house where the landlord lived were surrounded by his 'pride and joy' on all sides. The landlord was constantly making improvements to the garden. Mixed in among a grove of ornamental trees such as Japanese oaks, silver birches, southern magnolias, and maples, were fruit trees such as persimmons, peaches, and summer mandarins, in addition to showy varieties like fragrant olive trees, azaleas, and hydrangeas, all growing together in a jumble. The undergrowth was a mass of English-style flowering grasses with tiny white and blue blooms, and over the entrance to the premises was an arch with large roses.

'It sounds like a garden with no particular rules,' I remarked to Mr Nakano, who nodded in agreement.

'But, you know, Maruyama is enough of a scatterbrain to get caught up with someone like my sister, so he was easily taken in by that heartless landlord,' Mr Nakano said sagely, shaking his head.

If it was only that the rent was expensive, I'd say just deal with it, but Maison Kanamori's heartless landlord is hostile towards his tenants, Mr Nakano explained.

'Hostile?' I said.

'Yes, hostile,' he replied in an overdramatic, low voice.

The landlord and his wife were so crazy about their garden that if a tenant did the slightest harm to it, they held an implacable grudge. But they didn't just show hostility towards a tenant who had damaged the garden in the past, they even got really tough with the tenants who hadn't done anything. Mr Nakano went on, I hear that, when showing the apartment, they are terribly courteous, if anything they seem like a timid and naïve married couple, only to change their manner abruptly as soon as the lease is signed, scolding and rebuking for all sorts of things.

'Scolding and rebuking?' I repeated with surprise.

Mr Nakano laughed. 'For instance, you know, if someone parks their bicycle in a corner of the garden, less than an hour later, they might find it covered with stickers that say DO NOT LEAVE BICYCLES HERE or TO BE REMOVED, so I hear.'

'Stickers?'

'The landlord and his wife must have had them made up for just this purpose.'

Isn't that a bit scary? I said.

Mr Nakano nodded. 'And if that weren't enough, apparently those stickers are impossible to peel off.'

Why can't people leave their bikes there in the first place?

'They say it affects the way the sunlight falls on the grass, and the flowers might get crushed.'

Maruyama's not a very good judge of character, Mr Nakano went on gleefully, and stood up. Should we call it a day? he asked as he started to tidy up the things on the bench out front.

As a matter of fact, I already knew about Maison Kanamori. It was less than a five-minute walk from Takeo's house. Once, for some reason, I accompanied Takeo home (of course I didn't go inside or meet anyone there), and on the way, we passed Maison Kanamori. It did have the feeling of a dense and contained forest, and the landlord's garden – his 'pride and joy', as Mr Nakano put it – was certainly something to be proud of, which is to say that it was rather tasteful.

'This place seems like it belongs somewhere else,' Takeo said, staring deep into the garden.

'Should we go in?' I said, but Takeo shook his head.

'One mustn't enter someone else's garden without permission. My grandpa taught me that, a long time ago.'

Hmm, I said. I was slightly annoyed that Takeo had opposed my suggestion. I had thought about giving him a big wet kiss, right there on the spot, but I gave up on the idea.

So, what does this have to do with the landlord and the aristocrat's dog? I asked, but Mr Nakano was preoccupied with closing the shutter, and didn't seem to hear what I said. That's how he was. It's still hot even after the sun has gone down, I called out as I stepped outside the back door. Beside the half-moon hanging clearly in the sky, the same star that I had seen on the way home from visiting Mr Nakano in the hospital stood out white and glistening.

See you later, I called back towards the inside of the shop, but sure enough, there was no response from Mr Nakano. I could hear him humming over the clatter of the shutter.

In the end, it was Masayo who revealed the full details of the aristocrat's dog.

'I mean, the landlord and his wife's children have been independent for a long time already,' Masayo began, almost as abruptly as Mr Nakano, a few days after I heard the story of Maison Kanamori from him. For the first time in a while, Mr Nakano, Takeo, me, and Masayo – the so-called full members of the Nakano shop – were gathered together there. It's the first time since Haruo was in the hospital, isn't it? Masayo said as she looked around at us all.

'Speaking of which, what is happening to the woman who stabbed Mr Nakano?' Takeo asked.

'I think she's in detention,' Masayo answered briskly.

I see, Takeo replied. After that, nobody asked for any other details, such as when the trial might be, or what kind of charges were to be expected. It was less out of tact or restraint than because we were not well versed in discussing such worldly matters.

'So, going back to the landlord and his wife, they didn't know what to do with themselves, so they ended up getting an enormous Afghan hound,' Masayo continued.

I see, I replied this time.

'And that dog became even more important to them than their garden.'

I see. Takeo's turn.

'One time, Maruyama ran into the landlord and his wife while they were taking the dog for a walk.'

I see. Me again.

'Not only did they scowl at him, on top of that, they told him to go away.'

So, what did Maruyama do? Takeo asked.

'He went away, he said,' Masayo replied, and then after a moment she giggled. I laughed too. Takeo's mouth relaxed just the slightest bit. Mr Nakano was the only one who seemed annoyed for some reason.

Come on, come on, don't be such a lazybones. We've got Kabukicho, so jump to it, Takeo, will you? Mr Nakano said with the same annoyed look on his face. That day both Mr Nakano and Takeo were supposed to go on a pickup at an apartment in Kabukicho, the red-light district. Apparently there was only one item in the pickup, and ordinarily, either one of them could go and take care of it on their own, but according to Mr Nakano, there was something about this customer that seemed fishy.

'What makes you say that?' I had asked, and Mr Nakano had thought for a moment before replying, 'When he called on the phone, he was terribly over-polite.'

After Mr Nakano and Takeo left, Masayo stayed behind at the shop for a little while. Four customers came in, one after another, and all four bought something that Masayo casually recommended – a chipped plate, or a glass with a beer logo on it, or some such.

I hope everything is all right with that customer in Kabukicho, I said after a lull in customers. Masayo tilted her head and said lightly, Everything will be fine.

Maruyama's landlord and his wife sound like strange people, I said after another pause. Masayo tilted her head even more than before. They are, indeed, and Maruyama is a good man. I just hope they don't create any problems for him, she said, sounding deeply concerned now.

Masayo went home soon after that. Once she was gone, the customers suddenly petered out. With nothing to do, I tried to remember what an Afghan hound looked like, but I kept mixing it up with a borzoi or a basset hound, and I couldn't quite picture it.

That means that the landlord and his wife are keeping that Afghan hound inside their house, Masayo had said. People say that they even specially ordered a double-size futon, so that the dog can sleep with them. You mean a futon, not a bed? I asked, and Masayo had nodded.

As I was daydreaming about the idea of that big dog spread out on top of a futon, the phone rang. Startled, I jumped up from my chair. The person on the phone wanted to know how much they could get for a rice cooker from 1975 or so. I told them when Mr Nakano would be back and hung up. Until Mr Nakano and Takeo came back, there wasn't a single customer.

'Was a helmet,' Takeo said.

He was sitting on the yellow stool that had no back, as usual. I was on a chair that looked like something a primary-school student would sit on. This seat wasn't from Mr Nakano's shop; I got it at a church bazaar that was near the place where I used to live.

Over the course of visiting my place numerous times, at some point Takeo seemed to have fallen into the habit of sitting on the yellow stool. But whenever he sat down on it, he did so in such a cautious manner that I wondered if it might be the yellow colour of the chair that he disliked.

'A helmet?' I repeated.

'And, just as Mr Nakano suspected, the guy was a yakuza mister,' Takeo said, putting his elbows on the dining table.

'A yakuza mister?' I laughed – it sounded odd to call a yakuza 'mister'.

'Well, he's still a customer. And compared to some of the others, he seemed like a pretty nice guy.'

The yakuza mister's place was on the top floor of an elegant building that faced the street where the Kabukicho ward office was. They had looked for a parking spot but the streets were packed so tightly with black Lincolns and Mercedes and Presidents, there was nowhere to park. They had no choice but to put the truck in a distant car park, and Mr Nakano and Takeo ended up being late for their appointment.

'Mr Nakano was kind of freaked out,' Takeo said as he swung his upper body back and forth on top of the stool.

What's Mr Nakano like when he's freaked out? I asked. Takeo stopped swinging to and fro.

'He becomes terribly over-polite.'

No way, come on! You mean, just like the yakuza mister? I had a good laugh, and Takeo started swinging his upper body again. The cushioned part of the stool was making a squeaking sound.

In spite of their late arrival, Mr Nakano and Takeo were greeted politely. The yakuza mister's beautiful wife appeared, carrying a tray with fragrant black tea served in Ginori teacups which she offered to them. There was double cream and rose-shaped sugar cubes. Encouraged by their hosts, Mr Nakano and Takeo hastily drank their tea.

'I drank it too fast – I burned my tongue.' Takeo relayed this abruptly.

There was cake too. It was deep, dark black. It wasn't very sweet; it was made almost entirely of chocolate.

'You ate that too fast too?' I asked. Takeo nodded emphatically.

'Did it taste good?'

'Amazingly good.'

Takeo let his gaze briefly wander through the air. Takeo, I said, you like sweets, don't you? But he shook his head slackly. Was hardly sweet at all, it was so dense, he said. Stop making the cushion squeak, I said. Takeo looked surprised. Then his torso went limp and he stopped fidgeting.

Once Mr Nakano and Takeo had finished eating the cake, the yakuza mister clapped his hands together. A door opened suddenly, and two men carried in a helmet and a suit of armour laid out on a plank. The two men were wearing white shirts with dark trousers. One of them looked even younger than Takeo and wore a tightly knotted tie. The one without a tie had a shaved head and round John Lennon glasses. After they placed the helmet and the armour on the floor, the two men quickly left.

'How much would this go for, approximately?' the yakuza mister asked in a composed voice.

'Lemme think.'

Influenced by the yakuza mister's Kansai accent, Mr Nakano had assumed a similar intonation.

'Does Mr Nakano know how to value things like that?'

'Guess helmets and armour have a general market price,' Takeo said, looking down. Now that he could no longer swing his body around, he must be bored. I pretended not to notice.

Mr Nakano offered a price of 100,000 yen. I have no objection to that, the yakuza mister said in a deep voice. His beautiful wife instantly appeared, bringing out whisky. She poured it into shot glasses and served it neat, with a chaser of mineral water in a Baccarat glass. Takeo left his untouched but Mr Nakano drained three shot glasses full, one after another.

It might have been that the alcohol went straight to his head, but Mr Nakano grew bold. Do you have any other items to sell? he asked without any hesitation, which made Takeo nervous. The yakuza mister was silent, sinking into his easy chair. His wife piped up, 'I keep unusually shaped bottles that I came across at the bar.'

She went on, 'Glass liquor bottles are pretty, aren't they? I have a little collection.' She looked from Mr Nakano to Takeo.

'She was what they call a stunner,' Mr Nakano said to Takeo later when they were back in the truck. He speculated that she must have been a hostess in what they call the water trade. Mr Nakano went on, I bet she worked in the kind of bar that you and I will never go to, pushing the kind of expensive booze that we'll never drink in our whole lives.

Each time they stopped at a traffic light, Takeo could hear what sounded like things moving around in the back of the truck. The lightly packed helmet and armour were probably sliding around. When they got onto the Koshu Kaido road, Takeo pulled over onto the side. Mr Nakano had been dozing for a little while. Takeo got out and carefully positioned the helmet and armour in between the cardboard boxes that had been piled up in the truck. When he got back into the driver's seat, Mr Nakano was still asleep. His mouth was half open and he was snoring softly.

'This meal is really delicious,' Takeo muttered once he'd finished telling the story of the yakuza mister.

Really? I answered coolly.

I had put an unusual amount of effort into cooking that night's dinner. Shrimp au gratin. Tomato and avocado salad. Soup with shredded carrots and peppers. Since I rarely ever cooked a proper meal, it had taken me two hours to make it all.

'It's no big deal,' I replied, scooping up some of the gratin and bringing it to my mouth. It needed salt. Just a little bit more. Next I tasted the soup; it was too salty.

Takeo and I ate dinner, neither of us saying much. We finished two cans of beer. Takeo hardly drank at all that evening. Even though I still had half of my food left, Takeo had already finished. Was delicious, he said, swinging his torso a little bit. Then right away, he said to himself, Ah, and was still.

'Hey, what kind of a dog is an Afghan hound?' I tried asking Takeo. He said, Hmm, and knitted his brows together for a moment. Then he pulled over a memo pad that was on the corner of the dining table and did a quick sketch with a pencil. With a pointed nose and long legs, it was a perfect illustration of what an Afghan hound looked like.

'Takeo, you're so good at drawing!' I cried out. Not really all that, he said, and again started to swing his torso. Hey, so next, draw a borzoi, I asked and, still swinging his torso, Takeo ran the pencil several times over the pad. And in no time at all, the shape of a borzoi appeared on the page. Amazing! That's amazing, Takeo! I said, and Takeo rubbed the tip of his nose with the knuckle of his index finger a few times.

At my request, Takeo drew pictures on the memo pad of a basset hound, a rice cooker from the 1970s, and Masayo's doll creations, one after another. Just like that, we moved to the bed, where Takeo then began to draw me full length. Takeo sketched quickly as I posed like Goya's *Maja*. 'This is like his *Clothed Maja*,' I said, but Takeo didn't seem to know what I meant.

After sketching me for a while, Takeo suddenly let out a brief exclamation. What is it? I asked, and just at that moment he stood up and leaned over me.

Takeo quickly took off his jeans. As I tried to take my own off, Takeo took over. My jeans were a little tight so it took some effort, but he managed to get them off as though he was peeling a fruit. We had sex, briefly.

Hey, that was nice, Takeo, I said afterwards, and Takeo looked at me intently.

He didn't say anything, but he was still clothed from the waist up, so he took off his T-shirt. I was still wearing my T-shirt too, and I thought Takeo might take it off for me, so for a moment I didn't move. But he didn't. I debated whether or not to keep it on or to take it off. Takeo had a blank look on his face. I said his name, and with the same expression on his face, he said my name softly in reply.

We had several days of blazing summer heat. Just when I thought the searing heat would never end, it suddenly turned cool, like the weather in early autumn. The Nakano shop continued to thrive; the helmet and armour that Mr Nakano had bought from the yakuza mister had sold for just over a million yen, and the bidding for an ordinary-looking Daruma doll that cost 1,000 yen had gone all the way up to 70,000 yen in an online auction. 'At this rate, I'll be able to hire two or three more of you, Hitomi,' Mr Nakano gloated.

'But it's not as if our salary will go up, I bet,' Takeo and I had said furtively to each other, though at the end of the month when our wages were handed over, there was a bonus of 6,500 yen. There was something about the amount that was just like Mr Nakano.

On payday, Takeo and I went out drinking for the first time in a while. Lured by a happy hour offering 100-yen glasses of beer until seven o'clock, we went to a Thai restaurant in the same building as the train station. We drank until after eight, and Takeo ordered his usual rice to finish, scooping it up with nam pla-flavoured fried chicken. When we went to split the bill and leave, we saw that Masayo and Mr Maruyama were sitting near the entrance.

'Oh, my goodness,' Masayo said brightly. Takeo took half a step back.

'Have a drink with us before you go?' Masayo said. Before we could answer, she quickly moved around the table to sit beside Maruyama. Then she pointed to the chair where she had been sitting and to the one next to it.

'That's extremely mysterious,' Masayo started in as soon as we sat down.

What? We responded in unison.

'Lately, he says that he hasn't seen the dog,' Masayo says, bringing her mug of draught beer to her lips. A waiter was standing beside the table. Oh, I guess we should order. Is beer all right? A bottle, please. And not Singha – regular Japanese is fine, Masayo briskly instructed the waiter.

'Right?' When the waiter left, Masayo seemed to peer into Mr Maruyama's face, seeking a response. Maruyama nodded with his usual vague look.

'Is the dog she's talking about the Afghan at your landlord's place?' I asked Mr Maruyama, who nodded lightly.

'And what's more, the stickering is getting much worse,

isn't it?' Masayo said, peering at Mr Maruyama again. The waiter brought the beer. Masayo placed glasses in front of Takeo and me and swiftly poured some for us. It was all foam, and Takeo's glass overflowed. Masayo paid no attention and kept chattering away.

'Just recently, Maruyama here stopped for a few moments to admire the fragrant olive in the landlord's garden, and the next day, he says, there were three stickers stuck on his door.'

'Three stickers?' I said. Takeo meekly took sips of the foam on his beer.

'All of the stickers had "Be mindful of the plants and trees in the garden" printed on them,' Masayo said in an indignant tone. Mr Maruyama nodded again vaguely. I nearly burst into laughter, but since no one else was laughing, I held back.

'Where on the door were the stickers?'

'On the edge, underneath where they put the ones for the census or to show you've paid the NHK licence fee.'

Wow, Takeo said as if he were exhaling. Masayo glanced at Takeo pointedly. Takeo hastily looked down.

'It's difficult to remove them.' This was the first time Mr Maruyama had spoken. His voice was pleasant, deep and resonant.

'I suppose the door actually belongs to the landlord, so it's probably not illegal for him to put stickers on it,' Masayo went on animatedly. I see, I replied. Takeo was silent.

Mr Maruyama drained the beer in his glass mug. Masayo paused to catch her breath, and drank her beer. I picked up my own glass. It wasn't very cold. When I took a sip, there was only the strong taste of alcohol.

Mr Maruyama took a piece of fried chicken with his chopsticks. It was the same thing that we had eaten. Masayo reached with her chopsticks at the same time. While the two of them were eating the chicken, neither Takeo nor I said anything. Takeo was tapping his foot along with the beat of the Thai music that was playing in the restaurant. There was no distinct rhythm to the music, though, so the beat that Takeo's foot was keeping time with was on the late side.

Well, I guess we'll be on our way.

I stood up, since all I had been doing was watch Mr Maruyama and Masayo eat their chicken. Takeo got up too, as if he were being dragged. Masayo looked up at the two of us, with an expression that said, Oh, you're leaving already? Her mouth was full of chicken, so she didn't say anything.

I made a slight bow. Takeo did the same. Just as we were turning our backs on them, Mr Maruyama wiped his fingertips on his paper napkin and said, in his low and resonant voice, 'It seems that the dog has died!'

'Hitomi, do you like dogs?' Mr Nakano asked.

'Generally,' I replied.

'Losing a pet must be terrible,' Mr Nakano said as he flipped through the pages of the notebook.

'Do you think so?' I replied. I have never had a dog or a cat. When Takeo and I were on our way home from the Thai restaurant where we ran into Mr Maruyama and Masayo, Takeo had muttered, 'It's so hard when a dog dies.'

Did you have a dog, Takeo? I asked. Takeo nodded deeply.

'I started working at Mr Nakano's because my dog died.'

Really? I asked, but Takeo did not offer much further explanation. All he said was, The mongrel I'd had since kindergarten died last year. Then he fell silent.

I'll see you home tonight. Takeo had been so sad after our conversation about the dog that night that I had walked with him all the way to his house. By the time we got close to where he lived, Takeo had cheered up a little bit. Now it's my turn to see you home, he had said and started to turn back towards the station, but I stopped him.

Once Takeo disappeared through the gate, I turned on my heel and headed for the station. I should have made it to the station in about ten minutes, but at some point I found myself walking along unfamiliar streets. The surroundings all looked the same to me. I seemed to be a little lost.

I thought I was following a street with regularly spaced street lights when suddenly I was in the dark. There were rows of old-looking apartment buildings. There was no sign of anyone around. As I braced myself for a moment, wondering if this was a cemetery or something similar, I heard a dog bark in the distance. Just as I was about to turn back, I realized with a start where I was.

This was Mr Maruyama's landlord's property.

I just stood still for a moment. I recalled Takeo's voice, saying, It's so hard when a dog dies. Mr Maruyama's evasiveness also came to mind, albeit faintly.

Okay, let's go, I said out loud as I headed straight for the landlord's 'pride and joy' garden. All three of the apartment buildings were quiet, and I saw no lights on in the main house where the landlord and his wife lived. Passing under the arch with its roses, I strode into the landlord's garden. The night-blooming vines and creepers were entwined around the trunks of big trees, with huge white flowers in bloom. My shoes made a rustling sound as I stepped on the grass.

As I walked a bit further, I came to a place where the ground was piled up. The earth was heaped in a mound that was just about the length and width of a person lying down. It was the only place where there weren't any plants. There was the fresh scent of earth that has been dug up and then reburied.

I came to a stop right beside the mound. As I stared at it for a moment, my eyes adjusted. At one end of it stood a cross. Leaning against the cross, there was a photograph of a dog with a long snout. There was a sticker on the top part of the cross. Written on the sticker, it said, HERE LIES PES.

I let out a cry and leapt away from the earth. I hastily made my way out of the garden. I was aware that I was recklessly trampling the grassy undergrowth, but I broke into a run anyway. I was still walking at a quick pace when I reached the station. My fingertips were trembling as I reached into my wallet for some change to buy a ticket. Once I was on the train, the fluorescent lights were uncomfortably bright.

'I'm thinking of getting a dog,' Mr Nakano said with nonchalance.

'Sure,' I replied flatly. I hadn't told anyone about what I had seen that night in Maruyama's landlord's garden. Not even Takeo, of course.

The heat has returned, Mr Nakano said, stretching. When it gets too hot, the customers don't leave their houses.

Hey, Hitomi, if we go into the red, would you give me back that 6,500 yen? Mr Nakano laughed and stretched again.

Not a chance, I replied. Mr Nakano stood up and went into the back room. I hear Maruyama is moving, you know, Mr Nakano said from within. What? Is he going to live with Masayo? I asked. Nope, apparently the landlord's sticker offensive was too much for him, so he got scared and found a cheaper apartment nearby.

As I contemplated the fact that Mr Maruyama didn't strike me as someone who would be afraid of the likes of the landlord, a customer came in and I nodded in greeting. The customer stood in the corner where the picture frames were and sized up what was there. He was picking up each of the five frames that were lined up, one by one, turning them over and bringing them close to his face.

After a while, the customer held out a small frame and said, I'll take this one. Is the picture inside included in the price? he asked. I looked to see that the frame held a sketch of a woman holding a pose like *The Nude Maja*. It looked exactly like what Takeo had drawn when he had been over at my apartment the other night.

I let out a little cry. I thought the sketch he had done was a *Clothed Maja*, but the woman in the drawing in the frame was naked. I was disoriented, my mouth agape. Mr Nakano called out a welcome to the customer as he came in from the back. The glass of the frame caught the afternoon light, sparkling in reflection.

Celluloid

'The other day, I wasn't naked, right?' I said, and Takeo nodded lightly.

'At what point did you undress me?' I realized, after asking the question, that it was a strange one.

Not being naked – I was referring to that sketch he made of me. The one that had originally been like *The Clothed Maja*, but had, at some point without my realizing it, turned into *The Nude Maja* and shown up, of all places, inside a picture frame in the shop.

Being undressed without realizing it didn't quite express what I meant. It was impossible to take off or put clothes on the me in the drawing.

'When did I become naked?' I rephrased the question. It still sounded a little strange, but the way Takeo glanced up at me from under his brows annoyed me, and I couldn't think of the right way to ask him.

Takeo remained silent.

'Hey, this kind of thing, like, creeps me out.'

Takeo opened his mouth, but then closed it again. The *Clothed Maja* had resembled me, but the *Nude Maja* didn't just resemble me – it looked exactly like me. From the texture of my thighs to the spacing between my nipples, even the disproportion of my peculiarly long calves to the rest of my leg – he had captured me with shuddering precision.

'I mean, a customer saw it.'

Takeo still wasn't saying anything, so my voice grew high and forceful. I disliked myself for nagging him, and my voice was all the sharper.

That sketch, Takeo began.

That sketch, just what was it? Instantly I pounced. Takeo closed his mouth again. His glare was fixed on the floor, his eyes like a stubborn little creature that lives on a riverbank. C'mon, say something, I prodded, but Takeo held his silence.

In the end Takeo never did say anything about it. As he watched, I tore the sketch, 'Hitomi, After *Nude Maja*', into tiny pieces.

'Hitomi, you look tired these past few days,' Mr Nakano said. Yeah, I guess, I replied. It's just late summer fatigue. The air conditioning is broken in my apartment.

'Takeo could fix that for you,' Mr Nakano said. What? I asked. You mean, Takeo can fix air conditioners?

Mr Nakano said that last year, when the air conditioner in the shop's truck was acting up, Takeo cleverly fixed it. I don't know, Mr Nakano rolled his eyes as he explained, once he took it apart and fiddled with it this way and that, then it was fixed.

'Should I say something to him about it?' he asked.

'I'm fine.'

Even I was aware that my flat refusal of Mr Nakano's offer made me sound snappish and unapproachable. Mr Nakano regarded me with a look like that of a pigeon pecking at grains in the grounds of a temple. I thought he would ask me if I'd had a fight with Takeo, but instead Mr Nakano just tilted his head to one side.

Mr Nakano went out of the door and began smoking a cigarette in front of the shop. Masayo was always telling him not to leave ash in front of his own store, but that day was no different – he thought nothing of leaving his cigarette butt out there. Mr Nakano's shadow was trailing behind him diagonally. The dark and squat shade of high summer was no longer with us.

After the temporarily cool days of early September, suddenly we were having an Indian summer, despite the fact that it was almost October. The air conditioning in the Nakano shop was an ancient and hulking thing that made quite a racket when it got going.

This air conditioner is definitely female, Mr Nakano had said one day. It flies into sudden rages, you know. And with all that clanging – once it says what it needs to say, then it goes quiet. But just when you think it's done, there it goes again. With no warning, suddenly it flies into another rage.

Takeo had chuckled at what Mr Nakano had said. This was before the *Nude Maja* incident, so I had given a carefree laugh as well. Just then the air conditioner had started making loud noises, and the three of us had looked at each other and all burst out laughing again.

Mr Nakano was now lighting his second cigarette. His

shoulders were hunched – although the temperature outside must be close to thirty degrees, for some reason he looked like he was cold. It was quiet in the shop. Ever since the Indian summer arrived, customers had been staying away. The street in front of the shop was deserted – there wasn't a single car. I saw Mr Nakano sneeze. I couldn't hear it. I had thought that it was quiet but the air conditioner must have been even louder than I realized. My ears had got used to its hum, and probably couldn't even differentiate its sound any more.

I followed Mr Nakano's movements absent-mindedly, as if watching a silent movie. After wavering over whether or not to light a third cigarette, Mr Nakano returned the cigarette that had been in his mouth to the pack. But the packet was crumpled up and he had a hard time putting it back in. As Mr Nakano tried harder to replace the cigarette, his shoulders grew even more hunched. His shadow's shoulders grew round as well.

At last, unable to put it back in the packet, Mr Nakano once again put it in his mouth. Then he turned his head around. His shadow's head moved in unison with Mr Nakano but the shift was sharper than that of his body.

A cat darted in front of Mr Nakano. He called out something to the cat. Over the past few weeks, the cat had been peeing in front of the shop. Each time we had to clean thoroughly.

Cat piss stinks like hell! Mr Nakano would say with seeming annoyance as he scrubbed at it with a deck brush. While both Mr Nakano and I suspected this spotted cat of making a habit of peeing here, Takeo had been secretly feeding it. At the back door where the truck was parked, Takeo was leaving dry food in the upturned bowl of a small *suribachi*. The cat always came by just after four in the afternoon. By the time Mr Nakano got back from a pickup or returned from the market at six o'clock, the dry food had been eaten up.

Takeo called the cat Mimi. When he said 'Little Mimi', his voice sounded much more tender than when he said my name, 'Hitomi'.

One day, no customers came in at all. But the Nakano shop was not some high-class antique shop – no matter how slow a day it might be, there were almost always at least three or four people who would wander in to browse.

'You know what I mean?' Mr Nakano said just as he was about to close the shop. At the height of summer, there had still been daylight up until the moment when the shutter was closed but at some point the sun had started going down sooner than I realized. And once the sun set, the temperature cooled off a bit, unlike in the early days of September.

Yes? I replied. It had been a while since I'd heard Mr Nakano use his pet phrase, but today it evoked no mirth in me. Ever since Takeo and I had stopped speaking, I had been impassive to whatever I saw or heard. And I myself found this annoying.

'Are all women really so damned erotic?' Mr Nakano asked. As usual, he was abrupt and hard to understand.

Erotic? I asked. I had intended to ignore him, but I had hardly spoken all day, and I felt like making some kind of sound.

'I mean, I came across something, I mean, something strange written by a woman,' Mr Nakano said, plopping down into one of the chairs in the shop. It was an unusual item for the Nakano shop, a true antique. American, late nineteenth century. It had a slender frame with an open pattern on its back, but Mr Nakano was sitting on it very casually. No doubt he would complain were Takeo or I to sit on it.

'What do you mean by something strange?' I asked. When he said 'woman', he must have been talking about his lover Sakiko. Mr Nakano started nervously tapping his foot.

'It's, you know—' He broke off, falling silent.

'When you say something written, is it like a letter?' Mr Nakano still wasn't saying anything, so I tried prodding him.

'It's not a letter.'

'Could it be like a picture?'

'It's not a picture either.'

I tried to remember what Sakiko's face looked like. For some reason, I couldn't quite fix upon her face when I had met her in the hospital after Mr Nakano had been stabbed. Rather than what she looked like, I could only recall her sobbing, surprisingly heavy with emotion.

'She says it's a made-up story, but—' Mr Nakano finally began to speak again.

I did remember Sakiko's face from the moment when I saw her with Mr Nakano as they were going into the love hotel. She had suddenly turned around, probably only for a fraction of a second, and my impression of her face in that moment was embedded distinctly in my mind. But whether that was actually what Sakiko's face looked like, or if it had been jumbled and transformed within my unsteady memory, I couldn't say.

'A made-up story?'

'It's, you know, totally pornographic. A story of a woman doing it like crazy.'

What? I retorted. I did not follow the connection.

'What is the relationship between this woman and the story of doing it like crazy?' I asked.

You know what I mean? Mr Nakano said, taking his head in his hands as his foot kept tapping even more intensely. You know what I mean? She's writing it! Look, it's like, like one of those novels! A story about a woman who's doing it like crazy!

'What? You mean, Sakiko was a novelist?' I shouted without thinking.

What the hell, Hitomi? How do you know her name? Mr Nakano asked, stilling his foot for a moment.

'But, didn't we meet her at the hospital?'

'But, it's not as if I introduced her as my mistress!'

Well, it was pretty obvious. In the first place, she was crying her eyes out, wasn't she? I said to a dumbstruck Mr Nakano. I just can't, I don't understand her at all, I swear, he muttered.

'Does she have a pen name?'

'Listen – in the first place – I do not associate with novelists, I told you.'

'But you just said that Sakiko is writing a novel.'

'Not a novel – just something like it. Anyway, there's no plot at all.'

'How pornographic is it?'

It's really nothing more than scenes of them doing it. Mr Nakano gave a deep sigh.

It sounds like a script for an adult film, I ventured timidly.

'Do adult films even have scripts? Don't they just film them and then edit them?'

'No, I hear there are some that are quite artistic.'

'But, as far as adult films go, I prefer ones that are simple and easy to understand.'

The conversation had digressed. Mr Nakano was slouched carelessly in the chair, looking up at the ceiling. The back of the chair was bending. I was about to utter, Are you sure it's, uh, okay to do that? But I held my tongue. One time, Mr Nakano had been using the feather duster on a small jar that looked as though it was going to fall over. 'Look out!' I cried, just as the jar fell and broke into pieces. Mr Nakano didn't reproach me, but somehow I understood that it was better not to say anything to him in a situation like that. Rarely has the ability to foresee danger been of any use to me – that's why I spend money like water! This was something Masayo said all the time, whether or not it had any relevance.

Part of me wanted to know more details about the 'totally pornographic' thing that Sakiko was writing, but part of me didn't want to hear about it. Mr Nakano had lapsed back into silence. The back of the chair made an ominous squeaking sound.

The next day, Mr Nakano was going to the auction market in Kawagoe very early, so I was entrusted with the key to the shop. I opened the shutter when I arrived, and after quickly arranging some items for sale on the bench, I went to put the key away in the back room when I saw there was a note from Mr Nakano on top of the safe.

'Hitomi, read this and tell me what you think,' it said, and as my gaze glanced from Mr Nakano's scrawl written in blue

Magic Marker, I saw that he had left the manuscript pages there beneath his note. It was on the kind of paper that had been distributed in school during composition class: Kokuyo brand sheets lined in brown with spaces for 400 characters on each page.

There was nothing written on the first page. Picking up the manuscript and flipping through it, I saw that the writing began after five blank lines on the second page.

'Along the midline,' I read out loud at first. The hand-writing was beautiful. It was written in black ink with a fine-tipped fountain pen.

'Along the midline, without straying,' I continued.

'The forehead, the bridge of the nose, the lips, the chin, the neck.' This isn't pornographic at all, I thought as I read. But after the third line, I could no longer read it aloud.

Here is what kind of writing it was:

'Along the midline, without straying. The forehead, the bridge of the nose, the lips, the chin, the neck, the breast-bone, the solar plexus, the navel, then from the clitoris to the vagina and to the anus. Gently trace along with your fingertip. Slowly, over and over, without stopping, as if this caress will go on forever. But without letting your finger drift from the midline of my body.

For instance, when your finger reaches my breast-bone, you must not let your finger trail around my nipples, or trace the wisp of my waist.

Simply trace the midline with your finger, repeated-ly. I still have my panties on. Without leaving the midline, put your finger inside my panties and, even more carefully, trace along where my clitoris, my vagina, and my anus align.

You must not squeeze or rub, or apply any pressure. Only slightly heavier than a feather, just barely lighter than a stream of water – you mustn't break the rhythm.

Simply continue to trace the undulating line of my body, from the forehead to the sacrum, with your wanton middle finger, ever so slowly.'

I swallowed as I read. The eroticism was different from how I had imagined it. But this time, I clearly remembered what Sakiko's face looked like. Not only the moment I saw her turn around in front of the love hotel, but I also distinctly recalled her somewhat swollen expression when she had been sobbing at the hospital.

A customer came in. I hurriedly turned over the manuscript and laid it down next to the till. Welcome, I said, much louder than usual. The customer looked at me, startled. He was a regular customer, a student who lived in the neighbourhood. He stuck out his chin and reluctantly nodded a brief greeting. The student then took a turn around the shop before hastening out the door.

'Sorry, Hitomi, sorry,' Mr Nakano said, not very sincerely, as he slipped back into the shop.

Sorry – what for? I say, furrowing my brow.

'I realized when I was in Kawagoe, you know, that might have been sexual harassment,' Mr Nakano said, taking off his green beanie. Since September, Mr Nakano had been shaving his head. Finally, Haruo is really going bald, Masayo said, but once he started wearing his hair this way, it turned out that Mr Nakano had quite a nicely shaped head. Or better yet, you're the type who would look good as bald as an egg! Masayo said admiringly, which only incensed Mr Nakano.

'Legally speaking, it *is* sexual harassment,' I replied solemnly. Mr Nakano peered into my face. The scent of dust wafted from his shirt. Lots of things at the auction market have been in storage, so whenever Mr Nakano went there he always came back covered in dust.

'Apart from that, were you able to buy anything good?' I asked in a completely ordinary tone. Mr Nakano's face suddenly brightened.

'Hey, Hitomi, you know, what did you think?' he asked me without replying to my question.

Why, what do you mean? I feigned ignorance. I had spent the entire morning reading Sakiko's manuscript. Actually, I thought it was amazing. I wondered if the first-person narrator was really Sakiko. The sexual act – from the beginning or foreplay, up until the finish or afterplay – was catalogued in vivid, lascivious detail. The narrator came at least a dozen times. Phoof! I said to myself as I devoured the pages. Five customers showed up but, whether or not it was in response to my fervour, just like the earlier student each one of them had hastily retreated from the shop, and so today's sales were still at zero.

When I went to the convenience store to get a sandwich for lunch, I decided to make a copy of Sakiko's manuscript. I felt a little uneasy about it, but I justified it to myself that I wasn't the one who had asked to see it. As I held the cover of the photocopier over the manuscript, the narrow strip of white light that escaped from the gap was dazzling to my eyes.

'Don't be mean, Hitomi. You read it, didn't you? That there,' Mr Nakano asked, casting a sidelong glance at the manuscript which was neatly arranged next to the till. Yes, well, I nod. Do you always have sex like that? I asked, making my voice sound as nonchalant as possible.

'Hitomi, isn't that reverse sexual harassment?' Mr Nakano said, pouting his lips.

So, you don't? I pushed further.

'I mean, that kind of thing, it's too much.'

Really?

'When I have sex, I'm more, like – you know, conscientious and honest,' Mr Nakano said as he rubbed the top of his head with the palm of his hand. It made a faint scraping sound.

'Are there people – do they all have such complicated sex?' I asked as I looked Mr Nakano square in the face. The 'I' and 'you' in the story that Sakiko had written had licked every conceivable part of each other's bodies, they had tried every conceivable sexual position, they had made every conceivable lewd sound, they had indulged in every conceivable pleasure.

'I wouldn't know,' Mr Nakano replied with mild disappointment.

Now, you see, I'll lose confidence, with her writing that kind of thing, he went on, blinking his eyes. Suddenly another waft of the scent of dust drifted over from Mr Nakano.

So, you mean, your style of lovemaking is simpler? I ventured without thinking, driven by curiosity.

No, uh, even though I'm middle-aged – you know what I mean? – I still do all right. But, you know, what is it – pretentious? Or elaborate? I mean, really, that business with the finger, that's not my kind of thing.

Come to think of it, there was something about Sakiko's writing that was reminiscent of the way that Mr Nakano talked. 'This here, what is it, literary?'

By the way, what kinds of things were you able to buy today? I changed the subject.

Without even answering my question about his work today, Mr Nakano just maintained his vacant expression. At one point he moved as if to sit in that same antique chair but, wavering, he decided not to sit there after all. Instead, Mr Nakano sank down onto an unstable, three-legged synthetic leather stool which had long languished in the shop.

There was the sound of a motor at the back door. Takeo had probably returned. Masayo was most likely in the truck with him as well. Masayo had gone along with Takeo, under the pretext of gathering 'materials' for her new doll creations. That day's pickup had been at the home of a man who had been a diplomat for many years and had just passed away.

'There were two Shinsui Itos there,' Masayo said as she strode into the shop. Mr Nakano looked up absent-mindedly. Takeo came in behind Masayo. Mr Nakano glanced at Masayo and then lowered his gaze once again. I myself had turned away the instant Takeo walked in.

It had been about five days since I had looked Takeo directly in the face.

'Come now, what's happened here?' Masayo asked in a forceful voice. Takeo was standing behind Masayo with a blank look. When I looked up for a moment, my eyes met Takeo's. I glared at him reflexively, but Takeo remained impassive.

Back at my apartment, I was pouring hot water over instant *yakisoba* noodles when the phone rang. I grumbled as I answered, holding the receiver between my ear and my shoulder.

'This is Kiryu, is this Miss Suganuma?' said the voice on the line.

What? I asked in reply.

'It's Kiryu, this Miss Suganuma?' the voice said again.

What is this? I replied brusquely.

The caller was silent for a moment. What do you want? I added, even more bluntly. After another brief silence, I could hear a stifled cough.

'Ah, of course, your last name is Kiryu,' I said reluctantly, since Takeo still wasn't saying a word.

'Thought you knew, Hitomi.'

I have a faint recollection, I said. Actually, I knew perfectly well, but it aggravated me to tell Takeo this.

'Um, I'm sorry for drawing you naked without asking,' Takeo said in a monotone, as if he were reading a script. The way he spoke the words, it was as if he had rehearsed how to say them over and over, and actually practised speaking them, so that their meaning was already worn thin, for him at least.

'It's okay,' I replied softly.

'I'm sorry.'

'It's okay.' It was a little depressing to be apologized to repeatedly.

'I'm sorry.'

I didn't say anything. Neither did Takeo. I stared at the second hand of the small clock that was in front of the phone without really looking at it. It moved slowly from the six to the eleven mark.

'Well, my *yakisoba* is getting cold,' I said, at the same time that Takeo uttered, 'Uh, your naked body.'

'What about my naked body?'

'I think it's beautiful,' Takeo continued in a voice that was difficult to hear.

I didn't hear you, so say it one more time, I said. Can't, Takeo replied. I was in the middle of making *yakisoba*, I said. Yes, Takeo said.

I'm sorry, Takeo repeated for the last time before hanging up. I shifted the receiver into my hand and looked at the clock – the second hand had reached the six again.

I stood there watching the second hand as it continued to revolve, over and over. Remembering my *yakisoba*, I pulled back the lid and, just as I thought, the noodles had absorbed the rest of the liquid and were completely soggy.

The next day, it was suddenly autumn. The heat had gone, and the sky was impossibly clear.

Once summer reached its end, various markets popped up all over the Kanto region, which kept Mr Nakano busy. That day Takeo had also been recruited for the market. Even Masayo, who normally dropped by for a leisurely visit once every three days or so, was occupied with preparations for her doll creation exhibition, which would open in November.

We had an unusually high turnover – although we sold

only small things, the takings totalled more than 300,000 yen. Ordinarily, whenever Mr Nakano hadn't returned to the shop by closing time, I just left the money in the till and locked up, delivering the key to Masayo's house. That was the usual procedure, but I was concerned about leaving such a large amount of cash, so I hung around the shop even after closing up.

I went out the front to lower the shutter, then went around to the back door and locked it from the inside. In the back room, where we usually put an unsold *kotatsu*, if one was around, there was now a large low table. It was for sale, but each of us used it in turn for our lunch break. Don't worry if you spill soup or anything on it – that only gives it more charm, Mr Nakano liked to say.

I made a pot of tea and drank it at the table, first one cup, then a second, and even a third weak cup of what was left, but Mr Nakano still hadn't returned. I had left a message on his mobile's voicemail that I was still at the shop, and so I had expected him to knock on the back door when he arrived, but now I worried that I might not have heard him.

I opened the back door to check the garage, but the truck wasn't there.

I took out the copy of the 'something like a novel' that Sakiko had written from the cloth bag that I always carried.

I stared idly at the sentence: 'At first, when I came, my voice was high. Then, gradually, it grew lower, and deeper.' Come to think of it, since September began, it seemed as though Mr Nakano's trips 'to the bank' had been a bit less frequent.

The phone rang. I walked over towards where it was next

to the till, debating whether or not to answer it. The lights in the shop were turned off, so I walked slowly, trying not to kick any of the merchandise.

The phone rang for a long time. Even when I finally picked it up, after about fifteen rings, the caller had not yet hung up.

They spoke before I could even say, 'The Nakano shop.'

'It's me.'

Excuse me? I asked. The caller was silent. I had a hunch it was Sakiko.

'Mr Nakano isn't back yet from the market in Fujisawa,' I said, making my voice as neutral as I could.

Thank you, Sakiko replied. After another short silence, she said, This is Miss Suganuma, isn't it? Since I had started the job at the Nakano shop, only rarely had I been called by my last name, but now it had happened two days in a row.

'Yes, it is.'

'My . . . what I . . . you read it, didn't you?' Sakiko said.

Yes, I replied frankly.

'How was it?' Sakiko asked.

'Thought it was amazing.' I slipped inadvertently into Takeo's way of speaking.

Sakiko giggled to herself.

'Hey,' Sakiko said, as if we were girlfriends who talked on the phone all the time. 'You know those celluloid dolls? Don't you think there's something erotic about them?'

Excuse me? I asked in reply.

'I've always thought so, ever since I was little – when I see the way their joints move, their arms and legs going all around,' Sakiko went on.

I was silent, unable to reply with even a 'Yes' or an 'I see'. After that, Sakiko didn't say anything more either.

The next thing I knew, Sakiko had hung up, and I was standing there in the gloomy darkness, holding the receiver.

Celluloid, I murmured.

The *lulo* of celluloid was difficult to pronounce.

I replaced the receiver and returned to the back room. I never had any celluloid dolls. When I was growing up, most of the dolls were made of soft plastic – Jenny and Sara and Anna – for some reason they all had foreign names.

I glanced at Sakiko's 'novel' again, and the word 'pussy' jumped out at me. It was a scene in which the man forces the narrator to say this word.

I could imagine Mr Nakano doing such a thing, I thought to myself as I put the photocopy back in my cloth bag. The fluorescent lights were painfully bright, and I covered my eyes with the palm of my hand.

Sewing Machine

'A Seiko Matsuda came in, you know,' Mr Nakano was saying.

'When's it from?' Tokizo asked.

'Says here it's from the early 1980s,' Mr Nakano said as he flipped through the notebook. The words *Seiko* → *early 80s*, written in the notebook that we keep by the shop's telephone, were in Takeo's handwriting. Considering his typical demeanour, it was difficult to imagine that these delicate and well-formed characters were his.

'In any case, we'll attach a photo, and you can let me take care of the sales copy – send it by email to me right away,' Tokizo said briskly.

Masayo referred to Tokizo as 'Mr Crane' behind his back. I think it was because he was skinny like a crane, and also because he had the dignity of a lord.

'You know, it's rumoured that Tokizo went to Gakushuin University,' Masayo had once whispered to me conspiratorially. Oh yeah, Gakushuin? I replied blankly, and Masayo responded by matching my inane tone. 'Yeah, that's right.'

Tokizo was maybe about sixty-five years old, or past seventy, or he might already have been well into his nineties – it was impossible to tell. The other day he mentioned that he gets a pension, so he must be at least sixty-five, Masayo said. Hey sis, do you have a thing for Tokizo? Mr Nakano asked. Masayo tautly arched the perfectly groomed crescent moons of her brows as she retorted, What are you talking about? Mr Nakano answered, I mean, you're the one who seems to want to know things about Tokizo.

Don't be ridiculous, Masayo said, pouting and looking away. Hmm, is it really so ridiculous? I wondered as I stared at her profile without really looking at her. There was no soft downy hair at all on Masayo's face. Do you shave it? I had asked her once. I do not shave it, Masayo had replied. My hair is very fine. Hardly any grows there at all.

What? I raised my head in surprise, but Masayo wore an air of nonchalance. Mr Nakano too seemed indifferent. Such an odd pair of siblings.

'The Seiko Matsuda must be one of those rare life-size stand-up posters, but if it has a few flaws, the starting bid will probably be at the low end.'

'It's fine if it starts low, then it can go up from there.'

Mr Nakano and Tokizo were discussing the items that would be for sale in the online auctions that Tokizo was taking on. Lately the percentage of the Nakano shop's Internet sales had been increasing. It's risky to leave things to others, Haruo, so you had better learn how to use a computer, Masayo told him, but Mr Nakano wanted absolutely nothing to do with the computer, so from the start he had let Tokizo handle it all.

I think Tokizo is related to Sakiko, Takeo had told me a little while ago, so that might have been why.

If Tokizo is related to Sakiko, then Mr Nakano's circle is pretty small, isn't it? I said. Takeo thought about it for a moment and then replied, Mine is even smaller – you and my dog who died. Your dog who died, I echoed. My dog, he repeated. There was a certain contentment in the sadness I felt at that moment.

Takeo was the one who carried the life-size full-body photo of the 1980s pop star into the shop. Backed by cardboard, it had been part of an ad campaign for a sewing-machine manufacturer almost twenty years earlier.

'That's Seiko Matsuda, isn't it?' Mr Nakano asked cheerfully.

I was in the midst of explaining that one of my classmates in middle school had collected celebrity things but that this was a bit outside of what he might consider a collector's item, when Takeo brought it in sideways.

'People will be startled to come into the shop and suddenly see a full-sized cardboard figure appear before them,' Masayo said.

'I think these kinds of things are called life-size stand-up posters,' Mr Nakano replied, peering closely at the face of Seiko Matsuda.

'Did you get this for free?' Mr Nakano asked Takeo.

'Said he would sell it for 5,000 yen.'

'He didn't just give it to you? What a cheapskate!' Mr

Nakano shouted, slapping himself on the forehead.

Takeo didn't say anything and laid Seiko Matsuda down on the tatami. The hair around her ears and her fringe, curled and rolled up and out, had lost some of its colour and lustre on the posterboard.

'Seiko Matsuda is pretty, isn't she?' I said, and Mr Nakano nodded. I've got a few of her records, he said.

Is that so? I nodded matter-of-factly. Mr Nakano must have taken a little offence, because he said, 'It has a slightly different meaning for someone my age to buy her records.'

'Meaning?'

'Seiko has a certain kitsch about her.'

As Mr Nakano was talking, Takeo went out of the back door. Is that so? Once again I nodded matter-of-factly at Mr Nakano.

'For example, Hitomi, when you hear the word *ayu*, it calls to mind the delicately sweet fish and the pleasures of an otherworldly nature, does it not?' Mr Nakano went on.

Ayu, I murmured. By Ayu, you mean the singer Ayumi Hamasaki? I asked, purposely imitating the way that Takeo talked. Mr Nakano let both hands hang down loosely.

I was about to follow up by asking what he meant by otherworldly nature, but it wasn't the moment to tease Mr Nakano, so I thought better of it.

Well, that's enough, Mr Nakano said under his breath, and followed Takeo out. The life-size Seiko Matsuda was lying face up on the tatami. In one hand she held a sewing machine, while the other hand lightly pointed at her chest, and she wore a sweet smile.

Ayu, my lips formed the word one more time as I shook my head.

'Also need a scrubbing brush,' Takeo said.

A scrubbing brush? I asked.

'For cleaning.'

'But don't we have a deck brush?'

'You can work into it better with a scrubbing brush.'

The cleaning we were talking about involved scrubbing the cat pee from the front of the shop. Lately the cat had been peeing there more and more frequently, marking no fewer than three times a day. At the entrance to the alley right beside the Nakano shop, where the asphalt was cracked, tufts of foxtail grass were growing, and it appeared that stray cats were using it as a toilet.

'Who's going to use this scrubbing brush?'

'You, me, I don't know.'

'Ugh, not me.'

'Okay, then, I'll take care of it myself.'

Takeo looked at me with an upward glance.

'I didn't say I wouldn't do it, did I? Just that I don't want to use the scrubbing brush. I do just fine with the deck brush.'

'I got it.'

Even with his upturned eyes, his gaze was intense. Was he scowling at me, this guy? I was suddenly annoyed.

'Hey, are you still feeding it?' I asked. Despite the problem with the cat pee, Takeo was always leaving cat food at the back door.

'Cat who comes to eat is not the same cat who is pissing here.'

How can you tell? I retorted coolly. Takeo clamped his lips together. His shoulders stiffened. Instantly I regretted what I'd said.

We were making a shopping list. Masayo had written, *Planters, size #5 (two), clay pebbles.* Below that was Mr Nakano's writing, *Gummed linen tape, three rolls; black Magic Marker, broad tip; curry-flavoured curls.* The hardware store doesn't sell curry-flavoured curls, does it? I tried saying to Takeo, but he remained tight-lipped.

The phone rang. Takeo was closer to the phone so I waited and let it ring four times, but Takeo made no move to answer it. Hello, I said as I brought the receiver to my ear, and after a brief silence, there was a click as the line went dead.

'They hung up,' I said as brightly as I could manage, but Takeo still kept silent. The heat of Indian summer had finally ended, and the days had been clear and bright. The clouds were high in the sky. Mr Nakano was at another dealer's market that was being held in Kawagoe. I'll find out what the market price for Seiko is, he had said as he drove away in the truck.

'Cats are cute, aren't they?' It was a struggle to keep the conversation going, but I tried aiming for cheerfulness.

'Think so?' At last Takeo spoke.

'They're cute.'

'Not so much.'

'So why do you feed them, then?'

'No reason.'

What is this about? I cried. What is it that I said?

A bee had flown into the shop, through the front door which had been propped open, and it was buzzing around. With his face still lowered, Takeo was watching the bee's flight out of the corner of his eye. It soon found its way back outside.

'No reason,' Takeo repeated. Then he quietly folded up the shopping list and put it in his back pocket, turning his back on me. Do you have money? I called after him. I do, he said without turning around.

Takeo's voice was composed, which made me all the more angry. I had a tremendous urge to say something nasty.

'We won't see each other any more,' I said. Takeo turned around.

'Just the two of us, I mean, not any more.'

What? Takeo seemed to say, but I couldn't catch his voice.

He just stood there for a moment but then he turned his back again, and this time he hurried out of the shop even more quickly. I wanted to shout after him, Wait! But I couldn't find my voice.

I had absolutely no idea why I had blurted out such a thing. The bee came back inside. Just like before, rather than going straight back outside, it flew droning around the entire shop. The sound of its wings echoed loudly when it came near the till. I waved the towel that Mr Nakano had left on a chair. The towel only fanned the air. Flashing its wings sedately, the bee just kept flying around inside the shop.

'They said Seiko's campaign for Walkman II went for as much as 270,000 yen,' Mr Nakano said, opening his eyes wide.

At the market in Kawagoe, Mr Nakano had enquired with the other dealers he knew about the going rate for a life-size stand-up poster. 'Two hundred and seventy thousand,' Masayo said, her eyes popping too. Even though they were brother and sister, ordinarily Masayo and Mr Nakano didn't look anything like each other, but when they made this wide-eyed expression, they were like peas in a pod.

'They said that the ones Junko Sakurada and Kumiko Okae did for cold medicines also went for almost as much.'

Really? My goodness, Masayo said, nodding deeply. Under the pretext of preparing for her doll creation exhibition, Masayo had recently been coming to the Nakano shop every day. The inspiration wells up in me when I come to the shop, she would claim, and spend almost the entire afternoon there. Thanks to her, the past month's sales had been very good. For whatever reason, as long as Masayo is by the till, customers seem to make purchases as if they were under her spell.

'Wow, I wonder if our sewing machine Seiko will sell for as much as two hundred thousand too,' Masayo said dreamily. The Seiko Matsuda that Takeo had brought in was now standing in a corner of the back room. That girl sure makes it seem easy to hold up that heavy-looking sewing machine, doesn't she? Masayo said with admiration. These celebrities are so impressive! she went on. I still couldn't fathom Masayo.

'There's a big crease on her hip, you know, so two hundred thousand seems unlikely, but I don't see why it can't go for one hundred thousand,' Mr Nakano replied absently. Since the day before yesterday, he had swapped his beanie for a bobble hat like the one the old manga character Sho-chan wore. Soon it will be winter, one of the regular customers had said yesterday, eyeing Mr Nakano's hat.

What do you think, Hitomi? they asked me, and I raised my head. I had been texting Takeo all morning, but he hadn't replied. He hadn't come back after he went to the hardware store yesterday. I had lingered in the shop until eight o'clock, but he had never shown up.

Takeo had apparently come in early this morning to drop off the things he bought at the hardware store, and I had been late to arrive, so our paths hadn't crossed.

'That guy, he didn't buy my curry curls,' Mr Nakano said, pouting. His pom-pom wobbled. Should I go and get some? I offered. I hate to ask, Mr Nakano said, even as he was taking out some coins. If there's any change, buy something for yourself too. Masayo laughed at him. She's not an errand girl!

I walked over to an old bakery that was on the edge of the shopping district. I checked my messages as I walked. I didn't have a single new text. Preoccupied with my phone, I managed to trip over a parked bicycle.

I righted the fallen bicycle, and as I went to set the kickstand, it made a rasping sound. I looked and saw that the kickstand was bent at a strange angle. In my haste to get my hands off the bike, it fell over again. No matter what I did, I could not get it to stand up on its own. I had no choice but to lean the bicycle up against a utility pole and quietly leave the scene. Just then my mobile started to ring.

'Yes,' I answered it crankily.

'This Miss Suganuma?' I heard a voice say.

'Stop calling me by my last name.'

'Is the only name I want to call you by.'

So then don't call me on the phone, I yelled into my mobile. I heard a crash, and when I turned around to look, the bicycle that had been propped against the pole had fallen over again. Pretending not to notice, I took big strides as I began to walk away.

'Please don't yell at me,' Takeo said.

'You're the one who says things that make me yell.'

I was trying to remember what I had written in the texts I had sent during the morning. *How are you? I might have said some pretty strange things yesterday. If so, sorry about that.* Something along those lines.

'If that's not really how you feel, then please don't say things like that,' Takeo said in a low voice.

Huh? I retorted.

'Like, that we won't see each other any more.'

Come on, isn't it obvious that I didn't really mean that? My voice softened a little. My brow relaxed for a moment, but then my jaw tightened up again.

''Cause I'm mad at you,' Takeo said, keeping his voice low.

Huh? I replied again.

'Please don't call me or send me texts any more,' Takeo continued.

My breath caught.

'Okay, bye.'

The next moment, I heard the sound of the line going dead. He'd hung up on me.

I didn't understand what had just happened. I made my way to the bakery and bought some curls. With the change, I bought two mini croissants. I cradled the bag with the curls and croissants against my chest and walked the streets back to the Nakano shop. The bicycle was still lying on the ground. Mr Nakano and Masayo were in the back room of the shop, laughing loudly. Silently I handed the bag of curls to Mr Nakano, who looked at them and said, 'Ugh, no – I told you curry flavour, not consommé!' Masayo turned to him and said, 'Go and buy them yourself if you're going to be like that!' Mechanically I nodded. Mechanically I took the croissants out of the bag, mechanically I made some black tea, mechanically I brought the croissants to my lips, mechanically I chewed and swallowed. Takeo must have really been angry, I murmured into the air. But why – what was he angry about? I could keep muttering, there would be no answer. Without my noticing, Mr Nakano and Masayo had disappeared. A customer came in and I called out a greeting. Mechanically the sun went down. When I checked the record on the till, it said the total for the day had been 53,750 yen. I had no memory of ringing up that much in sales. Cold air blew in from the entrance to the shop. I went to close the glass door, mechanically moving towards the front.

'What has happened, my dear Hitomi, is that you have stepped on his tail,' Masayo said.

'His tail?' I asked in reply.

'You know how a dog or a cat, when someone steps on their tail, they get mad as hell? Almost absurdly so?' Masayo replied, her skin glowy and bright.

The night before, Masayo had tried a cucumber and kiwi mask that Aunt Michi had told her about. Masayo had informed me about it as soon as she came into the shop, and without my even asking, she gave me the recipe for a 'Kiwi Cucumber Beauty Treatment'. It was written carefully in light blue fountain pen on pale pink stationery.

Thanks, I said, quietly taking it from her. Masayo tilted her head.

What's wrong, Hitomi? You don't seem like yourself these days.

Well, yeah.

I started talking in bits and pieces, and before I realized it, my tongue had loosened, and I found myself getting advice from Masayo about the situation with Takeo.

'So it's not fair for him to really be so angry, when a girl was just giving tit for tat, after what he said,' I complained to Masayo, who took a moment to organize her thoughts, a serious look on her face.

'In your twenties, you can say girl,' Masayo said, her face still solemn.

What do you mean? I asked, confused.

'Once you're in your thirties, you ought not to refer to yourself as a girl.' Just when I thought she was going to give me some real advice, that was what she offered.

I don't see what's wrong with it, as long as that's how the person sees herself, I grumbled in response.

'And what about in your fifties?' Masayo asked, her expression growing even more serious.

In my fifties, well! In my fifties, I would definitely con-sider myself a woman.

In your fifties, well, would you? Masayo let out a sigh.

A customer came in. It was one of our regulars, a man

with a mane of white hair. Thick and full and white, that's the best way to go, Mr Nakano had once said with envy. I mean, compared with thin and black, or the usual salt and pepper.

Masayo stood up and called out a greeting to the man. They chatted for a while. We haven't had any plates come into the shop lately, she said. This customer bought a lot of platters, not quite antiques but outdated ones from the early twentieth century. They aren't the kind of thing that often comes into your shop, the customer told Masayo chattily, but the ones that do are cheaper and of surprisingly good quality, compared to other shops. Whenever this customer dealt with Mr Nakano or me, his taciturn and fastidious mien never even cracked.

The man bought a small, shallow dish from the late 1920s or early 1930s. Smiling, Masayo bowed in thanks. She maintained her graceful smile until the customer had left. As soon as he was gone from view, Masayo resumed her usual animated expression and asked, 'So, so, then what happened?'

He doesn't call or text me, I replied in a subdued voice.

'And what about you, have you called or texted him?'

But . . .

'But what?'

I'm scared to.

Scared? she said, nodding. Of course, I understand. Boys are scary. And for no reason at all, sometimes. Masayo nodded repeatedly.

That's it – I'm scared, I thought to myself. Right now, I'm scared of Takeo. Me, who half-mocked him, who didn't take him seriously.

So, is it right to call him a boy, rather than a man? Masayo asked.

Yes, he's a boy, definitely not a man, I replied. I hadn't actually told Masayo that it was Takeo we were talking about. Just what kind of boy is he, one of these young toughs around today? Masayo murmured with a certain amusement. He is definitely not one of those, I replied sullenly. Well, I don't ever want to see him again. I won't call or text him either. I could feel myself getting more and more furious as I spoke.

My goodness, Masayo said. These kinds of things depend on how the person who's involved reacts. There's nothing for me to say, she stood up as she spoke. Another regular customer, who was in her thirties, had just come in.

She's definitely a woman, isn't she? Masayo whispered softly to me, then she went to greet the customer with a beaming smile. Would you care for some tea with us? I was just about to make some, Masayo said merrily. Despite the fact that the two of us had just drunk three cups of black tea while we had been chatting.

I'd be delighted, the woman replied floridly, and in unison, Masayo and she laughed in the same way.

I had said that I wouldn't see him again, but I couldn't very well not see him at all.

'Good morning,' is all he ever said. But he said it every day. Besides that, he made no other conversation whatsoever.

'Good morning,' I replied, with deliberate politeness.

It was uncomfortable at first, but Takeo didn't linger in the shop the way he used to; as soon as he arrived he would head straight for the back door, where he'd be doing mainten-ance on the truck or packing up goods, so we were able to avoid the awkwardness of being in each other's presence.

That day was unusual in that Masayo didn't show up. I was alone for the afternoon. Without Masayo there, we didn't even get any window shoppers. Towards the end of the afternoon, a woman with a single item for a pickup brought it into the shop herself. She was carrying a rectangular white cube that looked heavy.

'Here,' she said, setting down the cube on the desk beside the till. She was a thin woman of about fifty. I had never seen her before.

'How much can I get for it, I wonder?' the woman asked. Her perfume was strong. It was sweet and floral, and didn't seem to suit her at all.

I can't say until the owner of the shop returns, I replied. Really? the woman said, looking around as if appraising the shop. The bottom of the cube was set on the edge of the notebook that was spread open on the desk. When I tugged on the notebook, it made a sound like *pfft*.

'Is it all right to leave it here?' she asked.

Yes, I replied. Please write down your address and telephone number, I said as I handed her the notepad and a ballpoint pen. She wrote down only her phone number.

Mr Nakano returned soon after. Takeo was with him.

'Hey, isn't that a sewing machine?' Mr Nakano said. Lately, when Takeo came back from pickups, he'd rush right home like the ebbing tide, without even pausing to wash his hands. But hearing Mr Nakano, he turned his attention to the desk beside the till.

'This customer said that she wanted a pickup,' I said, trying not to look in Takeo's direction.

'These kinds of machines are a pain,' Mr Nakano said as he took hold of the top of the cube with both hands and lifted it up. The cover came off, revealing the body of the sewing machine.

'Hey,' Takeo said.

'What is it?' Mr Nakano asked.

'Is the one from the stand-up poster,' Takeo said, and then clamped his lips together. His manner of speaking was curt, as if saying anything in front of me would put him at a disadvantage.

'Oh, right, this is the same sewing machine that Seiko is holding up,' Mr Nakano said with a vacant air, utterly oblivious to the war of nerves that was secretly playing out between Takeo and me.

The sewing machine was gleaming and white, as though it had been polished up. It looked even newer and brighter than the faded sewing machine that Seiko Matsuda was holding in the life-size stand-up poster.

'But you know, machines are a pain for me to deal with,' Mr Nakano repeated, grimacing.

'You get rice cakes from the rice cake maker, and sewing machines at the sewing shop, you know?' Mr Nakano muttered, not really to me or to Takeo. Neither of us responded.

Mr Nakano carried the sewing machine to the back room with its cover still off. He set it down beside Seiko Matsuda. The genuine article was only slightly bigger than the sewing machine in the stand-up poster. I guess it's not life-size after all, the real one is a little bigger, I said, in spite of myself. Hmm, they must have shrunk Seiko, Mr Nakano said. No, they just trimmed her down a bit, I replied, and Takeo made a pluffing sound.

I stole a glance over my shoulder and saw that Takeo was laughing. What are you laughing at? Mr Nakano asked, in a drawling voice.

It's just, something strange about shrinking Seiko, Takeo said, and he laughed again. It's odd, don't you think? Mr Nakano wondered. Definitely strange. Don't you think? Takeo said.

Mr Nakano put the cover back on the sewing machine. We should probably sell the life-size stand-up poster together with the sewing machine, Mr Nakano said as he went to close the shutter. I peeked at Takeo's face, using the sidelong glance that was Takeo's trademark. Takeo immediately stopped laughing. His face suddenly resumed its cold expression. Unable to speak, I just stood there, motionless.

We were different from each other in the first place – it's not surprising that two people with nothing in common would end up like this, I thought to myself as I threw caution to the wind and continued to steal glances at Takeo's face.

As it turned out, Seiko sold for no more than 50,000 yen.

'I wonder what was wrong with the sewing machine Seiko?' Mr Nakano lamented.

'I know, and even when a sewing machine is a basic necessity,' Masayo said, also sounding puzzled.

In an auction, it's always during the last five minutes that the number of bids surge, creating a sharp increase in the price, but our Seiko ended up selling for a bid that was put in late the night before. Mr Crane explained this when he came to pick up the packed-and-ready Seiko Matsuda.

It just so happened that the winning bidder was a man who lived very near to Mr Crane, so he was going to deliver it himself.

'Sure you can carry that by yourself, Tokizo?' asked Mr Nakano, who had assumed that Tokizo had come by car, but in fact the Crane had walked.

'Takeo, get the truck out,' Mr Nakano said, and Tokizo's laughter echoed through the shop.

Takeo headed straight for the back and brought the truck out. Still in the driver's seat, he gave a little toot on the horn. Mr Crane laughed again, and then he left the shop and stood beside the truck. Mr Nakano was laying Seiko down on the truck's flatbed.

Mr Crane rested his arm on the part of the truck between the door and the flatbed, and his body appeared to go limp.

'Can't you open the door?' Mr Nakano asked him, and Tokizo shook his head. I'm getting there. Just out of shape, this old man.

When he said 'this old man', it sounded more like 'soul man'. Before long Masayo appeared and stood near Tokizo. She remained still, just watching his movements. Tokizo was now in front of the door to the truck, and then he started to stretch his arms.

A customer had come in, so I went into the shop by myself. It was the same guy, the regular who always buys platters. When he noticed that Masayo was there, he craned his neck in her direction.

My mobile chimed. The customer turned around. I put the phone, which had been left out on top of the desk, in my pocket. Masayo seemed eternally glued to Tokizo's side, and when she didn't come back into the shop, the man ended up leaving in a huff. I pulled the phone out of my pocket.

I had an email. It was from Takeo. I hurriedly scanned it, but there was no subject or message. Just the name 'Takeo Kiryu' in the field for sender. Another customer came in. He bought two second-hand T-shirts and left. Tokizo, Masayo, and Mr Nakano were bustling about and chatting away in front of the shop. I couldn't really see Takeo.

I heard Mr Nakano's laughter. Feeling somewhat desperate, I sent a reply to Takeo's email. Just like him, I left the subject and body of my message blank.

Hey there, Hitomi, Masayo called out loudly from outside the shop. Yes? I replied. I still couldn't really see Takeo.

When you get old and long-sighted, you can't look your sweetheart in the eye from close up. You need a little distance, so that you can focus on each other. So that your faces don't look blurry – anyway, you need a little distance. Masayo said all this loudly enough so that I could hear her from inside.

I was mystified by this sudden pronouncement. Mr Crane gave a belly laugh. Masayo laughed too. Inside the truck, Takeo appeared to be completely still.

I brought my mailbox back up on the screen of my phone and read the message from Takeo one more time. It being blank, I suppose I should say I looked at it rather than read it.

The scene in front of me – Masayo and Mr Nakano and Tokizo, the three of them standing there chatting – seemed to loom and recede before my eyes. You can't look your sweetheart in the eye from close up, really, you can't, Masayo said again. Her voice echoed unpleasantly in my ears.

Takeo's was the only voice I could not hear. I never would have expected to fall for someone like him. What if you sold Sakiko's novel on the Internet? Masayo was saying. 'I'm not sure I can handle something like that,' Mr Crane said, his laughter resounding. His entire body trembled. The scene steadily loomed and receded. I had no idea whether that kind of full-body quaking felt good or if it felt weird.

The truck's engine stopped, and Masayo, Mr Nakano, and Tokizo continued to bustle and crowd around the shopfront. I couldn't see Takeo. Still clutching my phone, I turned my back away from the front of the shop.

Shifting from the brightness to the shadows, at first my vision couldn't make out the distinct contours of my surroundings. Soon enough I began to distinguish the actual sewing machine that was left behind after the life-size Seiko had been carried away.

The sewing machine appeared in the corner, dull and white amidst the dimness of the back room. I could hear Tokizo's resonant laughter, carrying remarkably clearly from the front of the shop.

Dress

I decided to call Takeo's mobile, just once, every day.

Today, I called at 2.15 in the afternoon.

I figured he would already be completely finished with the pickup. He had left in the morning, and it was in the next neighbourhood over, so even if the streets were jammed it shouldn't take more than an hour to get there. Then an hour to negotiate with the client and load the goods, with half an hour to stop for lunch. The weather was nice today, so he might doze off under the shade of a tree, and then, twenty minutes later, just as he is dazedly waking up, my phone call comes in – that was the timing that I envisioned when I tried calling.

Takeo didn't answer.

Maybe he hadn't taken a nap today. In which case, when I called at 2.15, he would be right in the middle of driving the truck. His phone had rung, so he must be in range of the network. Had he not heard it? That must be it – nowadays Takeo has become a stickler for etiquette, and he must be keeping his mobile on silent mode so that it doesn't ring in front of customers.

As my mind raced with these thoughts, I felt the energy suddenly drain from my entire body.

I wondered why Takeo wouldn't answer my calls.

Yesterday I called at 11.07 in the morning. He might still be sleeping, I thought to myself as it rang, and just as I expected, he didn't answer. I had no way of knowing whether he had actually been asleep, or awake and purposely did not answer.

The day before that I tried calling at exactly seven o'clock in the evening. It had been after four o'clock when Takeo left the shop, so assuming he didn't stop anywhere on the way, it was reasonable to expect that he would be home at that time. But he didn't answer. Might have been eating dinner. Or it's possible that he was taking a bath. Or, who knows, he may have been struck by the urge to race a *nanahan* motorbike around the streets at night. Then again, Takeo didn't have a motorbike.

I tried to imagine all of the situations in which Takeo could not answer his mobile when it rang.

Such as, when he went to push the button to answer, his finger slipped because of the grease on his hand from the cream bun he was eating (Takeo had previously revealed to me that custard-filled buns were his favourite pastry), and instead of hitting the answer button, he disconnected the call.

Like, he tried to answer the phone that he keeps in his back pocket, but he's recently gained a little weight and his backside is bigger so his pockets are tighter, and he had a hard time pulling out his mobile.

Or, maybe, an old lady he doesn't know fell down right in front of him, and he was in the process of carrying her to the hospital on his back, so there was no way he could have answered his mobile.

Or else, he was snatched away by a nefarious underground gang and he was being held captive in a cave, where even if he tried to answer his mobile, he couldn't see the buttons in the dark.

While I was imagining these things, I felt the energy drain from my body again.

I hate mobiles, I thought to myself. Who the hell invented something so inconvenient anyway? There has been no greater evil for love affairs – those that are going well as much as those that are going badly – due to the greatly increased ability to receive phone calls no matter where you are, no matter what the situation. In the first place, since when was I actually in love with Takeo? And just what was I trying to determine, by constantly calling him?

I spent the entire day thinking about things that I knew Masayo would chide me about for being so pessimistic. Five days already that Takeo hadn't answered my calls! The past day or two, I'd been feeling anxious about what I'd do if he actually did answer the phone.

Suddenly Takeo answered. My breath caught. But Takeo didn't say a word. I made another little sound, like an 'ah'. This time my voice sounded darker than before. Takeo still didn't say anything.

My fear made me want to run away screaming.

Takeo, I ventured in a murmur. That was the end of it.

Despair (it seemed to me like an iron ball about the size

of a dodgeball) felt like it was lodged in my belly and, as I crossed both my arms over it, I considered at what time tomorrow I should call Takeo. There were two pickups, so I would aim for the time in between. And because it was a bill-paying day, I should allow for extra driving time. So far I hadn't left any messages on his voicemail, but maybe tomorrow I ought to try to leave a word or two, in as nonchalant a voice as possible. So maybe the time to put it into play would be around 2.37?

Put it into play? What am I talking about? I'm still not sure whether or not I really want to keep calling Takeo if he's not going to answer the phone.

2.37.

In my empty head, I repeated the appointed time – once, twice, three times.

'Are you on a diet or something?' Masayo asked.

'Hitomi loses weight in the summertime,' Mr Nakano answered for me.

Even if she loses weight in the summertime, it's already the end of October, isn't it? Masayo laughed, and Mr Nakano did too.

After a brief moment, I tried to laugh a little myself. Eh heh heh – as I listened to my own voice, I was surprised that I was able to laugh at all.

I've lost three kilos, I said quietly.

Wow, I'm so jealous! Masayo's voice rang out.

I shook my head slightly. And then, realizing what I was doing, I tried to laugh again, 'Eh heh heh.' This time, it didn't go so well. The first and the last sounds came out sounding hoarse and husky.

Mr Nakano went out. Masayo settled herself in. Her exhibition of doll creations would finally take place the week after next. Nevertheless, Masayo had been spending all her time in the shop, her face placid, even as she admitted, 'It's a bit on the thin side – to put it bluntly, I don't have nearly enough pieces.'

'Will it be all right?' I asked Masayo.

'It'll be fine. After all, it's just a hobby – I make them for my own pleasure,' Masayo replied in a lilting tone. Had Mr Nakano ever suggested such a thing, Masayo would have probably flown into a rage, but apparently it was fine for her to say so.

A customer had hesitated by the entrance, debating whether or not to come inside. When this happened, the Nakano shop way was to pretend we didn't notice. With my eyes downcast, I opened and closed the notebook on the desk beside the till. Masayo was staring into mid-air, looking as if nothing had happened.

The customer did not come inside.

It was a beautiful day. The sky was clear, dotted with faint cirrocumulus clouds that looked as though they had been swept here and there.

So, Hitomi, Masayo said.

'Yes?'

'What's been happening, since then?' Masayo was still staring into mid-air. She asked without looking in my direction.

What do you mean, what's been happening? I asked in reply.

'With that boy.'

Oh.

'Oh is not an answer.'

Yes.

'Neither is yes.'

Well.

'Well isn't either. You like this boy, Hitomi, enough to lose weight over him.'

Isn't it misleading, to put it that way? I replied without much conviction.

'You must really have been in love with him, Hitomi, to lose this much weight over him.'

There seemed to be something quite ominous about her use of the past tense.

'So, is it still going on?' Masayo asked, her eyes opening wide. Masayo's voice, brimming with vitality, jarred my fragile eardrums. I wanted to cover my ears, but I didn't even have the strength to make that much effort.

'I'm not sure how to say, whether it's still going on.'

Masayo's curiosity-filled expression was drifting through the dry autumn air. It was all I could do to return her intense gaze listlessly.

'Are you seeing him?'

No.

'Are there phone calls?'

No.

'Emails?'

No.

'Do you still love him?'

. . . No.

'Well, then, it's good that you broke up, isn't it?'

I was silent.

What is that? Masayo laughed. Hitomi, my dear, take a little time off. Haruo says the same thing – Hitomi has been acting strange lately. I'm worried about her, he said. He has his good points, that kid does. But just as these words came out of his mouth, he goes on with, You know, it's almost like Hitomi is possessed by a weasel, or a badger, or a spotted seal – some kind of weird animal – don't you think? Oh, I'm sorry! He didn't mean it out of spite. Really, he can be insensitive, that kid. Even with a mistress! But in the end, he always lets them get away. I told him, It's not that Hitomi is possessed, she's just a young girl. And young girls and young boys – you see, everyone has their troubles. Just like Haruo and his mistress – they don't have thick skins. Well, the truth is, I've always known that kid is quite lily-livered.

Masayo's chatter was incessant, like clear water gushing forth from a spring deep in the forest. Before I knew it, there were tears trickling from my eyes. Not quite crying, it felt more like an automatic overflow of liquid.

There was something weirdly cosy and comforting about the sound of Masayo's voice. Oh, my dear Hitomi, what's the matter? I heard her say as my tears fell in big drops onto my lap. That cosiness reminds me of something, I thought. I know – it's like when you wake up with a hangover, without even the strength to puke but somehow you manage to throw up anyway – it was warm and fuzzy like that.

First of all, Hitomi, go to the back room. Then, you and I are going to have a nice hot lunch, Masayo was saying. As my tears spilled over intermittently, I heard Masayo's voice as if it were the autumn wind howling far off in the distance.

The tears made a faint pitter-patter when they fell on my lap.

Recently Mr Nakano had been obsessed with Chinese hanging scrolls.

'You know what I mean? These are easy money,' Mr Nakano said as he slurped up the soup from his *tanmen* noodles.

After taking a little break in the back room, my tears had stopped. Masayo had promptly fixed me 'a nice hot lunch'. As usual, that meant *tanmen* noodles.

'They're a little salty today, aren't they?' Mr Nakano said, exhaling the smoke from his cigarette.

'Stop smoking while we're eating!' Masayo said as she lifted her chin haughtily. Mr Nakano hastily thrust his cigarette into the ashtray. Then he noisily drank his soup. Each time he took a breath in between sips, he frowned. I would never understand him – don't drink the soup if it's so salty, then.

'The Chinese buyers, you know, they come here themselves to buy them.' Having polished off his soup, Mr Nakano relit the cigarette that he had stubbed out just a moment ago.

'Are these Chinese scrolls old?' Masayo asked.

No, they're pretty recent. I mean, not more than five hundred years old, Mr Nakano replied with his cigarette in his mouth as he carried his bowl to the sink, deftly catching the falling ash with the airborne bowl.

Lately the economy in China is booming, and more and more enthusiasts are buying up scrolls made in China which have managed to find their way out of there. What's more, it's not ones from the Ming and Qing dynasties – instead they prefer ones from after the Cultural Revolution that don't even really have much value.

'Hmm, I wonder, is that similar to the vogue in Japan for things from the Showa era?' Masayo murmured.

Don't be stupid, sis! You can't compare China and Japan – they're completely different countries! Mr Nakano scolded her.

You're the stupid one! Masayo retorted under her breath after Mr Nakano had gone out into the shop, looking over at me with a smirk. I had been drinking the tea that Masayo had brewed for me. Its warmth made my throat tingle.

'You know,' Masayo said.

Yes? I replied as I sipped the tea audibly.

'I've given it some thought.'

Yes?

'This boy is alive, isn't he?'

What? I exclaimed. Wh-what do you mean?

No, I just, Masayo started to explain.

When I was young, I always blamed everyone. When I was in my thirties too. Even into my forties. No matter if it was my fault or someone else's fault, I still blamed everyone else. Whether it was a lover or just a friend, when trouble arose that's always how it was.

But now that I'm in my fifties, I have found it easier not to accuse others when things happen, be it a difference of opinion, or a misunderstanding, or a quarrel.

Is that so? I replied distractedly.

'It is so. Even though it might seem simpler just to jump to accusations,' Masayo said as she used a toothpick.

Do people become kinder when they turn fifty? I asked, still in a bit of a daze.

'No, no, that's not it at all!' Masayo raised her brows sharply.

Then what do you mean?

'If anything, the older I get, the more demanding I become!'

I see.

'And kinder towards myself.' Masayo gave a little laugh. She looks pretty when she smiles, I thought to myself. Her smile sort of reminded me of a small animal, like a pretty white hamster, running in circles in its cage.

No, I just, Masayo continued with her explanation.

The thing is, there is always the chance that this person – the one you accused – might be dying.

When I was young, I didn't think about people dying. But when you get to be my age, people can drop dead, just like that. In an accident. From an illness. By their own hand. By someone else's hand. Or just naturally. People die much more easily at this age than when they are young.

They might drop dead right at the moment when you blamed them for something. They might die the very next day. Or a month later. Or smack in the middle of the following season. In any case, you never know when people of ripe age will just croak. It keeps you up at night.

Having to worry about whether someone is healthy enough to tolerate my fierce hatred or criticism before I decide to blame them – that's what I call getting old. Masayo gave a somewhat serious sigh. But she had a smile on her face. I would never understand her.

Masayo wrapped up by saying, 'That's why, when I haven't heard from someone for a while, the first thing that occurs to me is that they might have just keeled over.'

Keeled over. I repeated Masayo's phrase, in the same tone she had used.

'You know?' Masayo suppressed a chuckle as she peered into my face.

I-I don't think he's dead, I replied, shrinking back in my seat.

'Are you sure?'

I-I'm sure, I answered, even as my mind whirled, trying to think back to when I had last seen Takeo. I haven't seen him yet today. I definitely saw him yesterday. It was yesterday evening. He showed no signs of dying. But people usually died without any warning, didn't they?

A customer came into the shop. Mr Nakano was waiting on him, his voice loud. I crept over to the door that separated the back room from the shop. Still in my lackadaisical state, I flung open the door only to see the figure of Tadokoro jump out at me.

Why, young lady, I haven't seen you in a long time, Tadokoro greeted me amiably with a beaming smile.

Ah, yes, I replied instantly. And just like that, I hurried to put on my shoes and grabbed my coat and bag as I bolted out of the shop.

I myself didn't seem to know where I planned to go, but I ran off anyway. My legs felt weak. I couldn't just drop weight like this. What will I do if he's dead? I thought to myself as I staggered along. It appeared that I was heading in the direction of Takeo's house, but I couldn't be certain. Don't be dead, I repeated over and over in my head. I was getting out of breath. My repetition of 'Don't be dead' was punctuated by the occasional thought of 'What will I do if he's dead?' This loop was coupled with the conviction, 'He can't be dead!' But within that certainty, there was the subtlest pinprick of a notion that, if by some chance he were dead, I might just feel terribly relieved.

The pale autumn sunlight shone on the top of my head. I felt warm, I felt chilly – I really had no idea what I was feeling – while I kept on running, where to I wasn't sure.

'Ah, Mr Tadokoro,' Mr Nakano called out. Tadokoro had just come into the shop with Mr Mao.

Mr Mao was a buyer from China. This was his third visit to the shop. He was always accompanied by Tadokoro.

'Today I have gathered an assortment of especially high-quality ones for you,' Mr Nakano said, putting on a smile and clasping both hands together. I call that the hand rub, Masayo whispered in my ear.

Tadokoro, Mr Mao, and Mr Nakano went into the back. Shall I serve tea? I asked. Yes, if you don't mind. But it wasn't Mr Nakano who replied, it was Tadokoro.

I moved in slow motion as I made the tea. Takeo hadn't died. I had run into him on the street. Takeo was on his way to buy cigarettes. Been smoking a lot lately, Takeo said, averting his eyes. I would never have imagined that it was really possible to run into the very guy that things weren't going well with in the middle of the street. But that is almost literally what happened.

Mr Mao was tall and thin, and he had large ears.

'He seems just like someone from the Chinese under-world,' Tadokoro had told me in a whispered aside the other day.

I had tilted my head, The underworld? And Tadokoro had looked me right in the eyes and said, In Japan we call it the black market, young lady. The man was inscrutable to me. But in contrast to the creepiness about him, Tadokoro gave off a pleasant smell. Rather than any particular cologne, the aroma seemed to have more of a warm presence, something like fra-grant tea or freshly roasted rice cakes. The scent was completely different from the impression Tadokoro himself emanated.

That day I had called Takeo at nine in the morning. Of course he hadn't answered. This was the seventh call. It had been a week. I'd stopped wondering what might be keeping Takeo from answering his phone. It simply registered as, Hmm, he didn't answer again today.

Mr Mao used much more courteous Japanese than Mr Nakano or I did.

'You have arranged many wonderful pieces. I am extremely grateful for your efforts,' Mr Mao said, after attempting to sweep all five scrolls towards himself with one hand while grasping Mr Nakano's palm with his other hand. Right away Mr Nakano pulled his hand back. Then he hurriedly forced a smile and said, 'No, well, now.'

Mr Mao began to lay money out on the low table. He laid each 10,000-yen note flat. *Hi ... fu ...* Mr Mao counted. Once the table was covered with 10,000-yen notes, he started from the left edge again, placing a second layer precisely on top of the first.

Unable to find a place to set the teacups, I was idling, balancing the tray I had carried in on my knees, when Tadokoro turned to face me. How many women have fallen in love with Tadokoro? I wondered irrelevantly. It was completely beyond me how a woman could be in love with a man who doesn't love her back. And just how were those women able to fall in love with men other than the ones who loved them?

Following a similar logic, once I had fallen out of love, I became completely incapable of explaining why I had loved a guy in the first place.

What was it I saw in him?

Tadokoro had sidled up to me. Hey, Hitomi, that's a lot of money, isn't it? Tadokoro pointed towards the table top. As if spellbound, Mr Nakano was watching Mr Mao's fingertips as he arranged the money. Mr Mao handled the notes smoothly, as if he were the kind of person who spends his whole day laying out money.

'Seventy-seven notes – have you made sure of the amount yourself?' Mr Mao asked, grinning.

Uh, yes, Mr Nakano replied, sounding awed.

'That makes seven hundred and seventy thousand yen, isn't that correct?' Mr Mao asked.

'I'm sure that's enough,' Tadokoro said, as if covering for him before Mr Nakano could open his mouth.

Mr Nakano folded his arms, as if he refused to be talked into following Tadokoro's lead. But then immediately he replied feebly, That's enough, I guess that's enough, uh-huh, and he went on nodding his head repeatedly.

Mr Mao stood up. One by one, he tossed the hanging scrolls into a large holdall.

Ah, Mr Nakano gave a little intake of breath. Not even he would handle merchandise so roughly. Mr Mao paid no heed; when he had cast the last of the scrolls into the bag, like a conjuror he rounded up the 10,000-yen notes on top of the table with a flourish and thrust them into Mr Nakano's palm.

'I do hope you will please contact me if you have any more excellent deals,' Mr Mao said, bowing deeply. Mr Nakano couldn't help but bow in return. Tadokoro kept his head up.

The next thing I knew Takeo was standing behind us. Tadokoro glanced at him calmly. Takeo scowled at Tadokoro. Just like that, Takeo came up to me and quickly took the tray I was still holding in his own hands.

Hitomi, Masayo is calling you, Takeo said, roughly putting the teacups on the now bare table. Mr Mao was already putting his shoes on. Tadokoro grinned as he watched Takeo.

'So then, see you later, Hitomi,' Tadokoro said, following Mr Mao and Mr Nakano.

Ah, yes, I said, and this time Takeo glared at me. Why are you staring at me? I muttered, but I swallowed the words and they didn't come out properly. Takeo glared at me for another moment. Then he suddenly broke his gaze, looking down.

It's been a long time, I said once the three of them had gone. Ran into you on the street two days ago, he replied, his eyes still downcast. I could hear the sound of the truck's engine coming from the back. Takeo squinted his eyes, and his lips were pressed together firmly.

Still, I don't know, it seems as if it's been a really long time, I said again. Takeo nodded briefly, with seeming reluctance. I could hear fragments of Mr Mao's voice. There was what sounded like the truck's door closing loudly, and the engine soon faded away. Masayo's voice echoed inside the shop as she welcomed a customer. Takeo still stubbornly kept his head down.

'So, the girls you dated in the past, what were they like?'

'What were they like?'

'Is there one you still think of fondly, or one whose name you don't even want to hear?'

Takeo was pondering it for a moment. Masayo had asked us to make a bank deposit transfer for her. There was a light drizzle, and the shopping district was deserted. This was the first conversation I'd had with Takeo in a long time.

'Depends,' Takeo finally replied when we were in front of the police box.

The officer inside was staring at Takeo and me. Don't have umbrellas, do we? Takeo said. I don't mind, it's barely raining anyway, I replied.

'So, why don't you answer my calls?' I asked, once we were past the police box.

Takeo was silent.

'Do you hate me?'

Still silent.

'Are we not friends any more?'

Takeo moved his head slightly. It was impossible to tell whether it had been a nod or a shake.

Abruptly, I realized that I did love Takeo after all, though I didn't know why. Despite not having given any thought to such feelings since he stopped answering my calls. I love him, like an idiot. Love is idiotic, anyway.

'So, answer the phone!'

Takeo was silent.

'I – you know – I love you, Takeo.'

Silence.

'Do you not want this any more?'

More silence.

We were in front of the bank. Even though there was no one on the street, there were tons of people inside the bank. We joined the queue, and I held my tongue. Takeo was facing straight ahead. When it was our turn, Takeo and I stood awkwardly in front of the cash dispenser. Will you do it for me? I asked softly, and Takeo nodded. He performed the transfer much more smoothly than I would have imagined. My eyes were riveted on Takeo's fingertips. His fingers were slender and elegant. I found his right little finger, the one missing the first part, the most beautiful of all.

Once we had completed the transfer and left the bank, it was raining much harder. It's a downpour, I murmured, and Takeo looked up at the sky.

'Doubt there's anything that can be done about it, I guess,' I said in the direction of Takeo's raised chin. Takeo still hadn't said anything. Even petroleum is in limited supply, I thought, to say nothing of the terribly meagre resources of my love. How could it be expected to sustain this level of silent treatment?

We stood for a while under the eaves of the bank and watched the rain. It had developed into a storm.

'I guess I, still, have a hard time, trusting people,' Takeo said haltingly.

This – he waved his right-hand little finger as he said it – because of this. Then he quickly drew back his finger.

'Don't lump me in with that horrible old classmate of yours.' Despite myself, my voice sounded angry.

It's not that I put you in with him, Takeo said without looking up.

'Then, what is it?'

People scare me, Takeo said slowly.

When Takeo said the word 'scare', the fear that I had been feeling this whole week blew up inside me all at once. That's because it *is* scary. I'm scary. Takeo is scary. Waiting is scary. Tadokoro, Mr Nakano, Masayo, Sakiko, even Mr Crane – they were all scary. Even more frightening was my own self. Guess that's not surprising, though.

I thought I would say all this to him, but I couldn't. No doubt my fears were different from Takeo's fears.

The rain had not let up at all, but I started walking by myself. I was wondering how I would be able to make the love I felt for Takeo disappear. I felt as though, by falling in love with him, I had hurt him somehow. I hated the thought of that, more than I hated the idea of being hurt myself. Thinking I was making myself out to be such a good person, I had to laugh a little. The rain was torrential. I was quickly soaked, the water running down the nape of my neck. I narrowed my eyes to see past the wall of rain in front of me. The scene around me became blurry.

Before I knew it Takeo was beside me. We were walking along, at the same pace, side by side.

'Sorry,' I said, and Takeo looked puzzled.

What are you apologizing for, Hitomi?

'Because, I really do love you.'

Takeo suddenly took me in his arms. Now the water was not just coming down the nape of my neck, but also running off Takeo's body as it covered me, and I was drenched to the skin. Takeo held me in a tight embrace. I hugged him back, just as strongly. I thought about how what I felt for him now and what he felt for me at that moment must be totally and completely out of sync. Trying to imagine it made me dizzy.

It started raining even harder, and there were rumbles of thunder. Takeo and I were just holding each other, without saying anything. There was a flash of lightning, followed soon after by a thunderclap that sounded very close. We pulled ourselves apart and started walking, our hands gently extended towards each other, fingertips touching every so often.

Masayo scolded Takeo and me as we changed our clothes. Takeo put on a pair of Mr Nakano's jeans and one of his shirts, and I borrowed a flimsy dress that was for sale in the shop for 500 yen.

The rain soon stopped.

'Apparently the lightning knocked down a pine tree at the shrine,' Masayo said as she made her eyes big and round.

Before long Mr Nakano returned. It was raining like hell! he said, staring at me.

Please don't look at me, I said, and Mr Nakano laughed. That dress suits you – you should buy it. I'll give you an employee discount. Takeo was at the front of the shop, wringing out his sopping wet trousers. He let out a little cry and we all turned to look just as he pulled a rectangle, about the size of a half-eaten bar of chocolate, out of the pocket of his trousers.

'Your card,' Takeo said as he came into the shop. The card we had just used at the bank for the deposit transfer was now sodden and tattered.

Oh, no! Mr Nakano slapped his forehead. Forgive me, Takeo said humbly. Forgive me, my voice chimed in with his.

'Hey, you guys made up?' Mr Nakano asked, fixing his gaze at a point exactly in between Takeo and me.

Yes, no big deal. Again we spoke in unison.

'Weren't you having a fight?' Mr Nakano asked again.

Don't be silly, it's not as though they're in primary school, they don't have fights. Do they? Masayo said crisply. Takeo and I both nodded vaguely.

'I'll take the dress,' I said, turning to Mr Nakano. Takeo casually drifted away from me and went into the back. I'm not going to call him any more, I thought. If things were really over between us now, I would be fine with it. But I also knew that I wouldn't last. I was pretty sure that tomorrow I would still phone Takeo.

'All right, I'll mark it down to three hundred yen,' Mr Nakano said.

I took the 100-yen coins out of my wallet and placed them in Mr Nakano's palm. I recalled the way that he opened and closed his hand when he accepted the wad of bills from Mr Mao. When I thought about the idea of spending the rest of my life like this – going through my days in a fog of anxiety and fear – I felt so depressed I could have lain down on the ground and gone to sleep right then and there. But, despite all that, I loved Takeo. When I scrutinized love, I still found myself in a world that felt empty. My mind wandered through these thoughts.

My body, chilled and wet from the rain, had finally warmed back up and, feeling the urge to say something but unsure of what, I just stood there, fingering the faded pink fringe that was glued to the belt of the dress.

Bowl

Mr Nakano had screwed up.

Not a business mistake. A screw-up with women.

'You know what I mean? I'm thinking of tagging along with Kurusu to Boston.'

Masayo and I looked up because Mr Nakano had blurted this out of the blue. The reverberations of Masayo's show last month had lingered for a good while, even causing her to be somewhat manic, but just this past week she had finally grown quieter.

Considering that Masayo had said there were too few dolls in this exhibition, the pieces she showed were quite accomplished. I know absolutely nothing about dolls, but I had been astonished by the profound expressiveness of several of her creations.

Even Takeo had said, 'Masayo has become quite the doll maker!'

Do you think Takeo has been a little cheeky lately? Mr Nakano chided with a laugh, but I hadn't found any mirth in his words; instead I maintained a moody silence. Things between Takeo and me were still uncertain, even though more than a month had passed since that day in the thunderstorm.

Recently Masayo had become absorbed in French embroidery. Whether it was cross-stitch, or making her chain or outline stitches, she had been meticulously embroidering classic patterns on throw pillows – a girl capering with her dog, a boy in knickerbockers playing the flute – like the kind you would see sitting on a sofa in the home of an elegant granny with perfectly coiffed fluffy white hair.

'What do you use those pillows for?' I asked.

Masayo thought about it for a moment and then replied, 'I don't use them. They are purely for rehabilitation.'

Having poured all her energies into doll making, Masayo said she had become 'like a zombie'. At times like this, according to her, there was nothing like rote tasks. Actually, the more intricate, the better, Masayo explained with an earnest look.

Seems interesting, I said, peering over Masayo's shoulder as she gave me a detailed lesson on the basics of French embroidery. That would make a nice place mat, wouldn't it? she said, referring to the square of linen cloth on which I was stitching mushrooms of various sizes. One of the mushrooms was polka-dotted, another had a checked pattern, and yet another was supposed to be filled in with satin stitch.

'What will you do in Boston?' Masayo asked Mr Nakano, as she held the embroidery needle tightly between her thumb and index finger and inserted it into the cloth.

'Do you have the money to go to Boston in the first place?' she pressed him for an answer.

I have it, Mr Nakano said, and then he started whistling. It was the tune of *Rhapsody in Blue*.

'And why are you in such high spirits?' Masayo said.

Mr Nakano stopped whistling. 'But isn't that an American song?' he replied.

'Is it a buying trip?' Takeo asked. He must have come in the back door without my noticing him. The moment I heard Takeo's voice, gooseflesh stood up on my arm. Lately this had been happening to me, almost as if it were a conditioned response.

Right, right, Takeo, my boy. You are the only one who understands me! Mr Nakano said in a lively voice. In response to being called 'my boy', Takeo's left knee seemed to twitch. Neither Takeo nor I were much good at making conversation, but our bodies were oddly sensitive. Figuring at least we had this in common, I set about filling in the checked pattern on the mushroom.

'Kurusu, you know, says he found a great little-known spot for Early American things,' Mr Nakano said to Masayo, who was bent over her embroidery and didn't even look at him.

'Kurusu, you mean that shady character?' Masayo said a little later. She turned over the cloth, tied a knot in the thread, and snipped off the end with a pair of traditional Japanese scissors. I liked the way Masayo held those scissors. It was like she had a small woodland creature playing in her hand.

'I'm telling you, he's not shady,' Mr Nakano said, pressing the button on the right side of the till. The drawer popped out with a *ka-ching*.

'Tell me, sis – when did you start making such artistic dolls?' he asked as he got two 10,000-yen notes out of the till and slipped them straight into his pocket.

'Since always,' Masayo replied, indignant at first, then her features softened infinitesimally.

'This time, you know, I was really impressed this time.'

You can praise me all you like, nothing will come of it, Masayo said as she pulled two strands of thread from the six-stranded skein of embroidery floss. Nothing will come of it but . . . And with that, Masayo's critique also trailed off. I know how to handle my sister, Mr Nakano had once said. It's easy, so easy. And I guess he was right – Masayo was easy to handle. However, that did not in any way mean that Masayo was an uncomplicated person.

Masayo and I silently devoted ourselves to our embroidery for a while. Behind me, I was aware of Takeo getting ready to leave. Once I became aware of Takeo's presence, it felt as though there was a faint electric current running from him to me, and whatever part of my body that was facing him rippled like a shock. The moment Takeo opened the back door on his way out, it seemed as if the centre of my back were being yanked with a thread, and when he closed the door, just like that, the line was disconnected with a snap.

'Hm . . . enough already!' I said. I set the embroidery linen on my lap and gave myself a good stretch. Hm . . . enough already! Masayo said. She sort of mimicked my tone.

Please stop, I said, and Masayo laughed. But, I was just about to say, Hm . . . enough already, too! Masayo said, pouting her lips. I mean, really – enough already with this world! I said, now imitating her by pouting my lips. Ha ha ha, Mr Nakano gave a hollow-sounding laugh.

'Oh, my dear, you're still here,' Masayo said.

'I'm going, I'm on my way, to Boston and wherever, I'll soon be on my way,' Mr Nakano said in a strange, high-pitched voice, and he left.

'That kid, he's got another woman,' Masayo said, as if she had been waiting to hear the sound of the engine through the back door to be certain Mr Nakano had really gone.

'What? You mean, Kurusu is a woman?' I said with surprise.

Masayo shook her head. 'That's not what I mean. Kurusu is an old man! Apparently this one's name is Rumiko. Sounds like the name of a hostess in a bar, but I hear she's a friend of Sakiko's. She recently opened up a small shop on her own – she's in the same business,' Masayo informed me under her breath.

But, then, what about Sakiko? I said as I recalled Sakiko's face. A face as beautiful as a mask floating in the water.

'Does Sakiko know about it?'

'I think she does.'

'How awful!'

'Haruo can be really stupid!'

'This is incredibly stupid, though.'

But it wasn't from Haruo that I heard about it, Masayo went on. At least, he's not that much of a fool.

'Then how did you find out?'

From Rumiko, Masayo explained, with a dark look. You see, what's doubly stupid – well, if you add in his wife, I suppose it's triply stupid, or however many times stupid – you see, when you're racing horses side by side, you shouldn't be stupid enough to get involved with a horse who's likely to tell the other horse how the race finishes – that's where Haruo has really gone wrong! Masayo said, all in one breath.

Horses? I murmured.

Masayo thrust her embroidery needle roughly through the cloth, her face aflame. She must really love her younger brother, I thought to myself.

Just at that moment, I felt the strength drain out of me as the embroidery needle slipped from between my fingers. Without dropping to the floor, the needle dangled in mid-air, still attached by the thread through its eye.

'That's why the kid brought up the idea of going to Boston.'

'That's why?'

'In order to get away.'

'Away from Sakiko?'

'No, from all the women.'

I see, I replied. Masayo wore a somewhat triumphant look on her face.

'Mr Nakano is a lucky man, isn't he?' I said. Masayo made a little exclamation, raising both of her eyebrows. Once again I took up the needle that I had dropped and started to sew outline stitches for the border of a mushroom. A dark green mushroom. I recalled Sakiko's face again. Her expression was dreamy, but with a touch of melancholy.

I hate men, I thought as I swiftly embroidered the dark green mushroom.

The following week there were many customers, and we were busy from morning until night. Busy for the Nakano shop might not mean the same thing as busy for the greengrocer down the street – we were probably only a fraction as busy – yet there wasn't a single moment for Masayo or me to pick up our embroidery needles.

'Mr Nakano, when are you going to Boston?' Takeo was asking.

'You know what I mean? Depends on Kurusu,' Mr Nakano replied, having gone into the back room. Takeo looked as though his question had been sidestepped as he stood absent-mindedly near the front door. A young man came into the shop and bumped into Takeo. He was a first-time customer. He glanced at Takeo suspiciously.

'Uh, here,' the young man said as he placed the newspaper-wrapped package he had been carrying next to the till. It was about the size of a few smallish roasted potatoes bundled up.

'Haruo!' Masayo called out. Mr Nakano appeared, plodding in from the back room.

With a cigarette in his mouth, Mr Nakano watched as the customer opened the package. His ash fell on the floor. The young man paused for a moment, glancing at Mr Nakano with distaste.

'Is that celadon?' Mr Nakano asked, paying no heed to the customer's gaze.

'It's Goryeo celadon,' he corrected him.

'Ah, excuse me,' Mr Nakano apologized frankly. The young man's expression became more and more displeased.

'There are shops other than mine that are better at dealing with ancient things like this,' Mr Nakano said as he gently picked up with one hand the delicate, grey-green porcelain bowl that the customer had brought in. He then set his still-lit cigarette in an ashtray.

'I am not interested in selling it,' the young man said.

Mr Nakano peered into the young man's face with a quizzical look. The customer instantly averted his eyes.

The man had beautiful skin. Rather than a moustache, he had darkish downy hair growing on his upper lip. He had on what looked like a well-tailored navy suit with a tie in a similar colour, knotted neatly. Going by just his clothing, you might think that he was a thirty-something salaryman at the peak of his career, but in fact he was probably quite a bit younger than he appeared.

'We don't do valuations here,' Mr Nakano said, turning over the bowl. He was staring at its pedestal.

'Would you consider displaying it?' the young man said.

'Displaying it?'

'Not to sell it but might you just keep it here in the shop?'

Keep it here, you say? Mr Nakano said with a laugh. He took a look around the shop. Masayo and I both followed his gaze, a beat behind. Only the young man kept his gaze fixed on the bowl that he had brought with him.

'This doesn't really fit in with the shoddy items that are jumbled here in this shop, such as it is, does it?' Mr Nakano phrased it like so, despite it being his own shop.

The young man was crestfallen. Mr Nakano took his half-smoked cigarette from the ashtray and inhaled deeply. For a while, nobody said anything.

'Which antique shop do you usually go to?' Masayo asked.

'I've never been to one,' the young man replied, flustered.

'So, what about that piece, then?' Mr Nakano said. That's not really the way to speak to a customer, I thought inwardly.

'I got it from someone I know,' the young man said, seeming even more dejected.

It sounds like there is more to the story, Masayo said, as if trying to draw him out. The young man raised his head and looked at Masayo imploringly. Tell us about it, Masayo went on.

Slowly and tentatively, the young man began to tell us the story behind it.

The bowl had been given to the young man – he said his name was Hagiwara – by his girlfriend at the time. They had dated for three years. They had never intended to marry, they were just having fun together, or so he had thought, while three years went by. But then one day, his boss brought him a marriage proposal. The woman was a good prospect. Hagiwara immediately broke things off with his girlfriend.

His girlfriend had protested at first, but she seemed to acquiesce, and in the end she asked him to accept a gift as a memento. Had she told him that she wanted a memento of their relationship, he would have understood, but he thought it was strange that she was the one who wanted him to accept a gift. Nevertheless he did so without thinking it through.

It wasn't long before the offer of marriage fell apart. The young woman – who happened to be his boss's niece – eloped with a man with whom she had long been in love. Around the same time, Hagiwara broke his collarbone. He wasn't even exercising when it happened – all he did was roll over in his sleep and he fractured it. Things at work weren't going well either: a personnel change in management caused orders to drop off precipitously, and a woman in his department started a rumour that he had sexually harassed her. On top of all that, it was suddenly announced that the building in which he lived was to be demolished, and he was notified of his eviction.

All of these events occurred after he accepted the bowl as a memento from his ex-girlfriend. That being the case, he thought he had better get back together with her. But when he tried to get in touch, her mobile number had been changed. The same with her email address. She had moved house, and what was more, apparently she had even changed jobs.

At a loss, he asked a friend who was interested in fortune telling, who told him that he had to get rid of the bowl. There was a jinx on it, so he couldn't sell it, but he couldn't keep it around either. His only option was for someone to borrow it or keep it for him, though that wouldn't completely dispel the jinx. Still, it would be better than doing nothing.

Hagiwara relayed this story haltingly to Masayo.

'But if the bowl is really Goryeo celadon, it must have cost dearly. Someone who gives such a gift must be a good person,' Masayo said when she had listened to the whole story.

'That's not the problem,' Mr Nakano interjected. However, the moment Hagiwara had heard what Masayo said, his cheeks had become tinged with red.

'I know! Why did I ever break up with her?' Hagiwara said, his eyes downcast.

That's right. You should never have left a girl you were comfortable with so easily, Masayo said flatly.

Is that really the conclusion you reach? I thought as I

looked at the young Hagiwara. He was nodding vigorously. Mr Nakano, for his part, wore a baffled expression. He was most likely thinking about his own 'triple' predicament.

'So, Haruo, what if you took this to Sakiko's shop?' Masayo asked, her voice noticeably forceful. Mr Nakano looked from side to side awkwardly.

That's right, the Asukado is the right place for something like this, Masayo said, carefully wrapping the Goryeo celadon bowl back up in the newspaper. The young man was watching Masayo's hands as she did this. Without waiting for a response from Mr Nakano, Masayo picked up the receiver of the telephone. Asukado, Asukado, she murmured as she dialled the number. Mr Nakano was looking at her from behind, his mouth half open. Like him, Hagiwara and I were watching Masayo blankly.

Sakiko came over less than fifteen minutes after receiving Masayo's call.

'Hello,' Sakiko said.

Coming from her, that simple word could sound like either a powerful curse or a benediction. A hex? Or a blessing? I couldn't tell which it was now.

'This is the client,' Masayo said, gesturing towards Hagiwara with her chin. Compared to Mr Nakano, her words were polite, and yet her attitude still wasn't what would be considered appropriate for addressing a customer.

Sakiko opened the newspaper bundle. Not surprisingly, her manner of handling the porcelain was much more conscientious than Mr Nakano's or Masayo's.

'This is Goryeo celadon, isn't it?' Sakiko said at a glance. Hagiwara nodded.

'With this style of glaze, it's about three hundred thousand, I would say,' Sakiko went on.

'No, I don't want you to buy it,' Hagiwara said, after which Masayo took over and explained the gist of the story.

'A jinx,' Sakiko said softly, looking in Mr Nakano's direction, after Masayo had finished telling the tale. Mr Nakano was just standing around stupidly listening to their exchange, rather than withdrawing to the back room as he might have done in a situation like this.

'You know what I mean? You should display it for him at the Asukado,' Mr Nakano said. The 'You know what I mean?' began in his usual tone, but his voice sounded more timid as the rest tumbled out. Sakiko was regarding Mr Nakano impassively.

'I wouldn't be able to take in something with that kind of backstory,' Sakiko said, her face still expressionless. Hagiwara buried his head in his hands. Well, my goodness – everyone has their grudges, don't they? It's not such a big deal, is it? Masayo said brightly. Sakiko, who had shown no reaction to Mr Nakano's suggestion, instantly stiffened at Masayo's words.

'Please keep it for me!' Hagiwara begged Sakiko earnestly. Sakiko's expression quickly resumed its impassivity.

'What about in your shop?' Now Hagiwara was beseeching Mr Nakano. No way! Mr Nakano said, exhaling the smoke from his cigarette. Hagiwara looked away with distaste. I could have sworn that Hagiwara's displeasure was directed not at Mr Nakano's offhandedness but rather at his cigarette.

'Our shop can borrow it from you for twenty thousand, if that is acceptable,' Sakiko said softly.

What do you mean by borrow it? Masayo retorted in a loud voice.

Well, we can't buy it, can we? So instead we can borrow it for an extended time, as long as the lending of it doesn't eventually turn into a sale of any kind – that's what I have in mind, Sakiko explained, her face still expressionless.

This conversation was becoming less and less comprehensible. Both Mr Nakano and Masayo looked similarly confused, but because it was so hard to read Sakiko's expression, they held their tongues.

'You mean, uh, in other words, you'll keep it for me, and on top of that, you'll give me twenty thousand?' Hagiwara said. So, with that little twenty thousand it becomes like an unredeemed item in a pawnshop, you know, Masayo said in a low voice, but Hagiwara pretended not to hear her. Sakiko ignored her too.

After all that, Hagiwara wrote out a receipt for the 20,000 yen to the Asukado, and then he left. Without the bowl, of course. The Goryeo celadon was very elegant, about one size smaller than the kind of bowl in a set-lunch restaurant that comes out heaped with a *katsu* cutlet. It had clearly been passed down from generation to generation, rather than found as part of an excavation, and with only one small chip, it was truly a fine specimen.

Well, then, I guess that's . . . Sakiko said, holding the bundle, now swathed in a layer of bubble wrap in addition to the newspaper, close to her chest as if it were dear to her.

Without even looking at Mr Nakano, Sakiko swiftly left the shop.

'Sakiko sure knows how to do business,' Mr Nakano was saying with admiration.

'If only we could have kept it here, instead of calling the Asukado,' Masayo said, forgetting that she was the one who telephoned Sakiko.

No way! I don't want anything to do with any kind of grudge, Mr Nakano said, sipping tea. We were eating the sugared red beans that I had just brought back from the *wagashi* confectionery shop in the neighbourhood after doing the errands I had been sent out for. Mr Nakano had brewed the green tea himself; it was sharp and astringent.

It tastes good, I said. Mr Nakano paused, blinking weakly, and then he said, You're kind, Hitomi, it means a lot to me.

'If you keep doing such bad things, nobody's going to be kind to you any more,' Masayo said bluntly. Mr Nakano didn't reply, he just seemed to be staring off into the distance as he sipped his tea.

There were a lot of pickups that week, so Takeo and I hardly saw each other. With at least three pickups per day, it was probably past eight o'clock when Takeo got back each night.

I was sent out to do errands again at the weekend. As I was getting ready to go, I checked my wallet to see how much money I had left, when Mr Nakano came over. Don't worry, don't worry, we'll go together in the car, so you don't need the train fare, and I'll treat you to a meal too, he said. It's not the bank today, you know, I thought I'd take you along with me to the market.

The market he mentioned was an auction for other merchants; they dealt in all sorts of items, running the gamut from very affordable to very expensive. According to Mr Nakano, that afternoon's auction promised to be 'pretty good stuff', and so he had decided to bring me along instead of Takeo.

'How come? What's wrong with Takeo?' I asked.

Mr Nakano chuckled. 'In a place like that, it just seems more festive to have a girl along, you know?' he said. What kind of an answer is that? There's nothing festive about the auction, Masayo chimed in, but Mr Nakano just kept chuckling.

It was only after the auction had started that I learned the real reason why Mr Nakano had brought me along. I thought I sensed someone at the front staring fixedly at us; across the hall from where we were, there was Sakiko.

When a jar came up for sale, Sakiko put in a bid but soon dropped out, and she didn't participate in the rest of the auction. On our side, Mr Nakano had called out his bid loudly when an old clock came up for sale. A request from a regular customer, Mr Nakano told me during a break in the auction.

'Sakiko seems very reserved,' I whispered to Mr Nakano.

Mr Nakano shook his head. 'It's just that she doesn't see anything she likes here today. She's known for not backing down when she gets her mind set on something,' he whispered back.

The auction went on for about two hours before it finally broke up. As several of the antique dealers started moving towards the entrance, Mr Nakano said to me, 'Hitomi, you get on well with Sakiko, right?'

Well enough, I guess, I replied, but Mr Nakano wasn't listening to me. You know what I mean? Do me a favour, Hitomi. See if Sakiko will have something to eat with us.

I understand, I replied reluctantly. Mr Nakano smiled broadly. I'd heard the phrase 'a boyish grin', but Mr Nakano's grin was decidedly middle-aged. There was something scruffy about it. And yet, at the same time, it was also a winning smile. I suppose it's the kind of smile that women, as they age, can't resist, I thought to myself as I walked slowly over towards Sakiko, who was lingering by the entrance.

We got a bite to eat. I don't drink saké, Sakiko had said coolly, and we couldn't very well go against such a pronouncement, so we ended up at a nearby chain restaurant. This place is too bright, don't you think? Mr Nakano grumbled.

At first I had thought that they ought to have dinner just the two of them, but I soon realized that Sakiko's stubbornness was too much for Mr Nakano to handle by himself. But meanwhile, Mr Nakano's mood of abashment spread to me as well, so that by the meal's end, all three of us had lapsed into a sullen and complete silence.

'All right, I'm going. I'd like to drive you home, Sakiko, though I don't imagine you'll accept,' Mr Nakano said quietly after he had paid the bill at the till.

Sakiko had been scowling at him but, contrary to expectations, she replied, 'Take me with you.'

Instantly, he broke into a broad smile. The same scruffy, middle-aged yet winning smile from before. Sakiko averted her gaze.

It was quiet inside the truck as well. Mr Nakano sat in the driver's seat, Sakiko sat on the opposite side, and I sat in the middle, like a child stuck between two parents. Mr Nakano turned the radio on, but he quickly turned it off again.

It was not long before we arrived at the Asukado. Sakiko slipped out of the truck and started to head around to the back door, but suddenly she stopped and spun around.

'Come in for a minute.' Her tone was calm but left no room for debate. All right, Mr Nakano said as he and I lumbered out of the truck.

Inside the Asukado, the air was clear. Outside, it was just another crisp night, but in the shop the air felt cool and dry, like there was a bit more oxygen in it.

'You've put grasses in the jar,' I said, and Sakiko's expression relaxed. The area beneath her eyes was plump and full.

Sakiko opened a built-in cabinet below a display case and took out an item bundled in bubble wrap. The bowl she took from Hagiwara for 20,000 yen. It had been rewrapped even more carefully than when she took it from the Nakano shop the other day.

Without saying a word, Sakiko opened the bundle and, moving aside an antique plate with a design of swimming fish and an off-white, rough ceramic saké cup, she placed Hagiwara's bowl in the centre.

Sakiko narrowed her eyes and contemplated the bowl for a moment. Seeing it here in the Asukado, the piece looks even better, Mr Nakano said in a low voice, but Sakiko ignored him. She leaned over the cabinet once again and took out a small paulownia wood box wrapped in a cloth.

'Are there *magatama* beads or something in there?' Mr

Nakano whispered again, but this too was ignored. Sakiko adroitly opened the paulownia box. Inside, there were three cubes set on top of fluffy cotton.

'Dice?' Mr Nakano said, peering timidly – well, timidly for Mr Nakano – into the box. I too could not help but peek inside. They were opalescent yellowish dice, their corners slightly worn. Are these very old? I asked, and Sakiko leaned her head to the side. Hmm. I think they're from the late Edo period – the early- to mid-nineteenth century or so.

Sakiko set the dice beside the bowl. The three dice were scattered randomly, in an arrangement that, if you were to take a photo, would definitely be considered 'artistic'.

'Let's play *Chinchirorin*!' Sakiko said.

Huh? Mr Nakano retorted. Huh? I murmured, mimicking him. Sakiko smiled brightly. It had been a long time since I had seen Sakiko's smile. And yet, she was not smiling with her eyes.

Chinchirorin, Sakiko repeated once more, and the moment she said the word, the air inside the Asukado became noticeably more taut and strained. Mr Nakano and I shivered.

I'll be the parent. You and Hitomi, you're the children, Sakiko said calmly. When she said 'you' to Mr Nakano, there was the slightest hint of sweetness in her voice. As if maybe she didn't intend for it to sound sweet, but it came out that way from habit.

'*Chinchirorin* – I've never . . .' I started to say. Again Sakiko smiled brightly (though not with her eyes). It's easy –

you just roll the dice three times, she said, covering them with her hand. Mr Nakano didn't say anything.

'If I roll a four, five, or a six, then the parent automatically wins,' Sakiko said, holding the dice in her delicate palm and throwing them into the bowl.

'Oh!' Mr Nakano exclaimed.

'What?' Sakiko asked as she looked up at him. The area beneath her eyes seemed puffy, so that looking at her from above, her expression appeared relaxed.

'You don't think it will crack?' Mr Nakano said, pointing at the bowl. 'Isn't there something else we could use?'

'I paid twenty thousand to keep the bowl, it's fine,' Sakiko said flatly.

'But it'd be a shame.'

'It will be fine as long as we take care when we roll the dice.'

Sakiko shifted the brunt of her argument towards me. 'Hitomi, don't you think you're perfectly capable of taking care?'

I am not, I said nervously, looking back at Sakiko. Mr Nakano and I both stared at her.

The two of us, we both resemble something, I thought to myself. I've got it – we're like chicks waiting to be fed.

'Look! They're already all lined up,' Sakiko cried out softly, without looking at either Mr Nakano or me. Two of the dice in the bowl were showing threes. The other one was face up on the side of the five.

'Okay, it's your turn next,' Sakiko said, putting the dice in Mr Nakano's hand. Her voice was gentle but unyielding.

Seemingly against his will, Mr Nakano rolled the dice.

Sakiko had thrown them decisively from above, but Mr Nakano put his hand almost on the edge of the bowl and, rather than throwing them, it was more like he placed them inside with a gentle toss.

The dice tumbled with a dull roll. Two of them fell to the bottom of the bowl, but the other one leapt off the edge of the bowl with a rather irresolute motion.

'Tinkle tinkle!' Sakiko cried out this time. She laughed out loud. Mr Nakano had a sulky look on his face. Sakiko's laughter echoed around the dimly lit Asukado. Overwhelmed, I could do nothing but stand there stiffly.

'Tell me, why are we playing *Chinchirorin*?' Mr Nakano said in a murmur.

'It's a bet,' Sakiko replied.

'What? You know I don't have any money!' Mr Nakano said.

'It's not for money.'

'Um, do I have to bet something too?' I asked.

'Oh, no, Hitomi, you don't need to worry.'

Okay, now Hitomi rolls. Sakiko picked up the dice that had fallen outside the bowl along with the two that were inside and placed them all in the palm of my hand. Sakiko's hand was terribly cold.

Okay, she said again, as if egging me on. I shut my eyes and flung the dice.

There was a pinging sound as the dice spun along the wall of the bowl. The first one stopped and showed a one. The other two soon stopped, and I looked to see they both had fallen on the same side – ones.

'Snake eyes!' Mr Nakano's murmur sounded subdued as he exhaled.

Hitomi wins, Sakiko said. I see, I nodded, still clueless. Sakiko fell silent for a while. And as long as Sakiko wasn't saying anything, neither were Mr Nakano or I.

'I guess that's it,' Sakiko declared abruptly after about five whole minutes had passed.

Eh? Mr Nakano said. I stole a glance at Sakiko's face and was surprised to see that she was smiling. Even a little bit with her eyes.

That was a narrow escape, Haruo, Sakiko murmured.

Eh? What do you mean? Mr Nakano asked in reply, but Sakiko didn't say anything more.

Then we just got back in the truck and returned to the Nakano shop. Mr Nakano offered to take me home, but I felt like walking a bit. Maybe I thought I might run into Takeo on the street like before. For some reason, I had an intense desire to see him. I felt as though even now, we could still manage to make up with each other. Although I had no reason to think so.

I didn't see Takeo. A narrow escape – Sakiko's phrase – kept running through my mind as I walked the streets to my apartment. Soon it would be winter. The air seemed to grow clearer, the later at night it was. A narrow escape, I murmured, quickening my pace.

Say, say, Hitomi, well done! Masayo said to me one day about two weeks later.

I hear you saved Haruo by the skin of his teeth! Masayo laughed. What are you talking about? I asked. Come now, I heard about what happened that night from our dear Sakiko, Masayo replied. At some point Sakiko has gone from just plain Sakiko to 'our dear Sakiko'.

According to what Masayo told me, Sakiko had entrusted the fate of her relationship with Mr Nakano to the dice that night.

'Her bet?' I murmured.

'That's right, her bet!' Masayo nodded effusively.

If Sakiko won, they would break up. If Mr Nakano won, they would stay together. And if I won, she would wait and see.

'But in the end, you won, didn't you, Hitomi?' Masayo peered into my face as she confirmed this.

I don't even know how to play *Chinchirorin*, I replied. Masayo laughed again.

That same week, Sakiko stopped by the Nakano shop. Since Mr Nakano wasn't there, Sakiko simply handed a small parcel to Masayo, and then she hurriedly went to leave.

'Thanks for the other day,' Sakiko said, turning around just as she was going. It appeared that this was directed at me. Flustered, I tried to deflect it, and Sakiko smiled. Her eyes still didn't seem to smile, though.

I walked Sakiko to the door, and once we were in front of the shop, she stared at the typewriter displayed there without really seeing it.

'Um,' I began to speak. 'Can you ever forgive Mr Nakano?'

What? Sakiko said. I-I'm sorry, I didn't mean to, out of the blue, I said. Sakiko shook her head. It's okay.

'I can't forgive him,' Sakiko said calmly after a moment.

B-but you still won't break up with him? I asked. Sakiko held her tongue again.

Then she said, 'That's a separate thing,' in a measured tone.

And she spun around, turning her back to me. I kept watching as her figure receded into the distance, growing smaller and smaller. It reminded me a little of how surprisingly pleased she had been when the dice had all lined up.

Takeo the fool, I murmured and squeezed my eyes shut. After a moment, when I opened them again, I could no longer see Sakiko's figure.

Apples

'I let him get away!' Masayo said.

Takeo was just bringing in the load from the pickups while Mr Nakano was coming and going in and out of the back door, and I was in the middle of counting change at the till, so at first I wasn't quite able to catch what she was talking about.

The customer left and Takeo, ambiguous as ever – lately I had even stopped phoning him, but actually in the shop we are back on normal speaking terms – had rushed off, and Mr Nakano had just sat down heavily in a chair while mopping the sweat off his brow with the towel that was slung around his neck.

Masayo murmured it again. 'I let Maruyama get away!'

What? I looked up at the same time that Mr Nakano let out an expression of surprise in a strangely cheerful voice, only to see Masayo lower the tips of her brows with a troubled look.

*

'Is it about money?' Mr Nakano asked as soon as he realized what Masayo had said.

This was before Masayo had uttered even a single word of explanation – about when Maruyama had gone, or what had caused him to run off, or what she meant by him getting away in the first place.

'That's not it,' Masayo replied sharply, arching her lovely eyebrows, but only briefly, for they soon drooped again as if from exhaustion.

This was not the usual Masayo. She seemed completely lacking in vigour. Mr Nakano's mouth was open at an odd angle. Masayo slowly sat down in a chair, her brows still sagging. Mr Nakano started to say something but gave up and instead took off his brown bobble hat. Then he put it back on again.

The three of us sat there as if petrified until, unable to stand it any longer, I stood up awkwardly and sidestepped my way towards the back room. The shop was chock-full with the load that Takeo had just brought inside, so it was impossible to walk in a straight line.

'Oh, dear. Where are you going, Hitomi?' Masayo asked in a forlorn tone. I had never seen her this way.

Just to the toilet, I replied. Masayo sighed.

'Me too, I'm just going to do the same,' Mr Nakano said rapidly, as if not allowing room for debate. He opened the front door with a clatter and went out, moving in a similarly awkward manner.

Until the beginning of autumn we would leave the glass door open, but once November was past, it remained tightly shut. Going from being wide open to suddenly closed, at first it felt somewhat cold and formal.

'We always close it when winter comes around, and open it when spring arrives, but for some reason this year it seems awfully sad, doesn't it?' Come to think of it, Masayo had said this just the other day.

For a moment, it had struck me that this sounded rather faint-hearted for Masayo, but otherwise I had hardly taken any notice at the time.

In order to make it clear that we were doing business even though the door was closed, Mr Nakano had recently hung from the eaves a piece of cardboard on which he had written, WE'RE OPEN.

'Why does Haruo seem to insist on lowering the tone of his shop?' That was what Sakiko had said last week when she saw the cardboard sign. She had dropped in, saying that she happened to have some business that brought her nearby. Lately Sakiko had been showing up at the Nakano shop more often. It goes without saying that I didn't have the slightest idea what that implied about the state of her relationship with Mr Nakano.

Right? Sakiko sought consensus from Masayo. But Masayo gave only a half-hearted reply. At that point, I had yet to notice that Masayo was not herself.

At first, the words WE'RE OPEN were only written on one side of the cardboard. Mr Nakano had carefully outlined each letter, drawn with a thick green Magic Marker, in black. What do you think of this? Pretty artistic, isn't it? Mr Nakano had said, as he happily passed a string through the hole he had punched in the cardboard.

When Sakiko disparaged his efforts, Mr Nakano had indignantly taken the cardboard down from the eaves and flung it beside the till. I thought he had abandoned it there, but then he stormed into the back room, still cross, and emerged carrying a six-pack of thick Magic Markers.

Turning over the sign, he wrote out the words, WE'RE OPEN, in yellow letters. This time the words were even more ragged than the green lettering on the front. Next, he took the cap off the red Magic Marker and sloppily outlined the yellow, and as soon as he was finished, he marched back out to the eaves and hung it up again.

Sakiko watched the entire process with a resigned look but when, with a pout, Mr Nakano asked what she thought, she burst into laughter.

After a cup of tea Sakiko left the shop, saying to Mr Nakano, It's beyond me. He watched her depart, his hands on his hips in a triumphant manner. Just as she passed the eaves, Sakiko flicked the lower part of the cardboard with her finger. The sign swung back and forth two or three times and then was still.

'In any case, five hundred thousand, definitely,' the man said.

It was early in the afternoon, and Masayo had just gone out to have lunch. Usually she brought her own bento lunch, or she would whip up some ramen or fried rice in the back, but for the past week – since she had told us about letting Maruyama get away – she had taken her meal elsewhere every day.

Yesterday, trying to make small talk, I had asked her, Where do you usually go for lunch? Masayo had tilted her head and said apathetically, Hmm, what is that place again . . . before falling silent. Unsure of how to go from there, I had hurriedly wiped the till with a dry cloth.

'Five hundred thousand,' Mr Nakano parroted the man's words in a murmur, with one hand nimbly taking the brass lighter that the man had pulled out importantly from his bag.

'Oh!' the man exclaimed. 'Don't handle it so roughly!'

I'm sorry, Mr Nakano said, raising his other hand in a gesture of apology. The lighter itself wasn't really pocket-sized or portable; it was a short, fat, cylindrical design, meant to be kept on a table top.

'The burner is shaped like a pistol, isn't it?' Mr Nakano said as he stared at it.

'You have a very good eye,' the man replied proudly.

The part that stuck out like a rod from the body of the cylinder was in the shape of the barrel of a child's toy pistol. There they were, putting on airs and playing out their roles, Mr Nakano with his 'isn't it?' and the man replying with his 'you have a very good eye' – and yet even I could see at a glance what it was.

The customer explained that his uncle had served as an ambassador and been posted to Texas, where a local big shot had given him the lighter. It was from the pioneer days, he said.

'And, you say it's worth five hundred thousand?' Mr Nakano asked casually.

'I've had it valued,' the man replied, as he stuck out his chest.

'Valued?'

'You know, like on those antique shows on television, right?'

'Have you been on television, sir?'

'No, that's not what I mean, but an acquaintance of mine is close friends with one of the antique dealers who does appear on the show.'

I see, Mr Nakano said. We learned from his story that the person who had done the 'valuation' for the man was not actually an official antique dealer, but rather someone who appreciated antiques and had an entrée into that world, and what was more, this 'friend' was not actually a friend of the man himself but rather 'a friend of an acquaintance of one of his relatives'.

'I need a bit of cash, you know,' the man said as he puffed up his chest again.

'We don't really do full cash payouts,' Mr Nakano spoke slowly.

'I don't expect your outfit to buy it from me!' the man quickly responded. You couldn't tell when he was just sitting there quietly, but when he started to speak, a slight jitteriness seemed to show between the chinks in his confident appearance.

'I heard from a friend of a relative's friend that your shop has an online auction site,' he said, speaking even more quickly than before.

A friend of a relative's friend? Mr Nakano repeated, his tone deadpan. I had to admit, the guy certainly had a lot of indirect contacts. I nearly laughed out loud, but I restrained myself.

While it was true that the Nakano shop was selling some goods on the Internet, the fact was that Mr Nakano still didn't maintain the site himself – he had entrusted Mr Crane, also known as Tokizo, with selling everything for him. But Mr Nakano didn't go into those details now.

'So, you want me to sell this lighter in an online auction,' Mr Nakano said.

That's right. The man nodded. His eyes were swimming a little.

I see, Mr Nakano replied, assuming a solemn intonation.

What's it gonna be? Will you sell it for me, or not? the man asked impatiently. His back, once erect, was shifting towards a slouch.

The one who really knew how to deal with this type of customer was Masayo. But I doubted she could have handled him, the way she was now. It made me a little sad to think about. Not sad because I empathized with how she felt – I'm not quite sure why – I just felt vaguely sad, in a general sort of way.

Mr Nakano was talking idly with the man. The ineffective air conditioner made a strange hissing sound as it blew out hot air.

'That for sale?' Takeo asked. He was looking at the lighter, the one that the man's 'uncle who had served as an ambassador had been given by a Texan'.

In the end, Mr Nakano had accepted the lighter from the man, making sure to remind him, 'Only because it's for the online auction, right? But five hundred thousand is probably too much to expect, okay?'

'Takeo, you gonna buy it?' Mr Nakano asked in response.

Takeo was considering it with unexpected seriousness. I

stole a glance at his profile. Having to spy on him was annoying, though, so I quickly averted my gaze. Without knowing what exactly I found so irritating about it, I grasped the hem of my dress and fluttered it about with both hands.

It was the dress that Mr Nakano had sold me for a discounted 300 yen back on that day of the thunderstorm. The tag said that it was 100 per cent Indian calico, but I doubted that it was pure calico, because after washing it just once the length had shrunk dramatically. Since then I sometimes wore it over jeans in place of an apron when I was in the shop.

'Can I buy it?' Takeo asked.

Come to think of it, Takeo might not have ever bought anything from the shop. Mr Nakano made his eyes big and round as he said, You see how Hitomi takes advantage of the employee discount.

The employee discount that he mentioned was given purely on the spur of the moment and according to Mr Nakano's whims. It wasn't as if there was a specific set rate. Though I had to admit that I had procured plenty of daily necessities and furniture from the Nakano shop. Things like that yellow stool and this dress, sure, but what I bought most often were baskets. Large ones, small ones, open-weave ones, and tightly woven ones – I bought all sorts and tossed all kinds of things into them. Thanks to these baskets, my apartment was much less messy than it used to be.

'He said it's worth five hundred thousand yen.' Mr Nakano grinned as he said this to Takeo.

Takeo's face remained expressionless as he replied, I see.

Takeo fell silent, so Mr Nakano didn't say anything else either. Mr Nakano glanced over at me with a look that seemed to say, Did I say something wrong? Takeo just stood there, seemingly oblivious of Mr Nakano's expression.

I hate guys like Takeo! I thought to myself. Guys like him are always like this. Even though they hardly ever worry about other people, it's like they force others to pay attention to them.

'Don't have five hundred thousand,' Takeo replied after a while. His cheeks were slightly flushed.

Mr Nakano hastily waved his hand in front of his face.

'Well, this is going to be in an online auction, so you could put in a bid for it yourself.'

Takeo looked at Mr Nakano blankly.

'You don't use the Internet?' Mr Nakano asked, wagging the palm of his hand again.

'I use it,' Takeo replied tersely.

'All right, then, I'll tell you how the auctions work, see. First put in a bid. And if you win, then you don't even have to pay for shipping!' Mr Nakano said, restlessly playing with his hat. It was the same kind of fidgeting as when I was fiddling with the hem of my dress a little while ago.

I really hate Takeo, I thought to myself this time. I felt much stronger about it than before. Why should I be brooding over a useless guy like him? I even started to get angry at myself. I was going to forget all about Takeo, find a new guy to fall madly in love with and be able to say breezily, Takeo and I had some good memories . . . Yes, I would eat a diet rich in vegetables, seaweed, and legumes, and every day would be sparkling and bright, my life brimming with health and vitality.

While imagining this, I was again filled with a general

sort of sadness. I definitely wasn't sad because I was thinking about Takeo. Definitely not.

Speaking of which, I wondered if Masayo was all right. I hadn't seen her since three days ago. After the man with the lighter had left, I had waited and waited, but Masayo didn't return from her lunch. My sis, she's always done this kind of thing. She just suddenly disappears, and then at some point, as if it were no big deal, she shows up again, Mr Nakano muttered, as if to convince himself, while he was closing up the shop.

The way Mr Nakano called her 'my sis' that day was a bit different from how he usually referred to her. It's hard to say, but it wasn't like the impudent, middle-aged Mr Nakano; it seemed like what a not-yet-grown-up, still somewhat innocent kid would call his big sister.

'Should I go and check on Masayo at her house?' I asked Mr Nakano, who was still fiddling with his hat. Meanwhile I was trying my best not to look in Takeo's direction.

'Right. That's probably a good idea,' Mr Nakano replied with concern. Takeo made a slight movement. I hadn't the faintest idea what he was thinking right then. Even though I used to think that I could tell. Sort of.

'I'll stop by on my way home,' I said.

Mr Nakano made a gesture of thanks to me with one hand, and with the other he pulled out a 5,000-yen note from the register. Maybe you could pick up some cake or something, he said, pressing the note into my hand.

The money was wrinkled. Takeo was still just standing there.

*

Masayo was doing surprisingly well.

Oh, my, thank you for coming! she said as she showed me into her home. I held out the box of cakes from the Posy tea shop, and Masayo immediately opened the lid.

'Just like Hitomi – a pie series!' she laughed.

A pie series? I asked in reply.

Masayo raised her eyebrows. 'You know, the time Haruo told you to come over to scout out what was going on with Maruyama,' Masayo said, placing the lemon pie on the plate in front of her. Go ahead, Hitomi, take whichever one you like.

Now that she mentioned it, I had bought the same pastries from Posy when I came here before. It was already almost a year since then.

'Time flies, doesn't it?' Masayo said as if she had read my mind.

Yes, I blurted out, surprised.

'Cherry pie, of course!'

Yes, I said once more.

'You had cherry pie last time too.'

Did I? I said, falteringly. Masayo nodded deeply.

For the time being, we devoted ourselves to the pastries. Come to think of it, how much had Mr Nakano given me back then? Was it 5,000 yen? Or was it 3,000? I wondered about this as I sank my fork into the pie. I couldn't quite remember.

'So, Hitomi, do you think that sexual desire is important?' Masayo asked suddenly.

'What?'

'Without sexual desire, it's not interesting, is it?'

Unsure of how to answer, I chewed the crust from the cherry pie in silence, and swallowed.

'Hitomi, you must still have plenty of sexual desire. I envy you!' Masayo said dreamily as she poked at the meringue of the lemon pie with her fork. By the way, don't you think that the quality of Posy's cakes has gone down a little lately? she went on with a nonchalant air.

'I don't normally eat them, so I wouldn't know,' I replied courteously.

Is that so? Masayo said, breaking off a large piece of lemon pie and bringing it to her lips. My goodness, but today they are quite good! I wonder if it has to do with my physical condition. It's really no fun getting old!

Masayo chatted away in a strangely cheerful tone. Sexual desire. I tried saying the words inside my head. They seemed to have a similar timbre to the way Masayo had said them, with an oddly bright resonance. I don't really like cherry pie all that much, I thought. And yet, just like that I am drawn to its red gooey moistness, almost in spite of myself.

My mouth was filled with the scent of butter from the pie crust. Masayo's chin was moving as she chewed.

The story about Mr Maruyama began.

But first Masayo polished off the lemon pie. 'One more,' she said, and then devoured the millefeuille.

'So, anyway, Maruyama disappeared,' Masayo said.

D-did he really? I replied hesitantly. What will I do if this turns into some kind of life counselling session? I was thinking. I'm not much good at either giving or receiving advice.

'There were signs.'

Maruyama had left two weeks earlier, and according to

Masayo, for the preceding month or so there had been indic-
ations. Restlessness. Absent-mindedness. A lack of punctuality.
And yet, for some reason, he was in awfully high spirits.

'That is obviously the behaviour of a man whose affections
have shifted to another woman, right?' Masayo asked, seeming
to peer over at me.

Y-yes. All I could do was timidly stammer another reply,
since I know absolutely nothing about 'the behaviour of a man
whose affections have shifted to another woman'.

'Then Maruyama was gone. The end,' Masayo concluded
succinctly.

Th-the end? I asked.

'Well, he disappeared!' Masayo's voice sounded the way a
child's does when wheedling their mother for a sweet.

Unsure of how to reply, I placed the apple pie on my
plate. Posy's apple pie is very tart. They use Jonathan apples,
you know, Masayo had said at some point. Haruo can't eat
Jonathan apples. That kid, he hates tart or sour things. He has
the palate of a child.

I ate the apple pie in silence. Masayo placed one of the
last two remaining pastries – cream puffs – on her plate for a
moment, but then she put it back. I prefer cream puffs filled
with custard, not with cream, she said in a low voice.

'Has Mr Maruyama not been back to his apartment?'
I asked, just to be sure, after I finished eating the apple pie.
Mr Maruyama did not actually live with Masayo; he rented
his own apartment. Even if he had left his relationship with
Masayo, he would have been back at his own place, wouldn't
he? This thought occurred to me when I had finally composed
myself a little.

'That's right. He hasn't been back to his apartment at all either.'

I was on the verge of asking if she had been checking there every day, but I quickly stopped myself.

'He hasn't even called you or anything?'

'He's run off, so he's not going to call, is he?'

'He didn't leave a note or anything?'

Not a thing. He just suddenly disappeared, that's all.

Just suddenly, I repeated like an idiot.

'Did you have a fight or something?' I asked gingerly.

'No fight.'

'Did one of his relatives pass away?'

'If so he would have told me, don't you think?'

'Could he have been kidnapped?'

'Why would someone do that to a man with hardly any money?'

'Amnesia?'

'He always carries his pension book on him.'

Perhaps because Masayo's tone of voice was so easygoing, I began to feel as though we were discussing someone who didn't concern her. Who is to say that, one of these days, he won't just show up again? You know people, sometimes they just have this burning need to go off on a trip by themselves, don't they?

The next thing I knew, it was as if I were spouting off responses to my own advice. Masayo was even occasionally nodding along in agreement.

The time has come, I thought to myself, and I slid off the seat cushion so that I was kneeling on the tatami. Well, I . . . I began to say as I bowed my head, when I suddenly remembered.

Keeled over. The words that Masayo had used to describe it.

When I haven't heard from someone for a while, the first thing that occurs to me is that they might have just keeled over. This was what Masayo had murmured when Takeo hadn't been answering my calls to his mobile.

I had let out a little cry and then fallen silent again, and Masayo was eyeing me dubiously. I sat back on the cushion that I'd just slid off, but as I did so, the low table shook, and the aluminium foil that had been stuck to the bottom of the apple pie crinkled.

Chiri – that was the faint sound it made.

'Did you put in a bid for the auction?' Mr Nakano asked Takeo.

'Not yet, but plan to.'

Well, well, you're actually going to bid on it? Mr Nakano's eyes grew round. The lighter is really that nice, huh? Mr Nakano asked, despite the fact that he had been the one to take it on.

"S'nice, sure. Guess it's my type,' Takeo replied.

'Your type?' Mr Nakano's eyes became perfect circles.

The three of us – Mr Nakano, Takeo, and I – had gathered in the back room. Masayo was not there. Since the day after I paid her a visit, Masayo had been showing up again at the Nakano shop, but only to drop in for an hour or so during the morning or afternoon, and then she would soon return home.

'Why don't we have a debriefing session?' Mr Nakano had said a little while ago as he was closing the shutter. There's really nothing to report, I replied. I asked him to do something too, Mr Nakano said, raising his chin in Takeo's direction.

Takeo went to check out Maruyama's building for me.

Mr Nakano ordered three bowls of *katsudon* over the phone, then we sat under the *kotatsu*. It was a small model. It's new but I decided to trade up, said the customer who had come to sell it the day before yesterday. Items like second-hand gas heaters and *kotatsu* moved surprisingly well.

There were no newspapers or letters piled up in the mail-box at Mr Maruyama's apartment. The needle on his electric meter was moving. Any time I went there, the curtains were always drawn shut. Nothing much, otherwise.

Takeo gave his brief 'report', and then I gave my own. It's been a little over two weeks since Masayo had any contact with Mr Maruyama. He gave no advance notice that he was leaving. The cause of his disappearance is unknown (I did not relay Masayo's theory that Maruyama's affections had shifted to another woman).

It had been a long time since the three of us had been together like this. Before the summer arrived, sometimes we all used to go out for lunch. Back then, Mr Nakano would just lock the glass door and leave the shop, without a sign that said OUT TO LUNCH or anything. At the time, sales had been adequate; Takeo's and my salary were calculated differently from month to month. Recently and all of a sudden, the Nakano shop was starting to put its affairs in order.

'I went to the police,' Mr Nakano mumbled.

The police? Takeo asked in response, a nervous look on his face.

'To find out whether or not they had found a body.'

'Had they?' Takeo cried. Nope, Mr Nakano replied. All three of us let out a sigh.

But these days my sis seems a little better, doesn't she? Mr Nakano mumbled again.

Sure does – other day she called me 'our dear Takeo' for the first time in a while. Now it was Takeo's turn to mumble.

As for me, I recalled something Masayo told me when I had visited her house. It was after she had finished eating her millefeuille, as she was poking her fork at the slivers of pastry stuck to the aluminium foil.

You know, I thought sexual desire was the reason why I'm with Maruyama, Masayo had said. Right, Hitomi – men and women have carnal urges, and people fall in love with each other in order to satisfy those desires, don't they? We can call it love or passion or various other things, but you know, no matter how pretty the paper that you wrap it up in, when all is said and done, the primary force that drives people towards one another is still that same sensuality – that's what I've always thought.

I see, I had replied.

But you know, Masayo continued. The thing is, it may not have been desire that brought me to Maruyama. At that point Masayo arched her eyebrows. She stared directly at me.

I was feeling the way I used to during a private meeting with my teacher at school, and without thinking, I had replied with a precise 'Yes' as opposed to my usual vague 'I see'.

And, since Maruyama disappeared, I can't help but feel lonely. Masayo said this and sniffed.

Is there a connection between sexual desire and loneliness? I asked.

In my experience, until now, when I have sexual desire, I don't feel lonely – it's more about feeling agitated.

Agitated, I murmured.

At least at first. After a while, though, that's when I start to feel lonely.

That's the order of things?

That's how it goes. Really, it is, Masayo went on. But you know, this is the first time I have felt only loneliness, Masayo said with a simple and innocent expression. This is truly the first time for me.

If sexual desire wasn't the origin of Masayo and Mr Maruyama's relationship, then what was their love based on? I had silently pondered this as I walked away from Masayo's house.

There was a knock on the shutter. Mr Nakano leaned out of the back door and called to the delivery boy.

The *katsudon* from the soba shop tastes better than the one from the cutlet shop, Mr Nakano said as he bolted down his bowl of food. Takeo and I ate in silence, heads bowed over our own bowls.

The deadline for the online auction was eight o'clock the next evening. At the end of the day, Takeo went home and came back carrying an old-model laptop computer. He connected to the Internet at the shop and, under the guidance of Mr Nakano, he managed to put in a bid.

'Seems it's at one thousand one hundred yen,' Mr Nakano laughed as he looked at the screen that appeared when they were connected. Tokizo had created the site so that the lowest possible bid was 1,000 yen. The people who bid in these auctions were quite savvy about the value of the goods being offered, so the prices were hardly ever unreasonably high or too low.

'Is this a joke, with that hundred yen?' Mr Nakano said, clicking away with the mouse. Ash fell from the cigarette in his mouth, scattering all over the keyboard. Sorry, sorry, Mr Nakano said, cursorily brushing it away. Takeo twitched.

'What's more, there are only two bidders,' Mr Nakano said.

Even at five minutes to eight, there was still no third bid on the lighter. When the competition is high, the bidding is fierce up until the last moment, you know, but in this case you might just get it, Mr Nakano said, tapping awkwardly on the keyboard. See, take a look! Mr Nakano leaned to the side and Takeo peered over his shoulder.

'One thousand four hundred yen,' Takeo muttered. 'If nobody wants to buy it, seems like it would be better to take it back.'

'But, you know, the customer himself was the one who said to put it up for auction,' Mr Nakano said, his tone harsh as he gripped the mouse again.

Mr Nakano let out a little sound, causing me to peer over his shoulder too. The number beside the lighter now read 1,700. The first bidder had raised his price against Takeo's bid. Mr Nakano tapped on the keyboard again. Should I switch with you? Takeo said from behind him, but Mr Nakano replied tersely, 'It's okay,' without turning around. The number on the screen changed to 2,000. It quickly jumped to 2,500; Mr Nakano tapped on the keyboard again and it read 3,000.

I stood right next to Takeo, our eyes fixed on the screen.

How many weeks had passed since I had been this close to him? Takeo smelled of soap. It was the same scent as when he used to come over to my apartment.

Boing! A wall clock that was for sale in the shop sounded the hour. Good thing this won't go on for much longer, Mr Nakano said between his teeth. He had been sitting still in front of the screen for some time, but now he stood up and said, 'Takeo, want to try?'

Yes, Takeo said and sat down in the chair with a thump. Now that he was in a lower position, the scent of shampoo wafted upward.

Takeo was staring intently at the screen. He made no move towards the keyboard. Looking at the display at the top of the computer screen, the time said three minutes past eight. Quietly, I moved away from Takeo.

Ten or so minutes must have passed. 'Won it,' Takeo said softly. 'Four thousand one hundred yen.'

That guy with his five hundred thousand yen! Mr Nakano said with a laugh. Takeo pulled a crumpled 5,000-yen note from his pocket. He took a 100-yen coin from another pocket, and handed them both to Mr Nakano.

Takeo seemed lost in thought for a moment before he said, Don't need any change. You can tell the customer it sold for that price.

That's generous of you. Mr Nakano laughed again, then wrapped the lighter in newspaper. Takeo took it, and at first he put it along with his laptop computer into a large ruck-sack, but then he took the lighter back out. He ripped off the newspaper, and set it on top of the shelf in the back room.

Okay if I leave it here? Takeo asked.

Mr Nakano nodded, a look of curiosity on his face. Why keep it here?

Takeo didn't say anything for a moment, but finally he replied with, Don't smoke at home, so if I leave it here, everyone can use it.

Mr Maruyama came home.

He had been on the edge of despair, he said. 'And suddenly stricken with wanderlust.' Apparently this was the pure and simple explanation Mr Maruyama had given as to why he had just upped and left.

'Of course I don't believe him,' Masayo said.

The two of us were eating *tanmen* in the back room. It was Masayo's signature dish, the way she always made it. Masayo sniffed as she raised the noodles high with her chopsticks. When it's cold out, your nose runs more than ever when you eat *tanmen*, she said languidly.

'You don't believe him?'

'He's lying. I mean, Maruyama definitely ran off, I'm sure of that,' Masayo said slowly.

'How do you know he ran off?'

'Because I love him, that's how,' Masayo replied with perfect composure.

I love him, I parroted her words in a murmur.

'Am I wrong to?'

N-no, I said, hurriedly slurping my noodles. They were hot, and I almost choked on them.

We heard the sound of the truck's engine. It must be time for Takeo to go out. I glanced at the heavy brass lighter which he had left on top of the shelf. When the man had found out that the lighter sold for only 5,100 yen, he had complained a bit. I knew that anything could happen but . . . he had said, glaring at Mr Nakano.

But, sir, I noticed it said *Made in China* on the bottom of it, Mr Nakano said serenely after the man had finished his griping. The man had turned pale and then fallen silent.

'Love has made me scared,' Masayo said in a sing-song tone.

'You only just got scared?' I retorted.

'Oh, Hitomi, touché!' Masayo said, laughing.

'To think that a young woman like you can understand how it feels to find oneself in a precarious love affair when one's desire is almost gone!' Masayo said, slurping her noodles. I slurped mine as well.

After I had finished the *tanmen*, I stood at the sink and drank a glass of water. Masayo brought the empty bowls over and handed me an apple, saying, Here you go. I bit into it while I was standing there. It was tart. That's a Jonathan, Masayo said as she bit into one herself.

The truth was, I knew very well that Takeo worried about other people plenty.

And I could never hate him, after all.

I thought about this as I chewed the apple. The Jonathan's tartness was bracing. Masayo and I made crunching sounds as we ate our apples to the core.

Gin

Like in those medieval European oil paintings or something like that, a fat old man would be drinking straight from the bottle – right? Just like that – come on, you know?

Sakiko tilted her head, sceptical of Mr Nakano's description, despite his conviction that he knew what he was talking about.

You know, the father and son painted together, their name was Peter? Pieter or something, right? In these guys' paintings, there would be a festival or something in the village, and a guy would be swigging from a jug, his huge, hairy hand gripping it at its neck where it tapers – that's what I mean.

Peter? Sakiko tilted her head again. Peter is probably as common a name as Taro is in Japan, she said, squinting. The area under her eyes was as plump and full as ever.

I mean, you know what I mean – it starts with Bru . . . Bru-something. Bruegel? There's a painting with a bunch of middle-aged guys wearing codpieces or something, drinking and dancing around.

That painting – it might have been painted by Bruegel's studio, Sakiko said, now opening her eyes wide and staring Mr Nakano in the face. Mr Nakano met her gaze, but seemed to stiffen briefly.

The right side of my body was being warmed by hot air spewing from a gas heater that a customer brought in to sell a few days ago – it was a strange sensation. Despite the fact that winter had arrived, it still hadn't seemed cold until a sudden temperature drop which coincided with the new year, and now, with the only other heat coming from the Nakano shop's ineffective air conditioning unit, there wasn't much to be done about my freezing hands and feet.

We'll hang on to this and use it in the shop, Mr Nakano had said, as soon as the customer who brought in the heater had left. He sent Takeo out to buy kerosene, and then with seeming delight turned it on right away. He was like a child who has just been given a wind-up toy and insists on playing with it immediately.

Mr Nakano squatted down to let the blast of warm air hit him in the face. Nowadays, gas heaters are different from the ones they used to make. See, the heat from the flame doesn't burn your face! Masayo seemed equally impressed as she crouched down beside him.

You know, I saw a wine jug like that the other day. Mr Nakano had picked up where he left off and was chatting earnestly with Sakiko. For her part, though, Sakiko was responding half-heartedly as she turned over a basket woven from akebi vines to look at the bottom.

'That basket is pretty, isn't it?' I said. Sakiko nodded. It is. But it's practically brand new.

I chuckled at the way Sakiko said, practically brand new. Ours was a strange world, in which whatever was new and neat and tidy diminished in value. Mr Nakano stopped chatting suddenly, and was looking up at the ceiling. He stayed like that for a moment, his face turned upward, before he started to walk slowly – in the same posture, just moving his legs – over to a corner of the shop, where he fumbled for a bamboo broom that was propped up against the wall. Steadily, he returned to his original spot, and letting out a cry, he struck the ceiling with the end of the broom.

What's the matter? Sakiko asked, her lips slightly parted. They look like flower petals, I thought to myself.

A mouse, Mr Nakano replied. With any luck, it will be knocked out from the shock!

I doubt that's enough to make it lose consciousness. Sakiko laughed.

With no further reference to the mouse in the ceiling, Mr Nakano resumed the conversation about the medieval wine jug.

For some reason, I've suddenly decided I want it, you know?

How much is it? Sakiko asks.

A lot.

Like a hundred thousand?

It's two hundred and fifty thousand.

That's quite a price, Sakiko said with admiration, and she squinted again. Sakiko has various ways of squinting her eyes, and this time it made her look like a merchant. Oddly enough, the area under her eyes did not seem as full when she squinted, and her lips looked thinner than usual too.

It's pretty steep, Mr Nakano said.

Since I specialize in Japanese things, I don't know if that's what the actual market price is, Sakiko said, while the expression on her face clearly conveyed that she thought it exorbitant.

Mr Nakano knitted his brows together. I thought it was the price of the jug that was making him frown, but it was the mouse. Dammit, it's back! Listen, you can hear it again! Mr Nakano said in an anguished tone.

I shifted the position of the gas heater a little, so that the hot air wouldn't blow directly onto the right side of my body. Mr Nakano saw me do it and scolded me. Careful not to start a fire! he said. Yes, I replied. Mr Nakano scratched his head. Don't use such a sad voice! he said.

I'm not particularly sad, I said.

Mr Nakano scratched his head again. I'm sad, you know.

Why are you sad, Mr Nakano?

Because it's winter. It's cold. And I have no money.

Sakiko's legs were dangling as she sat in a chair that was for sale. She was wearing black tights, her legs long and slender.

Oh, the mouse! I said. Mr Nakano and Sakiko turned towards the ceiling at the same time. Just kidding, I admitted. With looks of disappointment, both of them returned to the way they were. The heater made a soft whooshing sound.

Mr Nakano remained unusually fixated on the jug.

In the midst of opening the shutter, his body bent over, he would mutter, 'It's really steep,' or at the end of a conversation,

I would think he was about to say something else, and he would say to himself, 'I'd like to know what the original price was.'

It got to the point where Takeo even said to me, 'Mr Nakano seems a little strange lately, doesn't he?'

'That's not a very nice thing to say, is it?' I said bluntly.

''Scuse me,' Takeo said, casting his eyes downward.

I didn't really expect you to apologize, I said, swallowing the words.

Takeo averted his gaze. He looked as though all the energy in his body was draining away. This kind of lifestyle isn't good for your health, I thought. Maybe I'll quit working at the Nakano shop. Recently such thoughts had occasionally crossed my mind.

Masayo arrived. Ever since Mr Maruyama came back, Masayo has been – how shall I say? – even more smartly dressed than before. Today she was wearing a purplish, folk-art style skirt that came down to her ankles, and hanging around her neck was a scarf dyed from trees and grasses. It was one that she had dyed herself.

'Listen, Hitomi – don't you think that Haruo has been strange lately?' Masayo asked as soon as she sat down in the chair next to the till.

'Strange?' Unsure how to answer, I repeated her word vaguely. Takeo let out a weird little sound. I turned around to see him, his head still hanging, trying to stifle his laughter.

'Strange, definitely strange,' Masayo repeated, abruptly hoisting up the hem of her skirt which was dragging on the floor. She overlapped the edges of the tucked-up hem at her knees, the way you would fold up a *furoshiki*.

'Is that really appropriate . . .' I started to say, but before I could finish Takeo burst into laughter, and it caught me too as I erupted into giggles.

Oh, my goodness, what is all this? Masayo asks. No, um, Takeo also . . . Mr Nakano . . . I mumbled. What about our dear Takeo and Haruo? Masayo enquired, turning to Takeo with a tone of naïvety.

No, I, uh – why Mr Nakano, strange lately. Takeo's words didn't really form an answer.

Very strange indeed – everyone in this shop, Masayo shrugged her shoulders. Takeo let out a whoop of laughter. I joined in, at the same time, but only laughed a little. I thought to myself, it's been a really long time since I've seen Takeo laugh so unguardedly. For whatever reason, Masayo started laughing along with us. Come to think of it, Takeo's shoulders seemed a little broader than when I first met him. Masayo let her hitched-up hem back down again and, still sitting, let her knees bob up and down, swinging her skirt. The parts where the purple colour is darker and lighter undulated in waves and, while I was looking at this, I started to feel sleepy.

Mr Nakano's strange behaviour was not limited to the jug.

First of all, he was going to the markets less often. And when calls for pickups came in, more often than not he declined them. And whereas before it was common for Mr Nakano to send Takeo on his own, now he made sure to go along himself to these whittled-down pickup locations. Once back at the shop, Mr Nakano would fall into a chair and, with a disappointed look on his face, he would grumble, There was nothing good to be had there, Hitomi.

'I think I might know what it is,' Masayo said one day.

'You know what it is?' Takeo repeats after her.

I know, I do. You see, when Haruo quit his job at the company and had just opened this shop, it was exactly the same, Masayo said in a whisper.

'The same?' Takeo echoed again. Come to think of it, Takeo's voice sounded clearer than it used to.

'Yes, it's a sort of unfocused tension, you know?' Masayo said, lighting a cigarette.

When afternoon came around, Mr Nakano would go out to the bank. Not 'the Bank' that Takeo and I used to use as a code word for Sakiko, but the actual place, the real bank.

'It wouldn't surprise me if Haruo were thinking about changing his business plans. That's what I think,' Masayo said, her voice still a whisper.

What? Takeo's breath caught. I still didn't really understand what Masayo meant, and I couldn't quite react yet.

'So, he won't need us?' Takeo cried out in a low voice.

Why do you jump to such conclusions? Masayo laughed. Contrary to all appearances, our dear Takeo is a worryguts!

Sorry, Takeo apologized.

There's nothing to apologize for, Masayo said, laughing again.

Is a habit of mine to apologize. Sorry.

'My, my – our dear Takeo seems all grown up now!'

When Masayo said this to him, Takeo wore a momentary look of astonishment. For no logical reason, I thought back to the time when Takeo slipped off my jeans. When did that happen? It felt like ages ago. As if it were five million years earlier, long before Takeo and I were born, before human beings even existed – that many ages ago.

'I wonder if that kid isn't borrowing money from the bank, so that he can renovate the shop,' Masayo said, exhaling the smoke from her cigarette deeply.

Think he'll do it? Takeo asked.

Mmm, it's just a guess, that's all, Masayo replied.

A guess, I repeated Masayo's words distractedly. I still couldn't fully comprehend the meaning of what Masayo said. One half of my brain seemed to be plastered with images of my brief sex scene with Takeo from five million years ago. The other half was woolly with an uncomfortable warmth, like the hot air from the gas heater.

I shook my head, trying to dispel the fuzziness, but it was no good. Takeo's naked back, and the pale blue colour of my inside-out jeans merely splintered into fragments and scattered through my whole brain.

Um, I'm going to take a little break, I said as I opened the front door and went outside. As soon as there was no trace of Takeo around me, my mind suddenly cleared. Maybe I really should quit, I thought to myself for the umpteenth time. In the spot where the cat used to pee all the time, there were ice needles melting. I stepped on them, and they made a crunching sound as they easily crumbled to pieces.

'I feel like I've just got to get my hands on that jug, you know?' Mr Nakano was talking on the phone. Yeah. Yeah. Right.

Twelve thirty. Yes. The Mita Line. I've got it. If I have any trouble, I'll call your mobile. Money? I mean, I don't have much but . . .

It seemed like he was talking to Sakiko. Every so often he was calling whomever he was talking to 'love', so that's what led me to think so.

'Hey, have you ever taken the Mita Line before?' Masayo asked once he was off the phone.

'Don't make fun of me-ee!' he replied – illogically – in sing-song. Oh, little Momo! Masayo said as she too broke into song. 'Don't make fun of me-ee!' Apparently they were waxing nostalgic about a pop song from the 1980s.

'A mistress with talents is a good thing to have,' Masayo said after she finished singing.

Mr Nakano snorted. Using her connections, Sakiko was taking Mr Nakano to a 'swap meet' in Tokyo, a gathering of prominent high-class Western antique dealers.

'What is a swap meet like?' Takeo asked.

'Well, even though they say it's high class, it's basically the same as the markets we always go to,' Mr Nakano replied.

'There's an auction?' Takeo asked.

'Right, it's an auction,' Mr Nakano said.

Takeo sometimes went along to the markets that were only for the trade, where dealers auctioned their goods. What kind of markets are they? I had asked right after I started working at the Nakano shop, when I was completely clueless.

Takeo had thought about it for a moment before replying. 'Like a shack filled with a bunch of middle-aged guys buying and selling stuff at slashed prices – that's what it's like.'

Mr Nakano would always come back from the markets

with incomplete sets of plates and bowls, old mirrors, mid-century toys, and whatnot – all bought for next to nothing. Small 'retro' items were strong sellers at the Nakano shop.

'So, swap meets and markets – not the same, right?' Takeo asked.

'Not the same.' Possibly Mr Nakano had grown tired of answering questions, because he mimicked the way Takeo spoke.

'How are they different?' Undaunted, Takeo piled on another question.

You think you're all grown up? Mr Nakano asked in reply, as if flummoxed.

'What?' Although Takeo spoke in the same tone as always, what was different from before was that he wasn't intimidated.

'In that case, maybe you should all come along?' Mr Nakano said, turning to face Takeo and me.

'Don't you think that's asking too much? When Sakiko has offered to take you to this private event?' Masayo reproached.

'It'll be fine, won't it?' Mr Nakano said with an unlit cigarette in his mouth. Anyway, I've got a mistress with talents, don't you know? he went on, biting down lightly on the base of his cigarette.

Oh, my – such a sneer on this kid! Masayo laughed.

That's not it! Mr Nakano pouted this time, still chewing on his cigarette. It will be a good experience for Takeo and Hitomi.

Experience? Takeo said, his mouth agape. He was back to the old Takeo. We'll leave around eleven o'clock tomorrow morning. Whoever wants the experience, don't be late, Mr

Nakano said, adopting the tone of a teacher. Takeo was still standing there with his mouth open. I was staring at the pom-pom on the top of Mr Nakano's hat, without really seeing it.

The wind was strong that day. So strong that it almost blew Mr Nakano's bobble hat off his head. The colour of that day's hat was dark red.

This wind seems to be blowing through the tall buildings, Mr Nakano shouted, and Mr Awashima replied in a low voice, It does. Sakiko was next to Mr Awashima, and Mr Nakano, Takeo, and I were walking diagonally behind them.

Mr Awashima was pale-skinned. His appearance was completely different from what I would have imagined when I heard the phrase, Western antique dealer – which for me called to mind a talented, swarthy man with well-groomed sideburns. He had said he was in his early thirties, but his hair was already thinning. He had a slight stoop and goggle eyes – he seemed like a fish swimming in the deep sea. There's something about Mr Awashima that makes me feel at ease, Takeo said later, on our way back to the Nakano shop after the swap meet was over. I had the same impression. But, hearing Takeo say this, Sakiko responded coolly, That's just the mark of a good dealer. If he can get you to let your guard down, then he has won.

Mr Awashima had gone into a building on the corner. Beyond the entrance, there was a carpeted area one step up. After bowing in greeting to the woman dressed in black who was standing at the reception desk, Mr Awashima removed his shoes and placed them in the shoe cupboard. The rest of us followed his example. There weren't slippers available, so we all stepped onto the carpet in our socks.

There were chairs lined up in front of a long table, like in a conference room, and people who seemed like dealers were eating in groups of two and three. In front of each duo or trio were rice balls from convenience stores, white Styrofoam deli containers filled with deep-fried chicken, cans of tea, and suchlike. Takeo's stomach growled audibly.

'Please do as you like until we begin,' Mr Awashima had said in a low voice, and had then walked off in the direction of someone he recognized.

The room where the swap meet would take place was about forty-five metres square. There were white floor cushions lined up along the walls, leaving the inner square completely empty.

Mr Nakano was looking around restlessly. Sakiko quietly took a seat on a cushion midway along one side. I sat down as well, leaving a cushion in between us. Takeo sat down next to me. Sakiko's hips and legs were slender, and when she sat on her heels like this, she seemed even more petite. She was almost a head shorter than Takeo and me.

There was a general stir in the hall. Mr Nakano was wandering around aimlessly. Takeo got up from his seat suddenly and followed Mr Nakano.

'Hey, Hitomi,' Sakiko whispered.

Yes? Sakiko's voice was low, so I tried to reply in a similarly muted tone.

'Are you going to quit?'

What?

'You're going to quit working at Haruo's, aren't you?'

No, I haven't . . .

I had not yet told anyone about the fact that I was ready to quit working at the Nakano shop.

Why do you say that? I asked Sakiko, keeping my voice low.

'I don't know, I just had a feeling,' Sakiko said. Her voice was mysterious – I could hear her perfectly even though she was whispering.

A feeling?

'Maybe it's because I'm thinking of quitting too.'

I cast a glance at Sakiko's face. The light in her eyes was brighter than usual.

When you say quit, quit what?

'Haruo,' Sakiko replied succinctly.

But you said before, you wouldn't break up, didn't you? I asked, my voice even lower. I could see Mr Nakano and Takeo on their way back.

'Yes. But at last I think I'm ready to quit him.'

At last? I retorted, before I could stop myself, but right at that moment, Mr Nakano sank down onto the cushion between Sakiko and me with a thud.

Sakiko turned her face towards Mr Nakano and smiled. It was a gentle expression. Her smile was soft and full, like that of the statue of a goddess from the Kamakura period I had once seen in her shop, the Asukado.

The items were placed on large rectangular trays, and the trays themselves made their way around. Once you had finished looking, you set the tray in front of the dealer beside you. One by one, like an assembly line, we looked at plates and lamps and etchings.

'This looks like you, doesn't it?' Sakiko said to Mr Awashima, who at some point had come over and was now sitting, Indian style, on the other side of her.

'Hmm, I do like it, but ones like this are awfully expensive now, so they just don't sell,' Mr Awashima said, his voice low, as usual. Still, he picked up the item that Sakiko had described as 'him' from the tray – an intricately coloured glass which fitted perfectly in the palm of his hand, and regarded it more closely.

'Is that a chip?' Mr Awashima said as he nodded to himself.

Takeo was handling each of the items as they made their way around. These expert dealers, Mr Awashima included, held everything casually and informally; Takeo alone was treating the goods with the utmost care.

'It's better to do it that way, of course,' Sakiko said in a gentle voice. The nape of Takeo's neck instantly turned deep red.

Mr Nakano, on the other hand, didn't touch any of the items that came around; he limited himself to peering down at everything, keeping his face right above the trays.

'If there is something you want, please let me know,' Mr Awashima said to Mr Nakano. Each time they spoke to one another, Sakiko, sitting between the two of them, pulled back and leaned on her arms behind her.

'Despite the bitterly cold weather, I hope that everyone is keeping well,' the auctioneer said, by way of introduction. Immediately after this brief greeting, the auction started. Not that I thought it would begin with a gong or a *taiko* drum, but since they had said it was so high class, I had thought it would kick off with something that felt more ceremonious.

'So simple, isn't it?' I whispered to Takeo, who nodded in agreement.

Yeah, it seems pretty much the same as the regular markets. Only thing is that it's in a building instead of a shack.

It had been so long since Takeo had spoken to me familiarly or without apologizing, I flinched. I felt a momentary surge of happiness. You idiot, I thought, while still thoroughly enjoying the feeling.

'It's starting,' I said, unsure of what to say, although Takeo seemed similarly tongue-tied. Idiot, I thought to myself again.

The swap meet began with an item whose opening bid was 3,000 yen. The auctioneer's voice was hoarse, and the way he spoke, it was hard to hear the beginning and end of his words.

Five thousand yen, 7,000 yen . . . the price rose briskly. Takeo was intently watching the auctioneer's hands.

Today has been pretty flat, overall, Mr Awashima murmured. There had been a few items that sold strongly, but lots more where the opening bid was 10,000 yen, with only two people calling out offers, so the bidding didn't go higher than 17,000 yen.

When the price had jumped steadily into the tens of thousands – or hundreds of thousands – of yen, the second-hand dealer standing diagonally behind the auctioneer would slowly move his head up and down in assent.

'Sold!' the auctioneer would say. After watching for a short period of time, I worked out that this nod was a signal that the selling price had been decided.

There were plenty of dealers calling out bids, but there were also items that only inspired sluggish offers. 5,000 yen, 7,000 yen, 10,000 yen, 11,000 yen, 15,000 yen – it was like the price had to be teased along.

A voice called out something.

What did he say? Takeo asked Mr Nakano.

'It means one-six-five,' Mr Nakano replied, without looking at Takeo or taking his eyes off the auctioneer.

'One-six-five?' Takeo repeated.

'In this case, it means 16,500 yen,' Sakiko said, looking directly at Takeo's face as she spoke.

'It means that we've moved up to the level where, once the bidding reaches ten thousand, it jumps straight up to 16,500 yen,' Sakiko continued her explanation. Takeo's mouth was agape again.

'If it reaches a hundred thousand, that means one hundred and sixty-five thousand.'

No way! Takeo said, his mouth still hanging open.

After the call that we had reached this level, the bidding crept to a halt. Too sluggish, Mr Nakano grumbled. But we're in a recession, and things don't sell, Mr Awashima replied, shaking his head. The second-hand dealer seemed dissatisfied with the final price, his brows knitted in a frown.

The auctioneer looked back over his shoulder, awaiting instruction from the second-hand dealer. When he saw the dealer make a slight wave of his hand in front of him, the auctioneer curtly called out, 'Fault!' and the item was withdrawn.

After the paintings had been sold, the auction moved on to porcelain and ceramics. It's Rosenthal, you hear, Rosenthal china. Service for five. Wait, what? Service for four. Like the one before, only for four. That's how it goes today, it seems. The auctioneer's pitch was light and witty.

Once the china was done, next came sundry items. Pink and blue decorative lamps, a set of two small framed portraits of aristocrats with their hunting dogs, and wine racks with wine glasses, all tightly displayed on a tray. That's right – enough to outfit two hotel rooms! the auctioneer called out.

30,000 yen, he called the opening price for the 'hotel lot' in his hoarse voice, but the bidding went nowhere. And just what kind of hotel does he think these will be used in? Sakiko asked Mr Awashima with a laugh. A super luxurious one, of course, Mr Awashima replied in his low voice. There was something similar about both of their voices. Even when they spoke in whispers, their words were very easy to make out.

'How much usually moves through a swap meet for Japanese things?' This time it was Mr Awashima who asked Sakiko a question.

'At last week's meet, I heard they turned over about sixty million,' Sakiko said.

'That's amazing,' Mr Awashima said blandly, not seeming all that amazed.

Mr Nakano had started to lean forward. Any time now, Mr Awashima said. I'm counting on you, Mr Nakano turned to Mr Awashima and bowed slightly. On one of the trays that had come around earlier, there was a bottle that looked like it had been daubed with soot, perfectly uninteresting as far as I was concerned. But something told me that this was Mr Nakano's sought-after jug.

It will be just a little longer, Mr Awashima said. Mr Nakano bowed his head again. He appeared to have completely forgotten the fact that when he went to the markets, he himself engaged in sharp tactics for the sake of a mere 1,000 or even 500 yen.

The auctioneer laughed as he said in a sing-song, 'What shall we do?' The price of the item went up. It was a paperweight decorated with a pug dog. You must buy this adorable dog and take him home, he said. 60,000 yen, a voice called out. In the end, the pug paperweight went all the way up to 150,000 yen.

And next, at last, was Mr Nakano's jug. When it had been passed around on the tray before the auction, a man and a woman – presumably a couple of buyers – who were sitting on two cushions next to Takeo had spent a long time holding and examining the jug.

'Changing lots!' the auctioneer called out. They had finished with the pug paperweight and the dealer's six other items that had followed. It seemed it was finally time for the second-hand dealer who had brought the bottle Mr Nakano has his eye on – now it was his turn.

20,000 yen, the hoarse voice rang out. Mr Nakano leaned forward in earnest.

The body and the neck had turned soot black, but when you turned it upside down, the bottom was rough and uneven and shone like a mirror. If you looked closely, you could see iridescence.

'Like the surface of a black pearl,' Takeo said.

'What a clever way of describing it!' Mr Awashima said, beaming as he looked at Takeo.

Mr Nakano had won the jug for 70,000 yen. As expected, the buyer couple who were sitting beside Takeo had bid quite fiercely for it but, as Mr Nakano explained to us in a still slightly excited tone once the meet was over, it was entirely the result of Mr Awashima's superior expertise as a merchant that he was able to acquire the jug for a bid far lower than he had anticipated.

'That's a gin bottle, you know,' Sakiko said softly.

Gin? Mr Nakano said dreamily.

'I love gin,' Sakiko said. It was a perfectly ordinary thing to say, but my heart started to race. Mr Nakano muttered a half-hearted reply.

As he patted the top of the box-shaped bag that the jug was in, having been bundled in newspaper he had brought with him in addition to bubble wrap, Mr Nakano repeated once more, Gin, you say? Sakiko was smiling. Mr Nakano looks happy, Takeo said with a touch of envy.

Looks happy, I almost murmured Takeo's words myself. Hurriedly I looked down.

What Sakiko had said to me before the auction began had been reverberating in my head this whole time.

At last, I think I'm ready to quit him.

A moment later, I looked back up and glanced at Sakiko. She winked at me, still smiling. When she closed her right eye, the right side of her lips turned up along with it, so that even though she was smiling, she looked as though she were crying.

Are you okay? I said without making a sound, only moving my lips.

Sakiko nodded. Fine, she replied, also only moving her lips. She drew in her smile and winked again. The right part of her mouth still turned up in exactly the same way, but now that she wasn't smiling, this time her expression looked, conversely, like a grin.

'Good luck to you too, Hitomi!' Sakiko said, speaking aloud. Her voice was louder than usual.

Taken by surprise, Mr Nakano looked at Sakiko. She returned his gaze, staring him straight in the face. Mr Awashima and Takeo were talking non-stop about something. The skin on Sakiko's cheeks was glowing with an inner light. Just like the bottom of the gin jug, they reflected a dusky and beautiful radiance.

It was about a week after the *Setsubun* holiday in early February when Mr Nakano announced that the Nakano shop would close temporarily.

It had been snowing on and off since the morning. It's called *kazahana*, when the snow is so fine like this, it seems as if it drifted in on the wind, Masayo said. Takeo went outside and stared up at the sky. He was still just standing there out the front, looking straight up above him. The boy looks like a dog, Masayo laughed.

Mr Nakano had shown up late in the afternoon, when the snow had already stopped.

'Employee meeting!' It was a strange command from Mr Nakano.

I had just been wondering why Takeo had been there since the morning even though there weren't any pickups. Mr Nakano explained very simply about the shop closing. He wanted to make a slight change in the kind of merchandise he carried. And to do so required money. He would temporarily lease the storefront to someone else, and for the time being he would only be doing business on Tokizo's website. He wasn't able to pay severance, but he would give us the month's wages plus a fifty per cent premium.

Mr Nakano had lost a little more weight since the beginning of the month. The other day I heard from Masayo that Sakiko had told him she wanted to make a clean break. It seemed to me that everyone – men and women, old and young – loses weight when a love affair is over. I have wondered about this.

Well, then, Mr Nakano said, and the meeting soon broke up. Masayo, Takeo, and I looked at each other in turn. Masayo's favourite scarf, dyed from trees and grasses, which she had been wearing since she started dressing more smartly, was wrapped several times around her neck that day. Her skirt was long and brown, worn with ankle boots, also brown.

'Hitomi,' Masayo said.

Yes? I replied.

Masayo curled her lips for a moment, as if there was something she wanted to say, but in the end she didn't say anything except for repeating my name once more. Yes? I replied again. Why don't you take the basket woven from akebi vines? This was all that Masayo said to me before falling silent once again.

I left the shop with Takeo. Mr Nakano didn't say anything. He just stood there in the same pose, with the same unlit cigarette in his mouth, at the front of the shop where he and Masayo had seen us out. When we turned the corner, I looked back and could see the pom-pom on Mr Nakano's hat. The colour of Mr Nakano's hat that day was the same brown as Masayo's skirt.

What will you do now? I said.

Takeo tilted his head and eventually replied, What about you?

The two of us walked along beside each other in silence. I tightened my grip on the old supermarket bag I was carrying the akebi vine basket in. The *kazahana* snow had started to fall again.

Punch Ball

For a moment, I didn't know where I was.

Pale sunlight was streaming through the gap in the curtains. The sound of the alarm clock on the bedside table gradually intensified. It went from an intermittent ringing to a continuous whir, until I finally reached over to turn it off.

In my not-yet-awake haze, I ruminated over the fact that the place where I found myself was no longer in the same neighbourhood as the Nakano shop. I now lived on the third floor of a tidy white building in an apartment that was even more cramped than the previous one but which was very conveniently located, a five-minute walk from the train station where I could transfer to the private rail line.

I moved here more than two years ago.

Slowly I got out of bed and, blinking repeatedly, I shuffled towards the bathroom. I splashed my face with water and brushed my teeth. I had left the cap off the tube of facial cleansing cream that I'd used last night. I looked around and saw that the triangular cap had fallen into a far corner of the washbasin. I picked it up and screwed it back on to the end of the tube.

I took out a can of tomato juice from the refrigerator. I opened the top with a clink and drank it straight from the can rather than pouring it into a glass. I forgot to shake it up, though, so the first sip was watery, and then suddenly it got very thick.

Drops of water fell from my fringe. I finished drinking the tomato juice, rinsed out the can and placed it upside down on the rack, and then went to peer into the small mirror that was next to the bed. The tips of my ears were tinged with red. I touched them with my fingertips. They were cold.

I opened the window and the wind rushed in. It was a cold, midwinter wind, full of moisture. I hastily closed the window and got dressed, pulling on a long-sleeved shirt, tights, a heavy skirt, and a thick sweater. From the top shelf of the wardrobe, I took out the beige coat I'd bought at a flea market the week before last and tossed it on the bed.

I turned towards the mirror again, put some foundation on my finger, and dotted it on both cheeks, the tip of my nose, and my forehead. Surprisingly quickly, I had got used to commuting on the overcrowded trains, to maintaining my distance from the permanent female employees, even to finding the best way to use Excel, but I just couldn't seem to get used to putting on 'proper' make-up every morning.

When I was at the Nakano shop, I barely even knew that something like foundation existed. I would dash some toner on my face and, if the mood struck me, maybe put on a little tinted lip gloss. Back then, that was the extent of it.

Almost three years had passed since the Nakano shop closed.

I'd been at this job for six months already. It was with a health food company located in Shiba.

My contract had been extended twice already, but it probably wouldn't be again. It had been a comfortable place to work, but there wasn't much I could do about it.

I lightly rolled my shoulders up and down while I haphazardly slapped on some blusher. My shoulders were very stiff, most likely from staring at a computer screen for so many hours a day. Maybe this Saturday, I ought to check out the new massage parlour that has just opened by the train station, I thought to myself as I continued to roll my shoulders.

A while ago, I'd been out drinking with Masayo, whom I hadn't seen in a long time.

'Look at you, Hitomi, a real office lady!' Masayo said as she poured herself some warmed saké.

'I'm not an official employee, I'm just a temp,' I said.

'What's the difference?' she asked.

When I explained, Masayo nodded as she listened. But I have no doubt she forgot it all immediately.

According to Masayo, lately she'd been 'as busy as a bee'. It seems that one of her doll creations had won a prize that was fairly well known in that world.

'The prize money wasn't much, 50,000 yen,' Masayo explained. 'But it adds prestige,' she said, raising her eyebrows halfway.

As a result of this new prestige, Masayo had been invited to lecture at the local cultural centre and, all told, she was to give three talks at various community centres.

'That's why I'm as busy as a bee! I don't love it,' Masayo said, taking a drag on her Seven Stars. She really didn't seem happy about it at all.

'But it's a good thing to earn money,' I said.

Masayo laughed. 'Hitomi, you sound like an old lady!'

'I am an old lady!'

'Oh, come off it! You're barely thirty!'

And then, even though we were already in our cups, we clinked a toast.

'Cheers to Hitomi, for becoming an old lady!' Masayo said, emptying her little saké cup.

'Stop it, please!' There was about a third left in my glass of *shochu* mixed with warm water, and I finished it in one gulp. I could feel the soft and faintly warm flesh of the pickled plum garnish as it slid down my throat.

I thought back to the last time I'd seen Masayo.

'You moved, didn't you?' When Masayo had first called me on the phone, I had recognized her voice immediately.

This had been right after I had moved from my previous apartment. Masayo said she had received my notice. I had sent handwritten change of address cards to ten or so people, including Masayo. After deliberating about whether to send them to Mr Nakano and Takeo, I decided not to.

'I spent what little savings I had,' I told her.

On the other end of the line, Masayo sighed suggestively. This whole time, I had thought that her voice sounded a little too beguiling.

'That's nice.'

'Do you think so?'

'I do. It's a good thing.'

It had been a perfectly ordinary exchange, but something about Masayo's voice had sounded different from usual. We made small talk and chatted about the weather, and just when I had decided it was time to get off the phone, Masayo had said, 'The wake is today, and the funeral service is tomorrow.'

What? I asked in reply.

'For Maruyama.'

For Maruyama? I repeated, like a parrot.

'His heart. I hadn't heard from him for three days so I went to see him. In this kind of weather, he was still in perfect condition.'

Since Maruyama's ex-wife Keiko has made the arrangements, I don't really want to go but . . . it's more of a social obligation. Haruo is going with me to the funeral service, but tonight, he has something that he absolutely must do for a client, so, Hitomi, would you consider going with me?

Her voice was smooth as silk. It was exactly the same tone Masayo had used when an unfamiliar customer came into the Nakano shop and she would talk them into buying some old random item.

'I'll go,' I replied softly.

'Ah!' Masayo sighed again, suggestively.

'The landlord at the building where he lived is making a terrific fuss, can you believe it? He really had the worst luck with that landlord!' This was the only time that Masayo sounded like herself.

But then she murmured strangely, almost innocently, 'Maruyama, he's really dead!' I had never heard her sound so bewildered.

'Anyway, congratulations on your move,' Masayo said, which was an odd way to end the call.

Maruyama, he's really dead! Like a broken record, Masayo's curiously charming and dispirited voice resonated in my mind.

Later, Masayo was already there when I got to the ticket barrier at the station where we had arranged to meet. She had on a brown coat with her brown ankle boots, and the same scarf dyed from trees and grasses that had been wrapped around her neck when the shop closed, but that night she wore it over her head.

'Is it all right to wear that to a wake?' I asked before I could stop myself.

Masayo nodded glumly, and the scarf shook lightly when she moved her head.

'If you wear excessively proper mourning clothes to the wake, it looks as though you were expecting the death, so this is perfectly appropriate,' Masayo said, and then she scrutinized my outfit. I was dressed head to toe in black mourning clothes – black stockings, even my coat was dark.

'I shouldn't have worn proper mourning clothes?' I asked nervously.

'You shouldn't have,' Masayo responded without hesitation, giving a nod.

The wake took place in a small funeral home which

was a fifteen-minute walk from the station. There were three wakes going on at the same time – the Midorikawa family, the Maruyama family, and the Akimoto family – and there was the steady hum of people talking as they came and went.

'I'm glad it's not empty,' Masayo said, hurrying into the queue.

Next to the altar, a middle-aged couple with two girls sat alongside a white-haired woman who seemed to be Mr Maruyama's ex-wife Keiko, all of them expressionless. Both of the girls were wearing uniforms from a local private primary school.

Without making eye contact with Keiko, Masayo performed the ritual of condolences and quickly turned her back towards the altar. Following Masayo, I made an offering of incense and, as I did so, I looked up to see that there was a colour photo of Mr Maruyama smiling radiantly. The photograph was from when he was quite young. There was not a single line on his forehead or around his mouth, and the contours of his face were slender and firm.

'Shall we have a drink before we go home?' I suggested once we had left the hall. Without replying, Masayo walked steadily along.

'I'm fine,' she finally said after a while. This was after we had been walking for about five minutes, so at first I wasn't sure what she was talking about, but I soon realized it must have been in response to my proposal when we had left the hall.

'He's gone, isn't he?' I said, and Masayo nodded again, silently.

We didn't stop for a drink. Neither of us spoke as we

walked the rest of the way to the station. Just as I was about to buy a ticket and head towards the barrier, Masayo said behind me, 'The one I love most in this world.' She didn't murmur, nor did she raise her voice – she spoke as if it were just a continuation of our conversation.

'What?' I asked as I looked over my shoulder.

Her face still glum, Masayo repeated herself, 'The one I love most in this world.'

I turned around to look at her directly, but Masayo didn't say anything more. It was the end of the workday, and several people coming through the ticket barrier had bumped into us.

'I missed the chance to say that to Maruyama,' Masayo said quietly during a momentary lull in the surging crowd, and she turned her back on the station and started walking.

The odd colour of the scarf dyed from trees and grasses which covered Masayo's head looked even stranger as it caught the light from the street lamps. Her back perfectly straight, Masayo receded into the distance.

Since that night of the wake I hadn't been in touch with Masayo, until the night I called my mother.

'I passed the second-level exam!' I said, and my mother whispered my name ever so softly. Then she remained silent at the other end.

'It's not really that big a deal,' I went on, but she still didn't reply; she may have been crying.

This is why . . . I thought to myself as I stifled a sigh.

'Were you really that worried about me?' I asked, my voice deliberately cheerful.

'I'm so happy for you, Hitomi,' my mother said, without answering my question. Her voice sounded gentle, the embodiment of maternal affection. Actually, she doesn't just sound tender; my mother is tenderness itself.

We had been out of touch for a long time when I'd called her suddenly last year to tell her I was doing a bookkeeping course, and to ask her to support me financially. Back then, my mother's voice had sounded anxious. Nevertheless, the money had soon been transferred into my account. I was somewhat dispirited to see that she had sent 150,000 yen more than I had asked for. It wasn't that I was embarrassed about her concern for me; it was more – how can I say? – it felt like a wake-up call, bringing me back to the reality of life. Of course I was grateful, but along with my gratitude I felt an odd sense of futility; it made me squirm in my seat. Since the Nakano shop had closed, whenever anything happened, the sensations resonated physically within me. Like they did now.

'Next, I plan to take the first-level exam,' I said in an even brighter voice. Finally, my mother sounded excited. Good for you, Hitomi! I always knew you would work hard and continue your studies.

I could vividly imagine the faces of my father and younger brother. Hitomi will never finish the bookkeeping course, she'll get sick of it and give up, I could hear them say. But my mother didn't mention any of this.

I miss Masayo, I had thought to myself. I called her up right after I got off the phone with my mother.

It's been such a long time! Would you like to go out for a drink? I said without any preamble, despite the fact that we hadn't spoken since that night of Mr Maruyama's wake two years ago.

I'd love to, Masayo replied, completely unfazed.

And so, there we were, having a drink together.

Masayo had got a little tipsy.

'Is Mr Nakano doing well?' I ventured. It was all I could manage to ask, afraid that she might reply, without batting an eye, that he was not doing well.

'He's fine!' Masayo replied crisply.

'Is he still doing the online auctions?' I asked.

'He went off on his own from Tokizo's and made his own website,' she said.

Saké, two more! Masayo called out. They don't need to be warmed, cold is fine. Just bring them straight away, she said in a rapid barrage. The server gave a perfunctory answer; it wasn't clear whether he had got her order or not.

'What's with that guy? He reminds me of our dear Takeo,' Masayo said, fluttering the menu in front of her face like a fan.

'That brings back memories, hearing you call him "our dear Takeo",' I said.

Masayo peered into my face. 'Tell me, Hitomi – were you and Takeo . . . like that?'

'Meaning what, like that?' I said, imitating the way that Takeo used to speak.

'Ah, now that brings back memories!' Masayo said, and

then she herself imitated Takeo. 'Meaning, you know, like that!' She didn't really sound like him, though.

'So, you know, Haruo told me he made such a healthy profit from the online auctions, he was able to get a small business loan.'

The cold saké arrived more quickly than expected, and Masayo poured it generously into a beer glass. The thick leftover foam from the beer floated wispily on the surface of the saké.

He's got a loan because of a healthy profit – isn't that a bit of an oversimplification? I asked.

Masayo fluttered her hand in front of her as she laughed, Oh, my, Hitomi – you really did pass second-level book-keeping!

With his loan and his profits, she said, Mr Nakano had decided to lease a storefront in Nishiogi and open a Western antique shop.

'That's amazing, isn't it?' I cried out softly.

Masayo gave a wry smile. 'I have my doubts, but with Haruo, you never know!'

We clinked another toast. Then we ordered a couple of plates of food, and we drank cup after cup of saké, and the night quickly grew late.

Closing time, we were told, and we left the bar. I was quite drunk myself now.

'You mean you haven't seen our dear Takeo at all?' Masayo asked in a loud voice.

You don't have to shout, I can hear you, I yelled back.

'You haven't seen him?' Masayo repeated. Her expression seemed half-smiling, half-angry, and wrapped around her neck was the very same scarf dyed from trees and grasses.

I haven't seen him, I answered flatly.

Really? Masayo said, disappointment in her voice. I wonder what our dear Takeo is up to? Have things worked out for him? I hope he hasn't died on the side of a road or anything, she said, knitting her brows together.

Heaven forbid, I hastened to say.

Masayo burst into wide-mouthed laughter. See, Hitomi – that's just what an old lady would say!

Well, I am an old lady – I told you so!

Yes, but, a real old lady doesn't call herself an old lady.

Hey, Masayo, have you put on a little weight?

I have, indeed! I get fat when I get busy – what can I do?

You must just be eating cake from Posy.

Say now, at Posy, since the son took over and became in charge, everything seems to have changed. All the cakes now have ridiculously long and pretentious names!

The moment I heard her say that the son had taken over at Posy, for some reason I felt the strength drain out of me. I tried to recall what Takeo's face looked like, but I couldn't quite picture it. I just kept seeing, in alarming detail, the severed tip of his right little finger.

The last train . . . I said, and I broke into a run.

Goodbye! Masayo said, drawing out the syllables. I got out of breath almost immediately but I kept running anyway.

The one I love most in this world. I had no one to say those words to. I hadn't even felt the desire to say them to someone, ever, I thought as I ran. There was still time before the last train, but I kept running all the way to the station, without stopping to catch my breath.

The next month, at the end of the accounting period, my contract term ended. The other women gave me a bouquet of flowers. It was the first time that had ever happened to me, and it practically brought tears to my eyes.

'What kind of company will you work for next?' a woman named Miss Sasaki asked. She was slightly younger than I was.

'It seems they have something to do with computers.'

'It seems so, does it? Miss Suganuma, you always do things your own way, don't you?' Miss Sasaki laughed.

My own way. Clutching the bouquet as I walked home, I repeated these words in my head. I had spent time with these young women for eight months. Some of them were a little mean, some of them were quite kind, some of them were slightly particular, and some of them were a bit odd. Did that mean that I was the one among them who did things 'my own way'?

It was as if everyone doled themselves out in such small portions. Never completely open, not all at once.

I reminisced about the people from the Nakano shop, brief scenes with each of them.

The whole bouquet did not fit into the vase I had, so I filled an empty mayonnaise jar with water and put the extra flowers in there. I would be starting at the next company at the beginning of next week. I would definitely try to go to the massage parlour tomorrow, I thought. I opened a drawer to retrieve the envelope that contained documents from my new office, and a scrap of paper fluttered to the ground.

It was one of the sketches that Takeo had done of me, the 'clothed' version.

So this is where it was, I murmured as I picked it up. I had on a T-shirt and jeans, and I was stretched out with an earnest expression on my face. It was skilfully done. Looking back now, I saw that Takeo was even better at drawing than I had thought.

Could Takeo have died on the side of a road?

That would serve him right! I thought at the idea of such a thing. But my smugness was soon dampened by the realization of how troublesome it was, just to feel that way – how troublesome it was, really, just to be alive. I wanted nothing to do with love! I wanted the stiffness in my shoulders to go away. I could probably put a bit of money into savings this month. These thoughts drifted by one by one, like tiny bubbles.

The flowers I had put in the vase looked as though they were artificial. And yet the ones in the mayonnaise jar looked like normal, real flowers.

I put the sketch back, under the envelope. I wondered if a computer-related company would have more computers around. Computers are rectangular. Microwaves are rectangular too. And the gas heater that we had been using when I left the Nakano shop was rectangular too, wasn't it? These incoherent thoughts went through my mind as I took off my stockings and crumpled them into a ball.

*

Instead of saying 'Miss Suganuma, this is your desk,' at a computer company of course they would say, 'Miss Suganuma, this is your PC,' I thought.

They may have said things differently, and this company was teensy compared to the health food company where I had worked before, but the substance of the work I did was not much different. I made copies, I ran errands, I filed vouchers, I created documents. I got the hang of it after three days, and it soon felt as though I had been at the company for a while. I may have adjusted to things there so quickly because the young women didn't all go out to lunch together. I find that kind of thing exhausting.

Everyone at this company – both men and women – was glued to their desk, all of them at their workstations in front of their computer screens. Sometimes you heard a voice ring out, 'Oh, no!' or 'Come on!' What's interesting was that the guys' voices sounded high-pitched, and the girls' sounded much lower.

I came and went at regular office hours, but plenty of people showed up for work late in the day, after I'd gone home. Or when I arrived in the morning, I'd see people who had worked all night, agitatedly peeling the shells off hard-boiled eggs from the convenience store.

It was about ten days after I had started working at this company that I happened to run into Takeo in the corridor.

'Hey, Hitomi,' Takeo said. He uttered it so naturally, as if we had been seeing each other every day, including yesterday.

I just stood there, breathless.

'What's the matter?'

What's the matter with you? I said at last.

I stood stock-still, right there in the corridor. Takeo was carrying brightly coloured files in both hands. Orange, yellow, pale purple, and green files.

'Hitomi, you're wearing make-up?' Takeo said in the same astonished tone as always.

What? I retorted. Hearing him speak in that same way had taken me right back to the Nakano shop.

The two of us just stood there in the middle of the corridor for a moment, rooted to the spot.

The invitation to the reopening of the Nakano shop arrived not long after that.

'Just like Mr Nakano, seems like a prank.' Takeo gave his verdict when I showed him the card I had received. The reopening was set for the first of April.

And the name had changed from 'the Nakano shop' to just 'Nakano'.

'It sounds like the name of a bistro,' was Masayo's assessment.

The day I ran into Takeo in the corridor, he had given me his business card.

'Web designer,' I read his title off the card in a monotone.

Please don't read it out loud! Takeo had said, fidgeting. The files started to slip, as if they were going to fall.

'Is this really you, Takeo?' I asked.

'It is,' he replied with a blank look.

'Oh, I doubt it,' I retorted.

'Why do you say that?' he asked.

'You're not even speaking the way you usually do.'

'Can't do that here,' he said, lapsing into his pattern. Just as he said that, two of the files slipped out of his hands. As I stooped to pick them up, Takeo also bent over, and I felt his breath on the top of my shoulder.

'This is like a bad soap opera,' Takeo grumbled as he retrieved the files. His shoulders were broader than before. That's not really him either, I thought to myself.

And then Takeo left, just like that. Apparently his desk, I mean his PC, was located in a room just across the corridor.

After I happened to run into him, Takeo didn't say anything to me for almost a week.

Well, he's just someone I used to know, I guess.

I left the office at the end of the workday, and while I was in my bookkeeping class, I tried to remember Takeo's face when we had run into each other in the corridor. It was his face, but not the one I was used to seeing.

How do you become a web designer? I had asked. Went to a technical school, Takeo replied.

I doubted this was the real Takeo.

As more time passed, I became increasingly convinced of this. I heard somewhere that human cells renew themselves every three years. His name might still be Takeo, and he might look just like him on the outside, but this guy was a totally different person.

It was about ten days later, just before the time I usually leave the office, when I suddenly noticed Takeo in front of my

PC, and I had the distinct feeling that the person standing there was a stranger.

Hello.

When I greeted this stranger, he blurted out, Uh, well, sorry about the other day.

And in that instant, the stranger turned back into Takeo.

It had been a long time, I said. Then I looked up at Takeo's face from the side.

His jaw was tense, and his stubble was a little darker. For a moment, Takeo turned up the corners of his mouth bashfully. You really are wearing make-up, Takeo muttered.

Yes, I am, I replied, turning up the corners of my mouth and imitating him.

The first of April was a Saturday.

In the meantime Takeo and I had had dinner together twice.

'The fulfilment is coming up, so I should go back to the office. I'd love to go out for a drink another time, hopefully when we can relax and enjoy each other's company.'

'Fulfilment? Our dear Takeo said that?' Masayo laughed uproariously when I relayed what Takeo had said, word for word.

'Nakano' was smaller than the Nakano shop. But it seemed much more spacious than the earlier incarnation.

'I've finally come to appreciate the beauty of empty space,' Mr Nakano said.

There were shelves all along the walls of the shop, with items arranged intermittently on them. He had bowls and vessels from the Netherlands, Belgium, and Britain, as well as kitchen utensils, glassware, and a few pieces of furniture, all of which ranged from the nineteenth to the twentieth century.

'It looks like a shop you'd see in a magazine, doesn't it?' I said.

'This place is better than a shop in a magazine,' Mr Nakano said as he adjusted the angle of his black bobble hat.

'How long do you have this space for?' Masayo asked.

'Let's see, I think about six months,' Mr Nakano replied with a grin. I would still never understand them.

Lots of people showed up on the day of the reopening.

There were some first-timers, but many of the best customers from the days of the Nakano shop were there too.

Mr Crane came by during the morning. He took one look around the shop and said, 'An old man like me, I can't relax in a shop like this, but I guess it's nice in its own way.' Then he gave one of his belly laughs.

After drinking two cups of tea that Masayo had made, he left with his wobbling gait.

The first person to arrive in the afternoon was Tadokoro. He took a long look around the shop, as if he were savouring each item, and as he calmly drank a cup of Masayo's tea, he said, It's a high-class shop.

'There are some very good buys in the glassware,' Masayo said with contrived cordiality.

Tadokoro shook his head and said in his typical serene manner, 'There is no leisure for the poor.'

Tadokoro lingered in the shop for close to two hours. He smirked as he watched new customers come in, one after another.

When I served him what must have been the fifth cup of now barely-tinged-green tea, which was really just for show, Tadokoro asked, 'Hitomi, are you working here again?'

No, I replied brusquely, and Tadokoro smiled and stood up.

'There's no need for such scorn, this old man will soon be dead,' he said, leaving me with those words.

Mr Awashima came by late in the afternoon. He cast a glance around the shop and declared plainly, 'Looks good, doesn't it?' He bustled off again without drinking the tea I served him.

Aunt Michi showed up with the patriarch who used to run the Posy tea shop. She presented Mr Nakano with a pouch tied with festive red and white *mizuhiki* cord on which was written, CONGRATULATIONS ON YOUR NEW SHOP! After taking a tentative look around, she hurried off.

Late in the afternoon, during a lull in the stream of customers, a young man arrived who looked familiar but whose name none of us could remember for the life of us.

'Who is that again?' Masayo asked in a quiet voice.

'Who is he, indeed?' Mr Nakano asked, his voice also low.

Hitomi, you're young, I'm sure you'll remember, the two of them said to me surreptitiously. His name is on the tip of my tongue, but I just can't seem to call it to mind.

'You stock Western things in this shop, I see,' the young man said, smiling pleasantly.

'Are you in the trade?' Mr Nakano asked, feigning nonchalance.

'No, I'm not.' Their conversation ended there, and while he gently sipped the tea that Masayo had offered him, it was completely silent in the shop.

When he had finished his tea, the young man stood up and looked around the shop a second time, as if he were patrolling the place.

'It's a wonderful shop,' he said at last.

It wasn't until about an hour after he left that I remembered – that was Hagiwara, the young man who had asked us to keep the Goryeo celadon bowl for him.

'The guy whose girlfriend put a curse on him!' I said. Then the three of us talked in a clamour for a while, until the door opened quietly.

Mr Nakano looked up. He let out a little sound. A moment later Masayo and I both looked up at the same time.

It was Sakiko.

'Hey,' she said, in her soft, well-projected voice.

'Hey,' Mr Nakano said. His voice was slightly timid, yet there was a hint of his fighting spirit in it.

Sakiko was silent for a moment as she looked Mr Nakano in the face. Masayo tugged on my sleeve, and I went with her into the small space at the back where there was a gas hob and a tap.

'The girl from Asukado is as pretty as ever,' Masayo said as she boiled some water.

'She seems even more attractive, doesn't she?' I said.

Masayo nodded deeply as she said, 'You thought so too?'

When I peeked out through a crack, Sakiko and Mr Nakano were smiling and chatting light-heartedly. Like grown-ups. Despite their history together at the Nakano shop, I couldn't help but think.

Sakiko stayed for just half an hour, and then she left. Mr Nakano saw her out, walking with her for a bit.

'It was good of Sakiko to come by,' I said to Mr Nakano when he came back in.

He sighed. 'She's quite a woman!' he murmured expressively. 'I really screwed that up.'

'Why not get back together with her?' Masayo asked.

'Doubt she'd be willing to, don't you think?' he grumbled.

A trace of Sakiko's sandalwood perfume still lingered in the air of the shop.

At seven o'clock, when they were about to close the shop, I went out onto the street, and there was a figure approaching. It was already completely dark out, but I soon realized it was Takeo.

Perhaps Takeo recognized that it was me, because he quickened his pace. I waved at him and he broke into a run.

'Is the shop already closed?' Takeo asked.

'Just about to,' I said, and he peered through the window into the interior.

Even though he'd been running, Takeo wasn't out of breath at all.

'It seems like you've become fit,' I said. Takeo laughed.

'Even your shoulders seem broader.'

You think so? Takeo said, laughing again. I've been going to the gym since I started working at the company.

'The gym?' I repeated with surprise. Takeo and the gym. Now there was a combination I never would have put together, not in a million years. But then again, this was the Takeo who had become a web designer without my knowing it, so I probably should have guessed that he was going to the gym.

'I like the punch ball,' Takeo said.

The punch ball? I repeated again.

'You know, like they use to practise boxing? It's a ball that you punch, it flies out and then springs back, like that.'

Ah, I nodded. Punch, spring. I was staring absent-mindedly at the dim shadow at the base of Takeo's throat as he explained.

'Oh, my, our, dear Takeo!' Masayo called out as she opened the door. Mr Nakano came outside too.

I hear you're doing very well, Takeo, Mr Nakano said. Like a hero returning home in glory, Masayo continued. Takeo scratched his head.

As the four of us went into the shop, Mr Nakano turned back to the front door and closed the shutter. Takeo took a look all around the shop. He wore the same dumbstruck expression as he used to.

There were only two chairs, so Mr Nakano brought a folding chair out from the back and he pulled over an antique chair that was for sale. Mr Nakano opened a bottle of wine and poured it into teacups.

'Haven't had a drink in a long time,' Takeo said.

'Because of the fulfilment?' Masayo asked impishly.

'Last in, first out. Low man on the totem pole,' Takeo said as he scratched his head again.

Without anything to go with the wine, the four of us finished it pretty quickly. Wine in the Nakano shop? Takeo said, his cheeks crimson. Mr Nakano opened a second bottle. We drink wine here! We do whatever we like! he boasted.

Masayo rummaged about in her bag and pulled out a half-crushed packet of soya bean snacks, which she put on a paper plate.

The second bottle of wine was soon empty as well.

Mr Nakano was the first one to fall asleep. He put his head down on the desk and started to snore. Before long, Masayo had nodded off. Takeo was yawning himself.

'Did you make the fulfilment?' I asked. Takeo nodded lightly.

This brings back memories of the Nakano shop, doesn't it? I said. Takeo nodded. Have you been doing well, all this time? I asked. He nodded again. The four of us together, it seems like old times, I said. This time, instead of nodding, Takeo opened his mouth. But he didn't say anything.

We fell silent for a moment.

Sorry, Takeo said in a low voice.

What?

I was awful to you, Hitomi. I'm sorry, Takeo said, and bowed his head.

No, I'm the one who acted like a child.

Me too.

Then we just sat there for a while, both of our heads bowed.

Maybe because I was tipsy, I felt moved to tears. My

eyes still downcast, I cried, just a little bit. But once the tears started, I was soon full-on crying.

I'm sorry, Takeo said over and over. I was so sad! I replied. Takeo put his hands around my shoulders and gave me a little hug.

Mr Nakano stirred in his sleep. Stealing a glance at Masayo, I saw that her eyes were half-open and she was peeking over at us. When our gaze met, Masayo hurriedly shut her eyes and pretended to be asleep.

Masayo! I called out her name. She opened her eyes wide and stuck out her tongue at me. Takeo quietly moved away from me.

'Don't stop! Hold her tighter!' Masayo said in a slurred voice, pointing her finger at Takeo.

Go on, hold her tight! Masayo said again.

Mr Nakano suddenly roused himself and joined in, Go on now!

We gulped down the wine that was left in our teacups. The four of us all exchanged glances and burst into laughter. I felt the wine coursing through my body again, and I felt as though I were walking on air. I looked over at Takeo, who was watching me too.

The Nakano shop is gone now, I said. Everyone nodded in agreement.

But the Nakano shop lives on forever, Mr Nakano muttered as he stood up. As if that were a sign, the four of us all started chattering, nobody sure what anyone else was saying. Completely bewildered, I looked at Takeo again; he was still staring at me.

Just then, for the first time, I truly felt love for Takeo. The thought inexplicably appeared in a corner of my mind.

The newly opened bottle of wine clinked against the rim of my teacup, sounding a clear ring.

Keep in touch with
Portobello Books:

Visit portobellobooks.com to discover more.

Portobello

STRANGE WEATHER IN TOKYO

Hiromi Kawakami

Translated by Allison Markin Powell

'Enchanting, moving and funny . . . a perfect love story' *Stylist*

One night when she is drinking alone in a local bar, Tsukiko finds herself sitting next her former high school teacher. Over the coming months they share food and drink sake, and as the seasons pass – from spring cherry blossom to autumnal mushrooms – Tsukiko and her teacher come to develop a hesitant intimacy which tilts awkwardly and poignantly towards love.

'A dream-like spell of a novel, full of humour, sadness, warmth and tremendous subtlety' Amy Sackville, author of *The Still Point*

'An elegiac sense of speeding time, and yawning distance, drizzles the story – sensitively translated by Allison Markin Powell – with a sweet sadness' *Independent*

'Tender, enigmatic . . . a portrait of an entire culture and a haunting, eccentric mediation on love and loneliness' Rupert Thomson, *Big Issue*

'Kawakami paints perfectly the lightness and delicacy of modern Tokyo, delivering a love story that breaks hearts' *Monocle*